"You won't want to miss this debut with Penelope Parish as she travels THE FERGUSON LIBRARY en Book bookstore in Merry HARRY BENNETT on has penned an irresistible cozy mystery that will delight your imagination and introduce you to a cast of interesting and quirky characters."
—*New York Times* bestselling author Paige Shelton

"A bookshop, lots of tea, a pub, and an English village filled with quirky characters—Margaret Loudon's *Murder in the Margins* has all the ingredients for a delightful read!"
—Marty Wingate, *USA Today* bestselling author of *The Bodies in the Library*

"Bookstores and tearooms and castles in England. Village fetes, charming police officers, and handsome aristocrats. Tea and Cornish pasties and fairy cakes. A town named Upper Chumley-on-Stoke. Plus a writer struggling with writer's block. What's not to like in this absolutely delightful new series by Margaret Loudon? I can't wait to see what Pen Parish and her friends at the Open Book get up to next."
—Vicki Delany, author of *Silent Night, Deadly Night*

"A lively series debut for an engaging heroine."
—*Kirkus Reviews*

A Fatal
Footnote

MARGARET LOUDON

BERKLEY PRIME CRIME
New York

BERKLEY PRIME CRIME

Published by Berkley

An imprint of Penguin Random House LLC

penguinrandomhouse.com

ISBN: 9780593099285

First Edition: July 2021

Printed in the United States of America

1 3 5 7 9 10 8 6 4 2

Book design by Gaelyn Galbreath

A Fatal
Footnote

ONE

꧁ ꧂

Penelope Parish's mother had told her, when she'd accepted the writer-in-residence position at the Open Book bookstore in Upper Chumley-on-Stoke, England, not to expect to hobnob with the nobility.

But here she was doing exactly that.

It was the night before the wedding of American romance writer Charlotte Davenport and Arthur Worthington, Duke of Upper Chumley-on-Stoke, who, despite being well down the line of succession to the throne, was the red-haired favorite of the queen.

The nobility did not wed without a certain amount of pomp and circumstance. In the case of Worthington and Charlotte that consisted of an afternoon polo match where the players graciously allowed Worthington's team to win; a casual dinner buffet that evening; the wedding ceremony itself the following day; the ceremonial carriage ride through town; the wedding breakfast (more lunch than breakfast if truth be told); and finally, that evening, a ball complete with fireworks and a bonfire on the lawn of the castle.

Thanks to her acquaintance with fellow writer Charlotte Davenport, Penelope was invited to all the festivities, which caused her no small amount of consternation given that her wardrobe was considerably subpar, consisting mainly of jeans, leggings, and shapeless but comfortable sweaters—hardly the sort of sartorial splendor expected when hobnobbing with said nobility.

Charlotte always looked impeccable whether she was wearing a pair of jeans and a crisp white button-down shirt or a priceless designer ball gown, and Worthington's bespoke vestments were all carefully made by a legion of devoted tailors in London.

There was nothing for it, Mabel Morris, the proprietor of the Open Book, told Penelope—she was going to have to make a trip to London and do some dreaded shopping.

With the help of Lady Fiona Innes-Goldthorpe, aka Figgy, the manager of the Open Book tea shop and Pen's best friend in Upper Chumley-on-Stoke, Penelope managed to acquire a wardrobe appropriate to the occasion—or, in this case, occasions.

Thus it was that Penelope found herself sitting in the drawing room at Worthington House, dressed in an unaccustomedly elegant gray pencil skirt and black V-neck cashmere sweater, rubbing elbows with the likes of the Duke of Upper Chumley-on-Stoke, Lord Ethan Dougal, Lord Tobias Winterbourne, and Lady Winterbourne—the former Cissie Emmott and onetime girlfriend of Arthur Worthington. The two had remained friends even after their romantic relationship ended.

It was clear that Worthington had a "type." Both Charlotte and Cissie were tall, willowy, and graceful blondes with great style who could almost be mistaken for sisters.

The drawing room, while quite large, felt as snug and cozy as a cocoon with a fire burning in the grate and the dark red velvet drapes drawn across the windows, shutting out the chill of the dark night.

Worthington was standing in front of the fire, one elbow resting on the mantel and one leg elegantly crossed over the other, a champagne glass in his hand.

Tobias, a short, stocky man with a red face and thick black eyebrows, approached Worthington and slapped him on the back.

"Good show today, old man. Leading your team on to victory like that."

Worthington assumed a modest expression. "You're way too kind. I played miserably. Now, if I'd had my lucky polo mallet . . . Darned if I know what happened to the blasted thing. Last I saw it, it was leaning against the wall in the boot room."

Tobias chuckled. "You're being too humble. You played brilliantly. No one can hold a candle to you on the polo field."

Worthington, it should be noted, did not demur further.

The women were clustered at the opposite end of the room—Penelope; Charlotte; Figgy; Jemima Dougal; Cissie; and Yvette Boucher, a petite, dark-haired French woman with a pixie cut who looked effortlessly elegant in a black jumpsuit and black suede kitten heels.

Penelope was perched on the edge of a chintz-covered sofa, attempting to maintain her balance even as its soft, enveloping cushions threatened to swallow her. She had a flute of Moët & Chandon in one hand and a water biscuit with a dab of potted mushrooms on top in the other and had come to the realization that if she bit the hors d'oeuvre in half, she was likely to wind up with crumbs all over her skirt. Eating the whole thing in one go wasn't an option either—it was far too large for that. Not for the first time in her life, she wished for a third hand with which to deal with the situation. How incredibly convenient it would be to be able to whip one out on occasions such as these.

Figgy, who by virtue of being the daughter of an earl had also been invited, was sitting next to Penelope and with a knowing look came to her aid by offering to hold her glass.

Penelope ate her canapé, one hand held underneath to catch the crumbs, and vowed not to accept any more from the butler who was circulating with a silver tray of tempting-looking morsels.

"Do give us a hint about your wedding dress," Jemima said to Charlotte in a teasing tone, one hand smoothing down her long plaid skirt. "I'm imagining something regal with a train that goes on forever."

Penelope thought that at the moment Charlotte looked as regal as ever in a pair of wide-legged cream-colored trousers and a matching cream-colored ruffled blouse. The spectacular diamond on her left ring finger sparkled in the light of the chandelier above.

Cissie, who was sitting cross-legged on the floor in front of the sofa, wagged a finger at Jemima. "It's a state secret. You'll find out soon enough."

Cissie owned Atelier Classique and had designed Charlotte's wedding gown herself. She'd been born in Upper Chumley-on-Stoke but had moved to London after having been sent down from university due to a singular lack of academic achievement.

Her mother had been a sort of royal hanger-on—her

great-grandmother having been a lady-in-waiting to the queen mother and claimed a distant relationship to the royal family. Her father had no pretentions—royal or otherwise—and had made a fortune in toilet paper thus earning Cissie the nickname "the Loo Paper Princess" in the British tabloids, where she appeared at least once a week.

"Just a tiny clue," Jemima wheedled. "I'm dying of curiosity. Is it satin or taffeta or lace?" She raised her eyebrows.

Cissie stretched out her legs in their slim trousers. A gold crest was embroidered on the toes of her black velvet smoking slippers. "It's one of my best designs yet," she said. "I *will* tell you that."

Penelope noticed Yvette shoot Cissie a look that was decidedly ominous. She nudged Figgy and Figgy whispered back.

"I saw that, too. I wonder what's eating her."

A butler stood in the doorway and cleared his throat. "Dinner is served," he said in solemn tones.

"I'm starving," Cissie said, getting to her feet. She patted her stomach. "Mustn't eat too much, though, or I won't fit into my ball gown tomorrow night." She glanced at Charlotte over her shoulder. "And you shouldn't eat too much either. There's no time to alter your gown again. Right, Yvette?" She shot Yvette a look.

Yvette gave a small nod.

The gentlemen followed them into the dining room, where the table had been set with a fine linen tablecloth and the Worthington china and monogrammed silver. Three ornate silver candelabras marched down the center of the table flanked by flowers clustered in low vases.

Food was spread out on the buffet—roast beef, asparagus, silver gravy boats filled with hollandaise sauce, and fondant potatoes. A magnificent chocolate biscuit cake stood on a stand off to one side.

Throwing protocol to the wind—the evening was meant to be casual—the men agreed to sit together on one side of the table with the women on the opposite side. Penelope was seated between Yvette and Figgy.

She turned to Yvette and introduced herself. "How do you know Charlotte?"

Yvette took a sip of her wine. "I work for Atelier Classique. I was part of the team that worked on Charlotte's dress."

Penelope couldn't help but notice that her tone was rather bitter and she had rolled her eyes at the word *team*.

"I'm only here in case last-minute adjustments need to be made," Yvette said, picking up her fork.

Penelope began chatting with Figgy, and by the time the main course was finished, she felt as stuffed as the Thanksgiving turkey.

The butler was serving the dessert when Cissie pushed back her chair and excused herself.

"I'll be right back. Don't wait for me," she said, waving a hand at the table.

Penelope had her back to the entrance to the dining room, but she was able to hear Cissie talking to someone.

"I'm afraid I have no idea who you are," Cissie said in the sort of tone one would use with a recalcitrant child or a servant who had gotten out of line.

"What was that all about?" Figgy cocked a head toward the door. "That was quite the put-down."

"I have no idea," Penelope said. "But it was certainly curious."

TWO

❧

The day of the wedding the weather cooperated nicely as if by royal decree—not too cold for February with blue skies dotted by a handful of puffy white clouds.

Penelope, Figgy, Mabel, and India Culpepper had agreed to meet at the Open Book before the ceremony. Mabel, the owner of the Open Book, had pressed one of her part-time helpers into managing the store in her absence. Fortunately, the young man had agreed—Penelope thought he must be the only person in Upper Chumley-on-Stoke not anxious to get a glimpse of Charlotte in her wedding gown.

Mabel had changed from the worn corduroys and warm cable-knit sweaters she normally wore in the shop into a powder blue suit and matching pillbox hat that set off her white hair very nicely. Figgy looked very proper in a burgundy dress and matching coat with an elaborate fascinator perched on her head, and only her black spiky hair and numerous ear piercings giving a glimpse of her true personality.

India Culpepper, who was related to Worthington and had a cottage on his estate, was wearing a dress-and-coat ensemble. The coat had a discreet fur color and smelled of mothballs. Penelope guessed it to be circa 1960. India was fidgety with excitement, continually smoothing out the fingers of her gloves.

Penelope herself had abandoned her comfortable and familiar uniform of leggings and a sweater in favor of an emerald coat and dress Figgy had urged her to purchase in London at Marks and Spencer. Figgy, who was quite artistic, had also created Penelope's hat—or fascinator as the Brits called them—a rather modest concoction at Penelope's insistence although it still felt odd on top of her head of curly and unruly dark hair.

The front door of the shop flew open and Gladys Watkins, who owned the Pig in a Poke butcher shop across the high street from the bookstore, rushed in. She wasn't wearing a coat and her face was flushed with the cold. The apron tied around her ample waist was smeared with blood.

"Don't you all look so lovely," she said, clasping her hands together. "You have to promise to remember every detail. If only I could go, but Ralph—that's me help in the shop—had his gallbladder out last week and won't be back for a fortnight. I'm all on me own at the moment."

Gladys hadn't been asked to the ceremony itself, but everyone in town had been invited to stand on the grounds of Worthington House and watch as the bride and her attendants arrived.

"Do you think the queen will be there?" Gladys asked breathlessly. "It's always been said that Worthington is a favorite of hers despite all of his escapades."

India assumed a superior air and looked down her nose at Gladys.

"I should doubt it. The queen is getting on in years no matter how well she looks and doesn't need to make unnecessary trips." She frowned. "I do hope that Worthington will have put all that self-indulgent nonsense behind him now that he's getting married."

"Not to mention about to turn forty," Gladys said, folding her arms across her chest.

"We'd best be going," Mabel said, glancing at her watch.

Her cheeks were pink and her eyes glowing. Penelope was surprised—Mabel had been an analyst in MI6 and Penelope would have assumed her to be impervious to the excitement generated by an aristocratic wedding even if it was right in their midst.

Figgy had offered to drive, but Mabel had rather firmly refused the offer, claiming there was more room in her car for Pen's and Figgy's suitcases, though Penelope knew it was because Figgy's driving scared them both half to death. Not that Penelope's was any better—she was still getting the hang of driving down the left-hand side of the road.

A crowd had already gathered outside Worthington House, bundled into warm coats with hats pulled down over their ears. Some of the women had dressed up—as if they were going to the wedding itself—and a couple of teenaged girls, despite being attired in distressed jeans and puffer jackets, were nonetheless sporting elaborate fascinators in honor of the occasion.

An attendant met Mabel's car in the drive and took over parking it for them. A valet followed behind him and removed Pen's and Figgy's suitcases from the trunk. Pen and Mabel were walking toward the Worthington House chapel when they became aware of a disturbance in back of them and turned around.

"What's going on?" Mabel said, craning her neck. "Is that someone shouting?"

Penelope, at nearly six feet tall, had a slight advantage. "It looks as if some woman is protesting."

"Good heavens! Protesting what?" India said.

"The wedding, I assume. She's carrying a sign, too." Penelope stood on tiptoe. "It says *Yankee Go Home*."

"I should imagine that's the first time a sign like that has been seen on these shores since World War Two ended," Mabel said. "What's happening now?"

"A constable is hustling the woman away."

"Dreadful impudence." India sniffed. "Trying to ruin Arthur and Charlotte's wedding day."

"Fortunately the bride hasn't arrived yet," Figgy said.

"We should probably hurry. We don't want to be late," Mabel said, shepherding them toward the door of the chapel.

The chapel was quite large, considering that it had been built only for the use of the members of the Worthington family. Today it was resplendent with all kinds of flowers. Penelope thought it gave the illusion of having walked into a garden.

"Most impressive," India said approvingly. She pointed to a vase overflowing with soft yellow flowers. "That's the Charlotte rose. Each blossom has up to one hundred petals. That's what makes them so lovely."

An usher greeted them and led them to their seats. They hadn't been seated long before there was a sudden rustling among the guests in the chapel. The organ swelled and began playing a piece by Handel and the assembled guests rose to their feet.

"There she is," India said, slightly breathlessly.

"She looks lovely," Figgy said. She turned to Pen. "Cissie was spot-on—the gown is downright regal."

Charlotte's silk gown had an off-the-shoulder neckline, three-quarter-length sleeves, and a trumpet skirt that flared into a long train that ran nearly the length of the chapel aisle. Her veil was simple and flowed in back of her.

In an unexpected move, Worthington had invited the local vicar from St. Andrews to perform the ceremony. Penelope thought that had been a shrewd public relations gesture on his part and the decision had been much praised by the residents of Chumley who were already unhappy that he had chosen an American to be his bride.

As soon as Charlotte reached the altar, Reverend Thatcher began the ceremony.

"In the presence of God, Father, Son, and Holy Spirit," he intoned, "we have come together to witness the marriage of Arthur Worthington and Charlotte Davenport, to pray for God's blessing on them, to share their joy, and to celebrate their love."

Finally, Reverend Thatcher was saying "you may kiss the bride," and the organ began playing the recessional. Worthington offered Charlotte his arm, she gathered her train in her hand, and they strode down the aisle, their faces stretched into broad smiles.

Penelope didn't think she'd ever seen Charlotte look so genuinely happy. She'd been through a lot since her arrival in England and Penelope thought she deserved all the happiness she could get.

The chapel doors were thrown open and the couple stepped outside into the sunshine followed close behind by the assembled guests.

An open landau with the Worthington crest on the side

was waiting in front of the chapel, the two horses pawing the ground and snorting great clouds of vapor into the air.

Charlotte and Worthington turned to face the crowd and waved before Worthington held out a hand and helped Charlotte into the carriage. The crowd roared their approval as they headed down the drive.

"That was lovely," India said.

Figgy made a face. "Hopefully now my mother will give up on the notion that I ever had a chance of becoming the Duchess of Upper Chumley-on-Stoke."

"And of course they know about Derek now," Pen said, pointing to Figgy's engagement ring.

"Yes, they've met him. They liked him. But I think my mother is still disappointed that I didn't snare someone with a title."

Figgy was engaged to a young man from a Pakistani family. Penelope found him charming, good-looking, intelligent, and caring. He had also secured a first in economics at Oxford and was very successful in his field. Personally, Penelope thought him quite the catch.

"I'm heading back to the bookstore now," Mabel said, putting on her gloves, "since I am not among the chosen." She laughed.

"I've only been invited to the wedding breakfast because I've come to know Charlotte," Pen said.

"And I've been invited as a courtesy because my father is an earl." Figgy rolled her eyes and put up a hand to straighten her fascinator. "That fact had my mother convinced that Worthington would seek me out to be his bride."

"I almost wish I wasn't going," Pen said. "I'm terrified I'm going to commit some sort of giant faux pas and let the American side down completely."

Mabel patted her on the arm. "You'll be absolutely fine. There'll be such a crush that no one would even notice if you dropped your entire meal into your lap. And we Brits are so polite, we'd look the other way and pretend it never happened."

Penelope laughed. She felt slightly better, but she still had the jitters as she and Figgy followed the guests to the entrance to the castle. Her knees were a bit wobbly and her stomach was doing flip-flops. She'd feel so much more comfortable in her accustomed leggings and sweater and without that ridiculous fascinator perched on top of her head.

The wedding breakfast was being held in the great hall of Worthington House—a vast space with a massive fireplace at one end, heraldic banners hanging on the walls and from the ceiling, and high arched windows with glass wavy with age.

Long rows of tables had been set with the finest linen, china, and silver Worthington House had to offer with each place setting positioned a precise distance apart. Penelope wondered if there was a single flower left in all of England, given the lavish displays on the table and around the room.

Penelope was dismayed that she and Figgy hadn't been seated together. Instead, she found herself next to a young woman in a moss green floral-print silk dress. Her dark hair was in loose waves past her shoulders and she had exceptionally blue eyes.

She glanced shyly at Penelope. "I'm Rose Ainsley. Are you a friend of Charlotte's or Arthur's?"

Penelope introduced herself. "I'm a friend of Charlotte's. And you?"

Rose hesitated. "I'm a friend of Cissie's actually. Cissie

Winterbourne. I met Arthur through her and we all sort of became friends." She fiddled with the handle of her knife. "I'm sorry I missed the dinner last night. I imagine it was gobs of fun."

They chatted briefly and then Penelope turned to introduce herself to the older woman on the other side of her, whose fascinator had become slightly askew. She gave Penelope a timid smile as she unfurled her napkin and placed it on her lap.

"Oh, dear," she suddenly said, her face crinkled with concern.

Penelope looked at her inquiringly. "Is something the matter?"

"I'm afraid I've left my handbag in the ladies' room. What a bother." She smiled apologetically. "It's difficult for me to get up. It's this pesky arthritis." She indicated the cane propped against the table next to her.

"I'll get it for you." Penelope pushed back her chair. "What does it look like and where is the ladies' room?"

Penelope followed the woman's directions out of the great hall and down the corridor. She remembered this part of Worthington House from the previous October when she'd been there during the annual Worthington fest.

She was passing the library when she heard raised voices. It was clear that someone was very angry, although Pen couldn't quite make out what was being said.

She paused briefly and peeked into the room. Cissie was standing with her back to the door—Penelope recognized the fascinator she'd worn to the ceremony. She was clearly arguing with someone. Her shoulders were set and her posture was stiff. The person with her moved slightly and Pen recognized Yvette Boucher from the evening before.

She tiptoed past the door and down the corridor to the ladies' room. She wondered what they had been arguing about.

Charlotte had insisted that Penelope and Figgy stay at Worthington House for the duration of the festivities— the ball that evening and a brunch to be held the following morning before everyone would see Charlotte and Worthington off on their honeymoon to the Seychelles.

They were sharing a charming bedroom with two carved mahogany four-poster beds draped in flowered chintz and piled with fluffy white duvets. There were two elegant slipper chairs, a small fireplace with an elegant marble mantel on one wall, and the door to an en suite bathroom on the other.

Penelope didn't know what she'd been expecting— something drab and cold perhaps—but of course this part of Worthington House had been thoroughly modernized and freshly decorated.

A maid in a black uniform with a frilly white apron had unpacked their small overnight bags that the valet had brought to their room and hung their dresses for the evening in the wardrobe.

Pen got out the voluminous garment bag housing her gown and laid it on one of the beds.

"I can't wait to see you in that dress," Figgy said. "We were so lucky to find it."

"Lucky indeed," Pen said. Her modest clothes budget was nearly running out when they came upon a sale at a tiny boutique. It was the first dress Penelope tried on and the last—both she and Figgy had agreed it was perfect for the wedding ball.

Penelope slipped it from the bag and, with Figgy's help, slid it over her head.

It was a long, slim column of navy blue velvet with a draped neck and spaghetti straps—simple but elegant.

"Now for your dress," Pen said, as Figgy got her garment bag out of the wardrobe.

Figgy unzipped it and the frothy pale pink confection that was her dress nearly burst out of it.

It was pure Figgy, Pen thought as she helped Figgy with the zipper. It had a full, tiered skirt in tulle and a high neck trimmed with feathers that fluttered just under Figgy's chin.

"I feel like Cinderella," Pen said.

"Hopefully we won't turn into pumpkins at the stroke of midnight," Figgy said as she bent down to peer into the mirror over the vanity.

"And Cinderella has already married her prince so there are no worries about that," Pen said. "Or I guess I should say duke, in this case."

Figgy turned to Pen suddenly, her hands on her hips. "Now what are we going to do about your hair?"

"My hair?" Pen touched a hand to her head of dark curls.

"I'm quite a whiz with hair," Figgy said, digging a hairbrush out of her suitcase. "I might have a pixie cut at the moment, but I've had every length of hair imaginable. At one point it was nearly to my waist." She pointed to the bench in front of the vanity. "Sit." She pulled a handful of bobby pins out of her makeup bag and laid them out.

Penelope did as she was told and watched in the mirror in amazement as Figgy transformed the unruly tangle that was her hair into a low bun with loose tendrils curling around her face.

"There," Figgy said in satisfaction.

"I think we're ready," Pen said, reaching for her wrap,

which she'd tossed on the bed. She felt a fluttering of excitement in her stomach.

"This should be exciting," Figgy said, linking her arm through Pen's as they headed down the corridor and toward the ballroom.

The ballroom glittered with light from crystal chandeliers, sconces along the walls, and flickering candles set out around the room. Flowers were everywhere, too, including the pale yellow Charlotte rose.

The assembled crowd gave off a sense of excited anticipation as they waited for Charlotte and Arthur to arrive.

Suddenly the doors to the ballroom opened and the couple arrived arm in arm. A gasp rose from the crowd as the newlyweds made their way into the room and the orchestra began to play. Charlotte was stunning in a white dress with a halter neckline and a mermaid skirt trimmed with marabou. Everyone gathered around as they began dancing and soon other couples joined in.

"I don't suppose we'll be doing much dancing," Figgy said, snagging a glass of champagne from a passing waiter. She grabbed Pen's arm. "Good heavens, look at that fellow."

"That's Tobias Winterbourne, isn't it?" Pen said squinting into the distance. "We met him last night at dinner."

"What on earth is he wearing?"

"It is quite something, isn't it?" Rose Ainsley had come up behind them. She smiled indulgently. "Tobias never did like blending in with the crowd."

Amid the sea of black dinner jackets and starched white shirts, Tobias stood out in a midnight blue burned velvet jacket and ruffled navy shirt.

"I rather like his style," Figgy said. She turned to Rose. "Speaking of style, did Cissie design the dress Charlotte's wearing tonight?"

"Yes. I have to admit—she is talented. Looks like she has it all—beauty, brains, and money." She gave a cynical laugh.

Rose wandered off and moments later, Pen noticed her dancing with Tobias.

She was glad no one had asked her to dance so far. With her height and long legs she always felt she looked like a flamingo on the dance floor.

"I suppose we should circulate," Pen said. "Otherwise someone might mistake us for one of the columns."

"You go ahead. I'm going to track down a waiter and get rid of my empty glass." Figgy began to move away. "And get another," she called over her shoulder.

Pen found Cissie; Jemima; and Jemima's husband, Ethan, clustered together near the French doors to the garden. Ethan had rather boyish good looks and hair that was long enough and shaggy enough to accentuate that impression.

"Lovely dress," Cissie said, looking Pen up and down, one eyebrow raised.

Pen thought she noticed a smirk hovering around Cissie's lips. She lifted her chin. She felt very elegant in her gown even if it didn't have a famous designer label attached.

Cissie waved a hand dismissively. "I'm going out for a smoke. Anyone care to join me?"

Everyone shook their heads and watched as Cissie made her way to the door.

Jemima rolled her eyes. "I guess she's still smoking that pipe of hers."

"A pipe?" Pen said in disbelief.

Jemima nodded. "Cissie always has to be different. Just like her husband." She gestured toward the dance floor where Tobias was again dancing with Rose.

Dancing continued until nearly midnight with a huge buffet set out around ten o'clock. Charlotte had insisted that she wanted the event to be fun, so the menu was unexpectedly informal with sliders, tacos, fish-and-chips, and Cornish pasties.

"I'm stuffed," Figgy said an hour later after several trips to the buffet. People were pushing back their chairs and moving toward the French doors to the garden.

"What's going on?" Pen looked around curiously.

Jemima was passing by. She stopped, put her hands on the table, and leaned down toward Penelope. She smelled of a heavy gardenia perfume mixed with whiffs of tobacco smoke.

"There are going to be fireworks and a bonfire on the lawn. It should be spectacular."

Figgy looked at Pen. "We don't want to miss that."

They got up and started to follow the crowd. They were almost to the door when they heard someone scream—a high, piercing scream that cut through the noise of the fireworks that had just started outside.

THREE

❧⚬❧

Penelope and Figgy looked at each other.

"What on earth?" Figgy said.

A woman had come rushing back into the ballroom, her gray hair in disarray, her mouth working but no sound coming out.

Worthington immediately broke free from the crowd and strode over to her. He put a consoling hand on her arm.

"I'm going to see what's going on," Pen said, beginning to move through the people clustered near the door.

The woman had finally found her voice and had started to talk. Pen sidled closer until she could hear what she was saying. She couldn't catch every word, but several were clear enough—*body . . . dead . . . Lady Winterbourne.*

Cissie was dead? Maybe the woman was mistaken? Penelope strained to hear, but the woman had lapsed into silent sobbing, her hands clutching and unclutching the folds of her gown.

Worthington cleared his throat and held up his hands to get everyone's attention.

"There's been an . . . accident, I'm afraid," he said finally, hesitating over the word *accident*. "Everyone please sit down. The authorities will be on their way shortly."

He spoke briefly to one of the men, who pulled a cell phone from his pocket.

The police? Penelope heard people whispering among themselves.

"They're calling the police," Pen said to Figgy when she rejoined her.

"What sort of accident requires the police?" Figgy said.

"Murder, that's what. It sounds as if someone has killed Cissie."

Figgy's eyes got rounder and she gasped. "You think Cissie's been murdered?"

"I don't know. That's what it sounds like, doesn't it?"

Worthington was standing at the front of the ballroom again, holding up his hands for silence. Slowly the chatter, which sounded like so many chirping cicadas, died down.

"Please help yourselves," he said, waving a hand toward the buffet table. "There's tea and dessert or brandy and port if you'd prefer something stronger."

A stout man, whose stomach strained the limits of his waistcoat, laughed. "I think we could all do with something stronger at this point."

Pen and Figgy began moving toward the buffet table. Penelope hoped the rest of the guests would follow. It would keep them distracted from what was going on out on the terrace.

"Look." Figgy pointed to a large cake placed in the middle of the table. *Congratulations, Charlotte and Arthur* was written in elegant script across the top layer.

Worthington pointed to the cake and had a whispered conversation with one of the waiters, who immediately whisked the cake away and returned with it in slices arranged on a platter so that the lettering was scrambled and the message no longer discernible.

"Worthington has such impeccable manners," Jemima, who was standing next to Pen and Figgy at the buffet table, said. "He and Charlotte have every right to celebrate, but I imagine he thought the message on the cake was inappropriate . . . if not in actual bad taste . . . under the circumstances." She ran a hand through her hair. "I can't believe Cissie is dead." She looked at Pen. "But then people always say that, don't they? No one can ever believe it." She fingered the sash on her tartan gown.

"Cissie—she was christened Cecelia after her great-grandmother—and I have known each other for ages—we were at school together." Tears glistened on her lower lashes and she swiped a finger under her eyes impatiently. "We were good friends and we went around with the same crowd." She massaged her forehead. "I wonder what happened? It's got to have been an accident, don't you think?" She glanced from Penelope to Figgy, a look of appeal in her eyes.

Penelope smiled. "Yes, of course. It must have been an accident."

"Although what sort of accident could have befallen her out in the garden, I can't imagine," Jemima said.

Heads began to turn toward the door.

"Looks like the police are here." Penelope jerked her thumb in that direction. "I think I recognize Constable Cuthbert."

Figgy poked Pen with her elbow. "There's Maguire." A sly smile spread across her face.

Penelope's breath momentarily caught in her throat. She and Detective Brodie Maguire had struck up a friendship—she wasn't ready to call it a romance yet—when they literally met headon while Penelope was driving down the wrong side of the street.

He wasn't a handsome man but there was something attractive about his face nonetheless. Penelope found him to be kind, honest, and trustworthy.

Cuthbert and the other constable led Maguire through the room and out to the terrace where the body had been found. The crowd had grown quiet upon his arrival but burst into animated chatter again as soon as he disappeared out the door.

Yvette walked over to Pen and Figgy, her long black chiffon gown swishing around her legs. "I do wish they'd tell us what's going on," she said, her French accent more pronounced than previously. "Is it true that Cissie is dead?" She looked at Pen and Figgy and cocked her head.

"It seems so," Penelope said. "But I'm going to see if I can find out if that's true."

Penelope made her way around the ballroom, looking for the woman who had come running in announcing that she'd found Cissie dead on the terrace. She thought she saw Charlotte help the woman into a room off the ballroom and headed in that direction.

The woman with the white hair was alone in the room. It was a small room—a sort of sitting room with a love seat covered in rose-colored damask and an armchair in a matching shade. An oil painting, badly in need of cleaning, of some long-dead Worthington relative was on the wall. Penelope supposed the room was meant for guests who might want to rest briefly when tired from dancing or socializing.

The woman looked up when she heard Penelope. Her expression was troubled, her eyes dull and slightly vacant, like those of a person who had suffered a bad shock. Her hand trembled as she raised an embroidered lace handkerchief to her face. There was a small glass of amber liquid on the table next to her.

She looked up at Penelope and gave her a brief smile. "I'm waiting for that detective to come and talk to me." Her voice shook slightly. "He's gone to see the . . . the body first." She tilted her head. "I'm Beatrice Russell," she said.

"Penelope Parish." Penelope sat in the armchair opposite. "Can I get you anything? That must have been a terrible shock for you," she said gently.

Beatrice nodded. "It was. I can't begin to tell you. To see her lying there like that . . ."

"I heard her say she was going out for a smoke," Pen said.

"Yes. I noticed her pipe lying on the ground next to her. She was known to smoke a pipe, you know. Cissie was unique." She smiled but it faded quickly.

So did the murderer know that sooner or later Cissie would leave the ballroom for a smoke break? Pen wondered. Had they been lying in wait for her outside?

"How could you tell she was dead and hadn't just fainted?"

Beatrice shuddered. "It was her head—all bashed in the way it was. I'm afraid I shall never forget the sight." She reached for the glass at her side and took a sip.

The image Beatrice described made Penelope suddenly feel sick to her stomach. She was glad she hadn't yet had a piece of Charlotte and Arthur's celebratory cake.

"Did you see anyone else outside? Or hear anything while you were out there?"

"No, I'm afraid not." Beatrice pleated her handkerchief

between her fingers. "I was so startled. All I could see was Lady Winterbourne lying there with—" She gulped and put a hand to her mouth.

She looked up at Penelope and Penelope was startled to see how blue her eyes were—nearly violet.

"Please, it's okay," Pen said soothingly.

"Her head," Beatrice said, balling up her handkerchief in her fist, "it was . . . it was horrible. It looked as if someone had hit her with something. Something fairly heavy."

Pen suddenly felt guilty. She really ought to leave the poor woman alone. Obviously, there wasn't much more she could tell Penelope.

Pen was getting up when she sensed someone standing in the doorway and turned around to look. It was Maguire. She found herself smiling at the sight of him.

He looked as if he'd been called out of bed—dressed casually in worn jeans, a plaid flannel shirt, and a brown leather jacket. His hair was slightly rumpled and his face was creased with sleep.

He stopped short when he saw Pen. "I didn't expect to see you here."

"I'll leave you two," Penelope said, getting up from the chair.

"Don't go far," Maguire said. "I'll need to talk to you."

He turned to Beatrice and introduced himself.

When Pen went back to the ballroom, she noticed that more constables had arrived. One was guarding the door to the garden and the other was standing in front of the door leading to the main part of Worthington House.

"They won't let us leave," Pen heard a woman in an elaborate sequin-trimmed gown whine fretfully to her companion.

People seemed to be milling around aimlessly, unsure of

what to do with themselves. Another constable was walking among the crowd with a notepad and pen in his hand. Penelope supposed he was taking down everyone's name and address.

"There are at least two hundred people here," Figgy said when Penelope joined her. "The police are going to have their work cut out for them questioning this lot. Most of them probably have their solicitors on speed dial."

Worthington walked to the front of the room once more and held up his hand to get everyone's attention.

"The police have asked that no one leave the ballroom for the moment. I am sorry for the inconvenience, but there's nothing to be done about it. My staff is putting out more coffee and tea, and if you'd like something stronger, please ask one of the staff and they will arrange it for you."

A certain amount of grumbling greeted Worthington's words but eventually died down and gave way to animated chatter.

"Truth be told, it's all rather exciting," a man standing near Penelope said.

"I'm positively exhausted," someone else said. "I wonder if anyone would notice if I slipped my shoes off? My feet are killing me."

Penelope and Figgy were joined by Jemima and Yvette.

"The police are asking if anyone saw Cissie go out on the terrace," Yvette said, wrapping her arms around herself.

Penelope could see the goose bumps forming on her arms.

"We did see Cissie out for a smoke, didn't we?" Jemima turned to Penelope, who nodded.

Yvette tilted her head in a way that reminded Penelope of a curious bird. "I did see Tobias go out," she said.

"Oh? Is he a smoker, too?" Penelope said.

Jemima shook her head. "No, he gave it up a couple of years ago. Not that he ever smoked all that much—with a cocktail perhaps or during intermission at the theater. It was more for something to do than a serious addiction."

Figgy put a hand to her mouth and yawned. "Suddenly I'm absolutely fagged out," she said. "I thought I might get a cup of tea. How about you?"

"That sounds like a good idea," Pen said while the others shook their heads.

They made their way to the buffet table, where a large urn held hot water with an array of tea bags set out beside it.

Penelope reached for the Earl Grey and handed one to Figgy.

A woman in a maid's uniform came out of the kitchen with a tray of clean cups and saucers and put it on the table. Penelope noticed she had a bandage wrapped clumsily around her left hand. The woman winced when she accidentally brushed it against the side of the table. Penelope felt sorry for her; she herself had certainly had more than her share of kitchen mishaps—she remembered the time she'd almost cut off the tip of her finger and another time when she'd grabbed a cookie sheet out of the oven without a mitt.

She smiled at the woman as she filled her teacup with hot water, added the tea bag and a generous amount of sugar—Penelope had been blessed with the sort of metabolism that made it hard for her to gain weight—and moved away from the table.

She looked around the room and noticed Charlotte coming toward her.

"Penelope," Charlotte said, taking Pen's hand in her own. "I need to speak to you, if you don't mind."

Pen put her teacup down on the nearest table and followed Charlotte. The constable at the door let them pass, which surprised Penelope, but then again, Charlotte was now the Duchess of Upper Chumley-on-Stoke and she supposed that had its privileges.

Charlotte led Penelope down a corridor, around a corner, and down another corridor until they came to a partially opened door. Penelope followed her inside and Charlotte closed the door behind them.

It was Charlotte's study—Penelope had been there before. The room was book lined, with an antique Empire desk, tall windows draped in moss green velvet, and a comfortable sofa and chairs.

Charlotte collapsed into one of the chairs. Penelope noticed her face was white and her hands were trembling slightly.

"This is just ghastly," she said.

"I'm so sorry this has ruined your reception," Penelope said.

"My reception?" Charlotte looked at her with a shocked expression. "The party doesn't matter. It's poor Cissie . . . She's dead. The police are saying someone killed her. I asked if there might be some mistake—that maybe it was an accident—but when they told me what her injuries were, it was obvious it was no accident." Charlotte shuddered. "I overheard that detective—Maguire—talking. He said the killer must have gotten blood on their clothes and he sent that constable off to go through everyone's things in case the murderer was someone staying here at Worthington House."

Charlotte was quiet for a moment, twisting her hands in her lap.

"Did you know Cissie very well?" Pen said.

"Not well, no. She was Arthur's ex-girlfriend, to be honest with you. It was long before we met. People seem to think her presence should bother me, but it doesn't. They stayed friends, but that's all it was, so why should I mind?"

Charlotte rubbed her forehead. "I don't know about you, but I could do with a cup of tea." She smiled. "I guess I'm becoming quite British after all. Tea—the cure-all for everything."

She reached out and pressed a buzzer hidden underneath the coffee table.

"Would you care for another cup of tea?" She leaned forward toward Penelope. "Or perhaps you'd prefer coffee or something stronger?"

Penelope was thinking longingly of the bottle of Jameson that Mabel kept under the front counter at the Open Book, but she wanted to keep her head clear and settled for the offered cup of tea.

Moments later there was a knock on the door.

"Come in," Charlotte said.

A butler stood at attention in the doorway.

"I hate to be a bother." Charlotte smiled. "But could we have some tea, please?"

"Certainly, your grace."

Charlotte gave a loud sigh and leaned back in her seat.

The marabou trim on Charlotte's dress fluttered slightly as she crossed her legs. She stared into the distance, a small frown wrinkling the skin between her eyebrows.

Penelope was quiet but she was curious. She wondered what Charlotte wanted to talk to her about. Was Charlotte having second thoughts about whatever it was?

A few minutes later there was a discreet tap on the door and the butler walked in with a tray laden with a silver teapot, bone china cups and saucers, silver spoons and a bowl of sugar, lemon slices on a small plate, and a pitcher of milk.

Charlotte picked up the teapot. She smiled at Penelope. "Do you know what the British sometimes say at tea?"

Penelope shook her head.

"Someone will say, 'Shall I be mother?' Which means they will handle pouring out the tea and handing around the cups. It's rather charming, don't you think?"

Charlotte smiled but the smile disappeared almost immediately, and Penelope noticed her hand was shaking again as she handed Penelope her cup.

Charlotte took a sip of her tea and then abruptly put her cup down. It clattered in the saucer. "I have to admit I'm worried about something." She kneaded the fingers of one hand with the other.

"What is it? Do you want to talk about it?"

"I don't know how to put it into words." Charlotte jumped up from her chair and began to pace the room. "I'm afraid you'll think I'm imagining things . . . or worse, that I'm crazy. One minute I think it's preposterous and the next minute, it scares me half to death." She gave a small laugh and looked at Penelope pleadingly.

"I doubt that. You're not the sort to imagine things— unless it's for one of your books, of course."

As Penelope had hoped, Charlotte laughed briefly.

"And as for being crazy—you're one of the most sane people I know. As my grandmother would have said—you have both feet firmly planted on the ground."

"Thank you." Charlotte bowed her head briefly. "Your support means a lot to me."

"Come on. Out with it then," Pen said. "Maybe I can help. At least I can try."

Charlotte gave a forceful exhale that fluttered the tiny hairs around her face. "Okay. You've managed to convince me. Here it is." She closed her eyes and wrinkled her forehead. "I'm afraid—" Her voice caught for a moment. "I'm afraid that someone mistook Cissie for me. We do look quite a bit alike, you know." Charlotte stifled a sob. "I'm afraid someone wanted to kill me but made a mistake and killed poor Cissie instead."

FOUR

❧⟋❧

"Why would someone want to kill dear sweet Charlotte?" Figgy said later when Penelope told her about her conversation with Charlotte.

Penelope shrugged. She massaged her forehead, which was beginning to ache. "I don't know. She said it's this feeling she has. She's convinced that we all hate her and that everyone wanted Worthington to marry someone else."

Penelope and Figgy were back in their room. Penelope sat on one of the brocade-covered slipper chairs and eased off her evening shoes. She groaned with relief as they dropped to the floor. She wasn't used to wearing high heels.

"That's not true," Figgy said. She gave Penelope a quizzical look. "I don't know why Charlotte would think that, although I suppose some of the people in Upper Chumley-on-Stoke do still resent the fact that Worthington chose an American to be his bride." She made a snorting sound.

"Which is perfectly ridiculous. I've become quite fond of Americans myself."

"But there was that woman outside the chapel," Pen said. "Remember? She was carrying that sign—*Yankee Go Home*."

Figgy's voice faded as her head disappeared inside the bodice of her pink dress. She struggled briefly, and then reemerged, her short hair tousled and standing on end. She tossed the dress on the bed with a sigh and pulled a pair of pajamas from the dresser and slipped them on.

Penelope had to smile when she saw them—the fabric was covered in a Wonder Woman print.

"I'm glad to be shot of that dress," Figgy said, collapsing on the bed. She wiggled her toes in freedom. "I don't know how the royals do it—prancing around day in and day out in all those fancy clothes. I don't envy them, that's for sure."

"Neither do I," Pen said from the bathroom where she was brushing her teeth.

Finally, they were both ready for bed and the lights were out. Penelope had been convinced she'd fall asleep the minute her head hit the pillow, but she was wrong. Thoughts chased themselves, one after the other, through her mind, which refused to shut down. She must be overtired, she thought. She couldn't imagine how Charlotte must feel.

She was almost dozing when a noise startled her awake. She sat up in bed and listened. She was positive she'd heard a door close somewhere down the hall. Or had she dreamed it?

A floorboard creaked. Someone was definitely walking around in the corridor.

Pen slipped from bed and tiptoed to the door. Figgy was sound asleep, curled into a ball with one hand under her cheek like a child.

Penelope eased open the door and peered out. Wall

sconces at either end of the corridor cast pools of light beneath them creating shadows everywhere else. Pen heard a door hinge squeak at one end of the hall and quickly glanced that way. She was in time to see a door being gently closed.

She couldn't see who had been in the hall but her impression was that the hand on the doorknob had been small—a woman's hand perhaps?

Penelope was quite sure she'd heard two doors open and close—was someone sneaking into someone else's room?

She got back in bed and pulled the covers up to her chin. Worthington House, despite all the updating and redecorating Worthington had done, was still quite drafty and she'd become chilled.

She burrowed under the covers and rubbed her feet together to warm them. Why was someone sneaking around the halls of Worthington House this late at night? Was someone—or two *someones*—having an affair?

And did it have anything at all to do with Cissie's murder?

Penelope finally fell asleep, tossing and turning with troubled dreams.

Suddenly, she bolted upright in bed. Where was she? She looked around the room and slowly remembered she was still at Worthington House. But what had woken her up so abruptly?

There were loud voices coming from outside. It sounded like an argument was under way. She tiptoed over to the window, pushed the curtain aside, and peered out.

The window looked out on the terrace and the sun-dappled gardens of Worthington House. The terrace and the area around it were roped off with crime scene tape that fluttered and snapped in the wind.

Tobias was arguing with the constable who was on duty guarding the area. Tobias's face was bright red, although whether from the cold or anger, Penelope couldn't tell. He was gesticulating wildly, flinging his arms out and waving them around.

He wasn't wearing a coat but did have on a tweed wool sport coat with leather patches on the elbows and there was a brown knit scarf around his neck.

At one point, Tobias attempted to lift the crime scene tape, and it looked to Penelope as if he was going to attempt to duck underneath it, but the constable grabbed him by the arm and spun him around.

Tobias shook himself free. He brushed off the sleeves of his jacket and straightened his scarf. His expression was clearly furious now. The constable, on the other hand, looked completely unperturbed by the confrontation, his face a bland mask.

Tobias stalked off and Penelope saw him wandering around the garden, his eyes on the ground, as if he was looking for something.

All very curious, she thought, as she let the curtain drop back into place and turned away from the window.

Penelope closed her suitcase, hauled it over to the door, and placed it next to Figgy's packed bag. They were having breakfast at Worthington House and then Pen would be heading home to her cottage on the high street.

Breakfast was being served in the dining room. The

room looked different in the daylight—the curtains were open and sun streamed through the windows. The cook had prepared a full English breakfast, or a "fry-up" as it was sometimes known—eggs, bacon and sausage, fried tomatoes, fried bread, mushrooms, kippers, and potatoes.

Charlotte was helping herself to some eggs and bacon. Penelope thought she looked tired—her face was drawn and there were telltale dark circles under her eyes.

Jemima was already seated at the table with a plate full of food, which she was attacking with relish. She seemed to be the only one with any real appetite. Rose was picking at the eggs on her plate. She looked almost as tired as Charlotte.

Yvette strolled into the room as Penelope was helping herself to some eggs. Pen couldn't help wondering how Yvette managed to make a simple pair of black pants, a black sweater, and a scarf look so impossibly chic.

Yvette stood and stared at the buffet.

"Is something wrong?" Charlotte put down her fork.

Yvette shook her head. "No. But I am not used to such a large meal in the morning—I normally have a cup of coffee and a roll or a croissant. I'm afraid I don't know where to begin."

"Help yourself to whatever looks good." Charlotte pointed to a toast rack on the table. "There's plain toast if you'd prefer."

Jemima looked up from her plate, her fork poised in midair. "Where is our groom this morning? Sleeping in, is he?"

Charlotte dabbed her lips with her napkin. "He's in his office, rearranging our honeymoon plans, I'm afraid. Unfortunately, the police don't want us to leave just yet and, although he tried, Arthur wasn't able to convince them otherwise."

"Speaking of police," Yvette said, spreading butter on her toast, "I noticed several had arrived this morning and were examining the terrace."

"Yes," Charlotte said. "Detective Maguire said they would be back in the morning to be sure they hadn't missed anything—although I have no idea what they're looking for."

"I should imagine they are looking for clues," Tobias said as he strode into the room.

He'd removed his scarf but was still wearing the tweed sport coat. Now that Pen could see it up close, she noticed that there was a purple thread woven in with the brown, cream, and black ones. After seeing Tobias's dinner jacket the previous evening, she wasn't surprised to find that his need to be distinctive extended to his everyday wardrobe and wasn't limited to his evening wear.

"Have they found the murder weapon yet?" Jemima said, returning to the buffet for seconds.

"I don't understand it," Charlotte said. "Who would want to kill Cissie?"

"Maybe it was an intruder?" Rose said. "Cissie was wearing some spectacular jewelry. So many of the ladies were." She appeared to be warming to the topic. "It was well-known that there would be a ball tonight. What better opportunity for some jewel thief?"

"But why go so far as to commit murder?" Yvette said. "It would be easy enough to simply hold a gun to her head and demand she hand over her necklace and rings or whatever."

"Maybe she fought back." Jemima speared a mushroom on her plate. "Cissie was quite tough. She was known for being ferocious on the hockey field when we were at school."

"Also, wouldn't the thief have simply shot her if he was

carrying a gun?" Yvette said, one hand on her coffee cup. "I gather the attack was very vicious."

Rose shuddered. "How awful to think about it. It's hard to imagine someone doing something like that."

"Well, someone did," Tobias said rather flippantly.

"He certainly isn't playing the grieving widower," Figgy whispered to Penelope as they took seats at the table.

What had Tobias and Cissie's marriage been like? Penelope wondered. Had they been in love at one time? Tobias certainly didn't seem to be terribly broken up by his wife's murder.

Tobias put his cup of tea down and slid into the seat next to Penelope. He, too, looked tired—as if he hadn't slept well. Penelope supposed that none of them had.

"You were up early this morning," Penelope said as she pierced the yolk of her fried egg with her fork.

Tobias jumped and his elbow caught his teacup, rattling it in its saucer.

"What do you mean?" He turned to Pen.

"I heard you outside early this morning. You were arguing with the constable guarding the terrace."

"How do you know that?"

"I saw you from the window of our bedroom—it overlooks the terrace and gardens." Penelope wiped her lips with her napkin. "You looked like you were searching for something."

Tobias's face flushed. "You're mistaken. I wasn't looking for anything. Merely getting some fresh air."

And with that he turned his back to Penelope and began to talk to Rose, who was seated on his other side.

She'd obviously touched a nerve, Penelope thought, as she finished her breakfast. She was positive Tobias had been searching for something. But why would he lie about it? Did he think it would incriminate him somehow?

They were finishing breakfast when Maguire stepped into the room. He looked less rumpled this morning although just as casual in jeans, a blue oxford shirt, and the same brown leather jacket. He glanced at Penelope and gave her an almost imperceptible wink.

"I'm sorry to have to disturb everyone but I have a few questions for you." Maguire gave a rueful smile.

"This is preposterous," Tobias muttered under his breath.

Jemima looked at him from across the table. There was a wicked gleam in her eye. "You'd better watch out, Tobias. The husband is always the first one the police suspect."

Tobias opened his mouth, but no words came out. A flush slowly suffused his face, turning it a mottled red.

"Worthington has been kind enough to lend us his office. I assume you all know the way?" Maguire raised his eyebrows. "I'd like to speak to you one at a time, if you don't mind."

"Do we have a choice?" Tobias muttered under his breath.

Maguire pointed at Tobias. "We'll start with you, Lord Winterbourne. If you don't mind accompanying me."

Penelope expected Tobias to make a snarky retort, but instead he got up from his chair and meekly followed Maguire out of the room.

One by one, Maguire called the house party into Worthington's office.

Jemima went back to the buffet and helped herself to another cup of tea. Her husband, Ethan, who had been quiet throughout breakfast, pulled out his cell phone and began scrolling through his e-mails.

Yvette sat and stared into space, crumbling the remains of her toast between her fingers. Rose was as still as a statue, the expression on her face unreadable.

Finally everyone had been questioned and it was Penelope's turn. She found her way down the maze of corridors to Worthington's office, pleased and surprised that she remembered how to get there.

Maguire was sprawled in an armchair, his legs stretched out in front of him, looking as if he had flung himself into it. He ran his hands over his face and then smiled at Penelope.

"You look tired," Penelope said, taking a seat.

Maguire blew out a puff of air. "I am. I was here all night. I only had an hour to go home and shower, change, and grab some breakfast."

"It must be tough."

Maguire shrugged. "It's part of the job." He smiled and nodded at Penelope. "I think you probably have the honor of being the most sane person I've talked to so far," he said.

"But Charlotte and Worthington . . ."

"Yes, of course. But aside from them . . ." Maguire shook his head. "Frankly, I think they are all lying about something. Either that or Cissie Winterbourne was the mostwell-liked person in the world."

"I don't suppose they would admit to disliking her," Penelope said. "Under the circumstances."

She'd taken a seat in the chair opposite Maguire. She found that his presence left her slightly breathless and she tried to will her heart to beat slower.

Maguire laughed. "True. The trick is to listen to what

they're not saying out loud. You'd be surprised how much people give away with their facial expressions and various mannerisms."

Maguire reached into his pocket and pulled out a small plastic bag with something in it. He held it out toward Penelope.

"We found this button in the garden alongside the terrace. You wouldn't happen to recognize it, would you?" Maguire wiped his hands across his face again. "We'll send it for fingerprint analysis, of course, but by the time we get the results back we'll likely have solved this thing."

Penelope took the plastic bag and examined the button inside. It was black onyx and carved into the shape of a rose. She handed the bag back to Maguire.

"It's not mine," she said. "And I don't recall ever seeing one like it before. It's very distinctive though."

"I knew it was a long shot." Maguire gave a weary smile. "No one seems to have seen it before. Of course it may belong to one of the other guests at the ball or even someone who had been at Worthington House at one time or another. I gather people can pay to take a tour."

Maguire shifted in his chair and yawned. "How well do you know these people—the Winterbournes, the Dougals, and the rest of them?"

"Me? Not very well. I know Charlotte and Worthington, but I met the others for the first time on the day before the wedding." Penelope hesitated. "I saw something curious out the window this morning."

Maguire's eyebrows shot up. "Oh? What was that?"

"I heard voices. It sounded like an argument to me. I looked out the window, and Tobias was near the terrace, arguing with the constable on duty about something. He even tried to duck under the crime scene tape but the constable stopped him. Afterward, Tobias appeared to be searching for something in the garden."

Maguire suddenly sat up straight. "I haven't spoken with the constable yet." He frowned. "That *is* interesting," he said. "I think I may need to have another talk with Lord Winterbourne."

Penelope was coming out of Worthington's office after her interview with Maguire when she ran into Charlotte.

"There you are," Charlotte said somewhat breathlessly. "I was afraid you'd already gone."

"I'll be going shortly," Pen said. Suddenly she was anxious to get back to her own cozy cottage.

"If I could talk to you for another minute," Charlotte said. She bit her lip. "I realize this isn't fair to you, but I'm afraid I need your help again." She began walking. "I was on my way to the kitchen to get a cup of tea. Would you like one?"

"Yes, thank you."

Penelope wondered why Charlotte was getting her own tea. Normally she had only to push one of the buttons hidden all over the castle and the butler or a maid would appear as if by magic.

"Sometimes I enjoy making my own tea," Charlotte said as if she'd read Penelope's mind. "It reminds me that we all put our pants on one leg at a time, as my old granny used to say when she thought I was getting too far above myself." Charlotte chuckled. "Although I'm afraid it always alarms the staff when I appear in the kitchen."

Penelope followed Charlotte down the hall and down a

set of stairs. She'd helped Charlotte once before—when Charlotte had been suspected of murdering the town gossip—but she couldn't see how she could possibly be of help this time.

The kitchen was a cavernous room with tiled walls and floor and stainless steel appliances. A long, stainless steel table with lights suspended over it ran nearly the entire length of the room and a huge Aga stove held pride of place between the massive refrigerator and deep double sinks.

The kitchen had been cleaned after the breakfast prep— the table and counters wiped down and the floor mopped. It was quiet and the only person in the room was a woman stirring a pot on the stove.

"It's so modern," Penelope said in surprise.

"Arthur had it redone a number of years ago," Charlotte said, nodding at the woman in a bib apron who was simmering a pot of stock on the Aga. "He entertains so frequently, he thought it would be a wise investment."

Charlotte went to a cabinet and retrieved several tea bags along with two cups and saucers. They were made of thick white pottery, which was a contrast to the delicate bone china served upstairs.

"Why don't we go sit in the conservatory? The sun will feel good on this cold winter day."

They carried their tea to the conservatory, where the sun streamed through the glass windows and ceiling, warming the moist, humid air. Enormous potted plants, small trees, and dozens of the flowering orchids Worthington cultivated gave the a room an exotic tropical feel that was enhanced by the high-backed rattan chairs arranged around a glass table.

"I feel like I'm always asking you for a favor," Charlotte said, as she put down her teacup and took a seat. "You were so helpful the last time we found ourselves in a . . . pre-dicament." She gave a sharp laugh. "People are soon going to think that Worthington House is cursed—two murders in less than a year."

Charlotte turned her teaspoon over and over on the saucer. "Arthur says it's good for business—more tourists will come to tour Worthington House now." Charlotte looked down at her cup. "But of course he's actually quite shaken by it even though he tries to make light of it for my sake. Especially this time—he'd known Cissie Winterbourne since he was in his twenties."

Charlotte put her hands on the table. "As I said before, either someone mistook Cissie for me—which Arthur doesn't believe is what happened and the police don't either—or the killer meant to target Cissie. Which is almost worse."

"Why?" Penelope took a sip of her tea.

"You know Cissie was Arthur's old flame. Apparently it was all over the papers at the time. People are saying that Cissie planned to write one of those tell-all books that everyone seems to love these days." Charlotte looked up suddenly. "Nothing criminal—just youthful hijinks that could prove to be embarrassing."

"Are you saying that Lord Worthington might become a suspect in Cissie's murder?"

Charlotte looked relieved. "Yes. I'm so glad you see it, too."

"I still don't understand what I can do to help." Penelope finished the last of her tea.

"You've solved one case already—Regina's murder in the fall."

And I nearly got myself killed, Penelope thought.

"I was hoping you would look into this one, too."

As Penelope headed back to her room to collect her suitcase, she was kicking herself for promising Charlotte that she would see what she could do. It had been sheer luck that she'd figured out Regina's murder one step ahead of the police.

Would she be able to do that again? And not get herself killed in the bargain?

FIVE

※⊙※

"D id Maguire ask you about that button they found near the terrace?" Pen asked Figgy as they checked the drawers in the dresser for any of their belongings they might have missed. "It was quite distinctive."

"He did, but I'm afraid I was no help. I didn't recognize it."

Penelope opened the last drawer in the dresser. Suddenly a thought occurred to her. She rolled it around in her mind for a couple of seconds. Did they dare?

"That button has to be relatively rare," she said. "I've certainly never seen one shaped like a rose before. I wonder if it came off of one of Tobias's jackets. He obviously goes in for unusual things. And I saw him poking around the garden this morning. It was clear he was looking for something, although he denied it when I mentioned it to him."

Figgy paused with her hand on the closet door.

"You're right. It looked like something Tobias would be partial to."

"How about if we sneak into Tobias's room and go through his clothes and check to see if any of his jackets have buttons like the one found outside?"

Figgy gave a little squeak and clapped a hand over her mouth.

"Oh, let's. It will give us something to talk about at cocktail parties for positively ages." Her eyes became huge. "Maybe we'll even crack the case—we'll be a regular Inspector Morse and Sergeant Lewis."

"Whoa," Pen said. "It might backfire. We might get caught. We'll have to be very careful and I don't think we should tell anyone about it."

Figgy looked downcast. "I suppose you're right."

"First we need to find out where Tobias is at the moment. The last I saw of him he was in the drawing room reading the *Financial Times*."

"Great. Let's go check his closet, then."

Pen shook her head. "We need to make sure he's still there reading his paper."

They set off down the corridor and headed toward the drawing room.

The chair Tobias had been sitting in was empty. Jemima was in the room standing with her back to them and in front of a small occasional table with a collection of antique snuffboxes arranged on it.

"Oh," she said, startled, when she turned around and saw Pen and Figgy.

"I was just . . . I was just going."

And she swept past them, leaving behind the scent of her gardenia perfume.

"That was odd," Pen said, glancing after Jemima.

"Yes, it was."

Penelope shrugged. "Well, it's obvious Tobias isn't here."

"Maybe we should abandon the plan?"

Pen shook her head. "Maybe he's gone outside."

A car started up just then. Penelope went to the window and peered out.

Tobias was behind the wheel of a late model Jaguar. As Penelope watched, he headed down the drive and out of sight.

"The coast is clear," she said to Figgy. "That was Tobias driving off."

"Supposing he's packed up and gone home?" Figgy said.

"We'll soon find out," Penelope said.

She had to stifle a giggle as they made their way back upstairs to the bedrooms. She felt like Nancy Drew in the books she'd read as a child, only minus the blue roadster.

Although the hall was empty and there was no one about, Penelope found herself walking along on tiptoe as they approached Tobias's room

"Here it is," Pen said.

"Are you sure?" Figgy whispered.

"Yes. I noticed him going into his room when we went up to change before the ball."

She opened the door slowly and peeked inside, then motioned for Figgy to follow her.

An enormous carved wood armoire was against one wall with a chest of drawers opposite it. The walls were painted a deep rich green that was echoed in the print on the curtains around the four-poster. It was unmade and all the pillows had been pushed to the center.

Figgy gestured toward it. "Looks like Tobias didn't waste any time spreading out into the middle of the bed."

"I'm getting the distinct feeling that he's not all that terribly upset by his wife's murder," Penelope said as she opened the door to the armoire.

Garments were hung on wooden hangers with shoes arranged neatly below. As Penelope flipped through them, the scent of Tobias's aftershave—something bespoke no doubt—filtered into the air.

"That's a relief," Penelope said. "Like you said, he might have already packed up and headed home but it looks as if he's just run an errand."

Penelope examined the other two jackets in the armoire but without any luck. The buttons were all ordinary—the sort you'd find on any men's jackets at Marks and Spencer or Turnbull & Asser.

"Where is that evening jacket he had on last night?" Figgy said, fiddling with the key in the armoire door.

"I must have missed it."

Penelope looked through the garments again.

"It's not here."

"Are you sure?" Figgy said. "Although I suppose it would be hard to miss."

"Why don't you look?"

Figgy went through the garments one by one, then turned to Penelope with a frown. "It's definitely not here. Has he thrown it over the back of a chair or something?" She closed the door to the armoire and began looking around.

"I don't see it," Pen said.

"Neither do I."

"Maybe he sent it down to be cleaned or pressed?" Penelope said, picturing scenes she'd watched on *Downton Abbey*.

"Or maybe he got rid of it." Figgy stood with her hands on her hips. "You said you saw him searching for something in the garden. Maybe it was the button from his jacket. He realized it was missing and that it would place him outside near the terrace at the time of the murder." She raised her eyebrows. "And if he didn't kill Cissie, maybe he saw who did." She snapped her fingers. "Or perhaps he hired someone to do the deed and wanted to make sure it had been done before he paid up."

"That makes more sense," Pen said. "If he'd seen the murderer himself, I would think he'd have told the police."

I'll be glad to get back to my little cottage," Pen said as she and Figgy got ready to leave Worthington House.

"I don't know," Figgy said, looking around. "I've rather enjoyed the luxury myself."

They were passing the drawing room on their way to the front entrance, where Charlotte had arranged for the chauffeur to meet them and drive them into town, when they heard voices—Charlotte and another woman. Charlotte sounded distressed.

Penelope paused by the entrance to the room and looked inside. Charlotte was talking to a maid holding a feather duster. There was a bandage on her left hand and Pen recognized her as the same woman she'd seen bringing out the tray of teacups at the ball the previous night.

"Yes, your grace," they heard the maid say as she left the room.

"Is something wrong?" Pen said, stepping through the doorway. The room smelled of lemon furniture polish, and all the wood pieces gleamed in the sun coming through the tall windows.

Charlotte's brows were drawn together in a frown and she was wringing her hands.

"A snuffbox has gone missing," Charlotte said, pointing to the small table next to one of the armchairs. "It's a rather special one. I bought it for Arthur to celebrate our engagement. He's been collecting them for years. I felt so lucky to find it." She smiled. "It belonged to a previous duke of Upper Chumley-on-Stoke and had been sold years ago when Arthur's grandfather racked up considerable gambling debts that needed to be paid off."

"It does sound very special," Figgy said.

Charlotte nodded. "It was silver with a drawing of Worthington House etched on the cover. Arthur was thrilled with it." She wrung her hands again. "And now it's gone missing. I can't imagine what happened to it. I asked Ivy about it—she is usually the one to dust and vacuum this room—but she hadn't noticed it was missing."

"Could it have been knocked off the table somehow?" Pen said, glancing at the armchair whose pleated skirt brushed the ground. "Perhaps under there?" She pointed to the chair.

"I've already looked," Charlotte said. "I even got down on my knees." She knitted her fingers together. "And yesterday I noticed the silver-backed comb was missing from the powder room." She looked around her as if expecting to see that something else had suddenly disappeared. "Nothing has ever gone missing before so I can't believe it's the staff."

Pen and Figgy looked at each other.

"That leaves our guests," Charlotte said. She shook her head. "But I can't believe any of them would stoop to stealing. . . ."

Charlotte made an obvious effort to smile. "I'm sorry. I didn't mean to trouble you with all this. I imagine you're anxious to get home. I'll have Tinley bring the car around."

"Do you suppose one of Charlotte's guests is a kleptomaniac?" Figgy said after Charlotte had left and they were waiting by the door.

"I suppose it's possible."

"A house party with a thief and a murderer," Figgy said, blowing out a puff of air and fluttering her short bangs. "It sounds like an Agatha Christie novel."

Penelope snorted. "Let's just hope it's not like *And Then There Were None*."

Penelope groaned as she opened the front door to her cottage. It really was good to be home. Mrs. Danvers, her tuxedo cat, came around the corner and stared at her balefully, clearly annoyed at Penelope's having left, even though she'd been in Mabel's expert care during Pen's absence.

She wound between Pen's legs, but when Pen bent down to pet her, she stalked off, tail in the air, and sat in the far corner of the room.

Penelope shrugged and put down her suitcase and looked around with satisfaction. The sitting room was small but charming with a large fireplace, windows that looked out onto the high street, and a beamed ceiling. When Penelope first saw it, she'd felt as if she'd stepped into Shakespearean times and it had been love at first sight.

The kitchen was equally charming with an old Aga that kept the room warm and cozy. Penelope filled the kettle and put it on to boil. She was going to have a cup of tea and then head down to the Open Book. She also planned to get some writing done on her third manuscript. Her second book was currently in the hands of her editor and she was in the nail-biting stage of waiting for the editor's suggested revisions.

The teakettle whistled and Penelope rinsed out her mug with hot water, then added a tea bag and the boiling water from the kettle. Mrs. Danvers seemed to have gotten over her little snit and had come into the kitchen. Either that or she was wondering if food was on order, Penelope thought. This time, though, she did let Penelope scratch behind her ears and under her chin.

Penelope finished her tea and checked Mrs. Danvers's food and water dishes, which were both full. She carried her suitcase up to the bedroom and checked her watch. She'd have to hustle if she was going to get to the Open Book on time.

The Open Book was as charming as Penelope's cottage with its timbered exterior; diamond-paned windows; and low, beamed ceiling. It was warm and welcoming and Penelope always felt like she was coming home when she walked through the door.

"Come to join the hoi polloi, have you?" Mabel said with a smile.

She was behind the front counter, looking more familiar in her corduroy trousers and cable-knit sweater.

"So how was hobnobbing with the nobility? You haven't become too good for us commoners now, have you?"

Pen laughed. "Hardly. I'm thrilled to be back in the normal world. The air in that one is too rarefied for me."

India sidled up to the counter. She came to the Open Book nearly every day and sat in a corner in one of the armchairs Mabel had scattered around, flipping through a stack of books. Penelope knew she lived alone—she supposed she was lonely and enjoyed the convivial atmosphere of the bookstore. Besides, Figgy often gave her goodies from the tea shop—a freshly baked scone, a few pieces of shortbread, or a slice of Victoria sponge cake.

"I missed you at the ball last night," Penelope said to India. Surely India had been invited—she was a relative of Worthington's, even if only a distant cousin.

India waved a hand. "I hung up my dancing shoes years ago, I'm afraid. I was tucked up in bed before the ball even started."

"Was it splendid?" Mabel said, leaning her elbows on the counter.

Figgy had wandered over to join them.

"Didn't you hear? There was a murder."

Both Mabel and India gasped.

"No, really?" Mabel's eyes were wide.

"Yes," Pen said. "I suppose it will be in all the afternoon papers. Someone hit Cissie—Lady Winterbourne—over the head with something and I'm afraid she's dead."

"It couldn't have been an accident?" Mabel said.

Penelope shook her head.

"Poor Arthur." India fingered her pearls. "Having his wedding ball ruined like that."

"I have to say the ball was quite spectacular up to that point." Figgy fiddled with one of the gold studs in her ear, turning it around and around.

"It certainly was," Pen said.

Figgy sighed. "I need to get the tea things sorted," she said. "I'd best get back to work."

A bell jangled as someone pushed open the front door. Gladys came in like a whirlwind, her hair wind whipped and her hat slightly askew.

"There's a right ruckus going on down the street," she said breathlessly. "In front of the stationer's. Did you see it?"

"No." Mabel frowned. "What's happening?"

"Someone was standing in the road—I couldn't tell whether it was a man or a woman dressed in all those baggy clothes as they were. They were waving a large sign with *Yankee Go Home* in black letters dripping with red paint. It gave me quite the fright—for a moment I thought it was actually blood."

Gladys paused to take a breath and snatch off her hat. "Constable Cuthbert got them to move along, but quite a crowd had gathered by then."

Penelope shuddered. Someone had been holding a similar sign in front of Worthington House right before the wedding. She knew that the residents of Chumley resented Worthington's choosing an American to be his bride—many of the mothers had been hoping that their daughters would catch his eye.

But she hadn't expected anyone to actually protest—and with such a gruesome and graphic sign.

Maybe Charlotte had been right and the killer had mistaken Cissie for her and Charlotte had actually been the intended victim all along.

As soon as the members of her book group left—they had been reading and discussing *Jane Eyre*—she carried her laptop into what she called her writing room—a tiny space off the salesroom of the bookstore. There weren't any windows, which was perfect because Penelope didn't want any distractions.

She opened her laptop and powered it up. She hadn't

checked her e-mail since before she'd gone to Worthington House. No doubt her in-box would be full of the usual advertisements, notes letting her know that there was an account with her name on it and a million dollars in it if only she'd hand over her bank account number.

Penelope scrolled through the e-mails. There was one from her sister, Beryl, complaining that the housekeeper had neglected to vacuum under the sofa. Another one was from her mother, wondering when she was going to come home and get serious about finding a husband. Pen sighed. Everyone seemed to have a different vision for her life than the one she had in her own head. She was enjoying her time in Chumley and had no intention of cutting it short.

She was about to click out of her e-mail folder when another one popped up suddenly. Penelope closed her eyes and groaned. It was from her editor, Bettina, in New York. She peeked at the e-mail notice. There was an attachment. She groaned again.

The dreaded request for revisions on her second book, *The Woman in the Fog,* had obviously arrived. Penelope sighed—there was no way of avoiding it—she'd have to read the e-mail sooner or later.

She decided that later would be just fine and powered off her laptop and closed the lid.

SIX

❧

Penelope had been about to summon up her courage and tackle her editor's e-mail when the telephone rang. She couldn't lie—she was glad of the diversion. And she was even happier when the caller turned out to be Detective Maguire inviting her to dinner.

Fortunately, Penelope wasn't the sort who needed a lot of time to get ready to go out. She brushed her hair, checked her sweater for any spots—there were none—powdered her nose, cleaned her glasses, put on her jacket, and headed out the door.

Since the restaurant was within walking distance for each of them—Pen coming from home and Maguire from the police station—they agreed to meet at the Sour Grapes.

It was a wine bar that yearned to be trendy and probably had been twenty years ago but could no longer compare to the up-to-date places in bigger cities like Birmingham, Leeds, or London. The residents of Chumley didn't care—

anyplace that served wine and had a cheese platter on the
menu was bloody slick in their opinion.

Penelope approached the Sour Grapes with a sense of
anticipation. She always enjoyed the time she spent with
Maguire—their relationship was friendly verging on the
romantic. Penelope was still getting over her breakup with
her longtime boyfriend, Miles, and, even though she'd been
planning to dump him, had been quite stung when he'd
dumped her first.

The weather had turned colder and the night sky was
clear with a scattering of stars. Penelope walked briskly,
the frigid air freezing the tips of her ears and turning her
fingers numb. She pulled her collar up and tightened her
scarf around her neck.

The windows of the Sour Grapes were fogged over and
the blast of heat felt heavenly when Penelope pulled open
the door.

The restaurant wasn't terribly crowded—a few people
at the granite-topped bar that ran the length of the room
and several of the best tables already occupied.

Penelope was unwinding her scarf when she felt a gust of
cold air and turned around to see Maguire coming through
the door.

He smiled when he saw her.

"Am I late?" he said breathlessly after planting a brief
kiss on her cheek.

"Not at all. I just got here."

A hostess, in a long skirt and a billowy blouse with
menus tucked under her arm, appeared and led them to a
table toward the back.

"This way you won't feel the cold air when the door
opens," she said as she plunked the menus down on the
table. "It's right bitter out tonight. They say we might even

get a few flurries." She put her hands on her hips. "Would you care for a drink?" She looked at Penelope, her head tilted.

"I'll have a glass of your house red, please."

"And you?" She turned to Maguire.

"A pint of Newcastle Brown Ale for me." He smiled sheepishly at Penelope. "I'm not much of a wine drinker, I'm afraid, even if this is a wine bar."

"It's actually more pub than wine bar," Penelope said, looking around. "I'm beginning to think that every establishment in Chumley turns into a pub at one point or another."

Maguire laughed. "You could be right."

A waitress in black pants and a white shirt with a short apron tied around her waist brought their drinks.

Maguire took a sip of his ale and then licked the foam off his upper lip. Penelope felt her heart flutter just a bit. There was something so endearing about Maguire— certainly a big dose of charm along with a boyish quality and a lack of self-consciousness, which was a change of pace from the sophisticated and hard-driving men she'd known in New York.

"I heard there was quite a scene earlier—someone standing in the middle of the high street protesting."

Maguire ran a hand over his face and Penelope heard the slight rasp of a day's growth of beard.

"Yes. It seems the woman resented the fact that the new Duchess of Upper Chumley-on-Stoke is an American." He whistled. "She was quite the nutter. Put up a real fuss when Constable Cuthbert tried to bring her in."

"Did you arrest her?"

Maguire tapped his glass with a finger. "We could have. It would have been within our rights—creating a public nuisance. But we decided against it. The poor thing needs psychiatric help, not jail time."

"Did you just let her go?"

"Not exactly. A social worker arranged for her to get an appointment with a doctor and a counselor."

"So you don't think she's dangerous?" Penelope hesitated. "Charlotte is afraid that the killer might have actually meant for her to be the target."

"Worthington mentioned that. We don't think it's very likely, but we're looking into it."

"I imagine this is all keeping you very busy," she said.

Maguire let out a gust of air. "Yes. The murder at Worthington House has us all on our toes, that's for sure." He ran a finger down the condensation on the outside of his glass. "It seems that the decision has been made that we're not to be trusted with such a high-profile case. They've decided to call in one of the big boys from the Met—the Metropolitan Police—to take over the investigation."

"Do you think that's Worthington's doing?"

Maguire leaned back in his chair. "Oh, that's almost certain. He wants this cleaned up and fast." He gave a bitter laugh. "He has a honeymoon to go on, after all." He sighed. "He's demanding someone with big-city experience."

"But you used to work in Leeds before you came to Chumley," Penelope protested. "Isn't that a big enough city for him?"

An odd look came over Maguire's face. It made Penelope think of a shade being drawn down or a book closed.

Just then the waitress appeared at their table with a pad and pen in hand.

"Have you decided?" she said without looking at them.

Penelope got the distinct impression that Maguire was quite relieved by the interruption.

* * *

Penelope felt a spark of delight at waking up in her own cottage. Worthington House was terribly grand and filled with beautiful antiques and other expensive furnishings, but she preferred the coziness of her little home on the high street.

Today she was heading to the Open Book to work on a display she'd promised Mabel she would put together in honor of the wedding of Charlotte and Worthington. She was planning to gather an array of titles dealing with princesses and knights in shining armor from Cinderella to Meg Cabot's contemporary take in *The Princess Diaries*.

Mrs. Danvers scowled at Penelope as she retrieved her coat from the closet in the foyer and slipped it on.

"I'll be home again soon enough," she told the cat, who turned her back and stalked off.

Penelope did a last check of Mrs. Danvers's food and water bowls to be sure they were sufficiently full—Mrs. Danvers viewed a half-full bowl with disdain—and then closed the front door of the cottage and headed off down the high street.

She'd decided to walk—she wanted to stop in at the newsstand on her way to the Open Book. The wind was being playful today—lifting the ends of her scarf and blowing them over her face as if it was some sort of childish game. It wasn't as cold as the day before, and Penelope held her face up to the sun that was shining down from a clear blue sky.

She passed the estate agency next to the apothecary and was about to pass the newsstand when she remembered to go in. She thought she would see if the London papers were covering the murder at Worthington House—the local news was usually relegated to the weekly Chumley paper, but this was a fairly high-profile story.

Pen pushed open the door and paused to catch her breath. The place smelled of newsprint and the slick glossy paper of the high-end magazines like *Tatler* and *Horse & Hound*.

Mr. Channa was behind the counter, wearing a bright orange turban. He greeted Penelope with a respectful nod of his head.

Penelope scanned the stacks of London papers and chose the *Daily Telegraph* and, for something more sensational, the *Sun*.

Mr. Channa nodded again as Pen dropped some coins into the palm of his outstretched hand.

"That's a shame—what happened yesterday," he said, shaking his head. "Just because the Duke of Upper Chumley-on-Stoke took an American to be his bride?" His expression was troubled. "It brought back bad memories of when I came to this country."

"Oh? I'm sorry."

"They did not want us here—the British. Many Indians were immigrating to England at the time. There were protests and riots. One young man—Sanjay Banerjee—was even murdered. It was a terrible time for us."

"I didn't know," Penelope said.

Mr. Channa smiled. "As in the famous song by the Beatles, 'all you need is love' to make the world a better place."

Penelope thanked him and was about to leave the shop when a rack of travel brochures caught her eye. She thought she'd take a few home to study—she really ought to see more of England while she was here.

She tucked brochures on the Cotswolds, Stratford-upon-Avon, and the Yorkshire Dales into her tote bag and was about to turn to leave when another brochure caught her eye. She pulled it from the rack. There was a photograph of an impressive home on the front and beneath it the text read *Winterbourne Abbey*.

Penelope began to read. The abbey had belonged to the Winterbourne family—purchased by the first Earl of Doveshire-on-Tweed, Lord Charles Winterbourne—until recently when it was sold to the National Trust.

Now that was odd, Penelope thought as she left the newsstand. Why would the Winterbournes give up the family home?

W hy did they sell? That's easy," Mabel said, when Penelope joined her in the bookstore. "The Winterbournes probably needed the money. A lot of those old families found their bank accounts running dry for various reasons—gambling debts, bad investments, rising costs—running those large houses isn't cheap. There's a whole host of reasons why they might have had to sell."

"But to sell the family home . . ."

"I'm sure they sold off everything they could before resorting to that," Mabel said as she straightened a stack of books on the counter—Charlotte Davenport's latest title, *The Regency Rogue*. "Like artwork, the family silver, bigger and bigger pieces of their land."

"So in other words—"

"In other words, Tobias Winterbourne has a title but no money." Mabel raised an eyebrow. "Although he'll have plenty now thanks to his marriage to Cissie Emmott. She inherited more than enough from her family and I'm assuming some of that will go to Tobias."

"So she got a title and he got a fortune," Penelope said, scanning a nearby shelf for any books that would work for her planned display on princesses and their knights. She pulled a title from the shelf and glanced at the back cover.

"It's not as common as it used to be, but it still goes on," Mabel said, coming out from around the counter. She glanced at the book in Penelope's hand. "Interestingly enough, a lot of the matches involved Americans—women with money sent abroad to find a husband with a title. They were known as dollar princesses."

Mabel leaned against the bookshelf. "It started in eighteen seventy-four when Jennie Jerome—an American—married Lord Randolph Churchill."

"Any relation to—"

Mabel nodded. "Yes. She gave birth to Winston Churchill, the future prime minister." Mabel brushed a speck of lint from her sweater. "The trend continued up until the Second World War. Marriage to a British nobleman was seen as a shortcut to social acceptance for the women and a welcome infusion of cash for the impoverished nobility."

"You don't suppose that Worthington chose Charlotte—"

"Oh, no," Mabel said. "The Worthingtons kept a close watch on their fortune. Worthington has no need for Charlotte's money, which I gather is rather substantial." She tapped the book in Penelope's hand. "Like your fairy-tale princesses', theirs is a love match."

Pen grabbed a copy of M. M. Kaye's *The Ordinary Princess* and added it to the stack in her arms.

Mabel glanced at Pen. "Did you find a copy of *The Princess Bride*? I think that would be a good addition to your selection."

Pen carried the books to the display table set up at the front of the store. She'd covered it with a length of gold cloth she'd bought online. She arranged the books on stands and placed the sign Figgy had made—she was very artistic, Penelope had discovered—in the center along with a rhinestone-covered tiara she'd ordered from a costume shop.

She stood back to examine the display. She rearranged a couple of the books and straightened the cloth where it had bunched up slightly.

"What do you think?" she called to Mabel, who had just finished ringing up a sale.

Mabel came and stood next to Pen. "I like it. It was a wonderful idea, given all the excitement over the Worthington wedding. Very clever." She smiled at Penelope and gave her a quick hug. "I honestly don't know what I did without you."

Penelope felt a warm glow. She reached out and tweaked the position of one of the books.

She had a sudden thought. "Do you suppose it was a love match between Tobias and Cissie? In spite of what they each gained because of it? They seem oddly mismatched somehow."

Mabel brushed a strand of white hair off her forehead. "I don't know. I don't really know anything about them other than that she was known as the Loo Paper Princess in the tabloids. Rather cheeky of them, if you ask me."

As soon as Pen was satisfied with the display, she grabbed the papers she'd bought at the newsstand and sat down at the table in the corner where she held her writing group.

She opened up the *Daily Telegraph* and scanned the headlines on the front page. There was no mention of the murder of Cissie Winterbourne. She found a discreet headline on the second page and quickly skimmed the article. It was short and there wasn't anything she didn't already know.

Hopefully the *Sun* would have something more interesting. A glaring headline in seventy-two-point type was splayed across the front page—Loo Paper Princess Cissie Winterbourne Murdered.

Penelope began reading. The paper recounted the murder in lurid detail—some of it accurate and some of it not but all of it sensational. The story detailed Cissie's early life—schooling at the Oakwood School for Girls, a year at the University of Bedfordshire, and her arrival in London where she became a muse for designer Molly Goddard, who was known, appropriately enough, for her chiffon "princess dresses."

It went on to her life in London—various romances with high-profile men; the opening of her own design studio, Atelier Classique; and finally her marriage to Lord Tobias Winterbourne.

Several paragraphs were devoted to Tobias as well: his illustrious lineage—descended, albeit somewhat distantly, from King William III—his schooling at King's College London, his clubs—Brooks's, the Beefsteak Club, and, rounding it all out, the Turf Club.

The article was lavishly illustrated with photographs—the Winterbourne wedding; the Worthington wedding; Tobias and Cissie in evening dress attending the premiere of the new James Bond film; and one of them at a party, holding glasses of champagne. The picture brought Penelope up short. Cissie was standing facing Tobias who was shoulder to shoulder with another woman. Penelope realized with a start that the other woman was Rose Ainsley.

And in the picture, it looked very much as if Tobias and Rose were a couple—not Tobias and Cissie. Had they been?

She wondered if Charlotte had any idea. Penelope pulled her cell phone from her pocket and punched in Charlotte's number.

Charlotte answered on the third ring sounding somewhat breathless.

"Am I interrupting you?" Penelope said, folding up the newspaper.

"I've just come back from a run," Charlotte said. "I had to get out in the air to clear my head. My protagonist is being difficult, but I came up with a solution fortunately."

Penelope laughed. "I know what you mean." She thought of the e-mail from her editor still sitting in her in-box but banished the thought. She'd get to it later.

She asked Charlotte if Tobias and Rose had ever been an item, but Charlotte said she didn't know. She suggested Penelope talk to Jemima, who had been friends with them a lot longer than Charlotte had.

Penelope clicked off the call and sat drumming her fingers against the table.

Had Tobias been dating Rose when Cissie came along? Had he dumped Rose for the loo paper heiress? And did that make Rose mad enough to kill?

SEVEN

~◦~

Penelope hoped she'd be able to catch Jemima while she was still at Worthington House. She didn't have her cell phone number but instead called Worthington's main number.

A very solemn-sounding butler answered the telephone and promised that he would find Lady Dougal for Penelope.

Pen pictured him tirelessly traversing the maze of corridors that made up Worthington House, peering into rooms and around corners for Jemima. The image made her giggle.

Five minutes later Jemima's throaty voice came over the line. She suggested they meet for lunch—she was starving and absolutely dying for a pub lunch—and offered to pick Penelope up in twenty minutes.

Penelope straightened up her things; put on her coat, hat, and gloves; and went to stand outside to watch for Jemima's car. It was windy and the wooden sign over the Open Book creaked on its pole as it was buffeted back and forth.

Penelope stamped her feet and blew on her hands to

warm them. She was about to go back inside when a sleek black Mercedes drew up to the curb and stood, purring in idle.

The car was low-slung and Penelope had to bend nearly double in order to slip into the front passenger seat.

Jemima put her hand on the gearshift, her massive diamond engagement ring shooting sparks in the sunlight, stepped on the gas, and they pulled away from the curb with a loud roar.

"There's a lovely pub just outside of town between Upper Chumley-on-Stoke and Lower Chumley-on-Stoke called the Wolf and the Weasel. They do an excellent ploughman's lunch and a truly magnificent steak and kidney pie," Jemima said, glancing in the rearview mirror. "Rather plebian fare, but sometimes one wants something straightforward and simple—the sorts of things that Nanny used to make for us in the nursery."

She took the road leading out of town at a brisk clip, but her hands were steady on the wheel. The sports car hugged the road as they rounded the sharp curves in what had become a country lane with fields on either side where cows grazed, blinking lazily at them as they sped by.

There were a handful of other vehicles in the parking lot when they pulled in—two muddy pickup trucks; a Vauxhall Astra with rust around the wheel wells; and an older model Mercedes station wagon with a saddle, riding boots; and a friendly-looking English sheepdog with a lolling pink tongue in the back.

A wooden sign, similar to the one over the Open Book, hung outside with *The Wolf and the Weasel* in Gothic lettering and an outline of the two animals.

Jemima pointed to the sign as they walked toward the pub.

"In the old days, most people couldn't read. Schooling was only for the wealthy—hardworking farmers had no need for books. The pictures on the pub signs became a way of identifying them—the white horse, the red rooster, and so forth. Even if you couldn't read, you would recognize the pictures."

The interior of the pub was dim with a ceiling crossed with wooden beams, a large stone fireplace, and simple wooden tables and chairs. The brass handles of the beer pumps gleamed in the low light and bottles were lined up in a row on a shelf above them.

Two men in worn and stained overalls sat at the bar, their calloused hands wrapped around their sweating tankards of ale. Two women in jodhpurs, tall leather boots, and heavy sweaters sat at one of the tables.

"Will this do?" Jemima said, pulling out a chair at a table near the front window. She took a seat and slipped off her coat.

A waitress appeared at their side as Penelope was sitting down.

Jemima pointed across the room. "The menu is on the board there. I highly recommend the steak and kidney pie."

The word *kidney* was a bit off-putting, Penelope thought, but nothing ventured, nothing gained, as her grandmother used to say.

"Now," Jemima said, straightening the silk scarf around her neck, "what is it you wanted to talk to me about? I have to admit to being intrigued." She laughed. "As if we haven't had enough mysteries already." She crossed her arms and settled her elbows on the table.

Penelope cleared her throat. She had no idea how Jemima would react to being questioned about her friends. Fortunately the English rarely created a fuss, and if they did, they did it quietly. It was unlikely that Jemima would embarrass her in a public place.

"I've been thinking about Cissie's murder."

Jemima rolled her eyes. "Haven't we all? I do wish they would find out who did it. Surely it was some stranger who'd wandered onto the grounds?"

"But why kill Cissie?"

Jemima shrugged her shoulders. "Who knows? Perhaps they'd planned to steal her jewelry—she was wearing that magnificent diamond necklace Tobias bought her as a wedding gift—but they were scared off by the start of the fireworks."

"I was, ahem"—Penelope cleared her throat again—"actually wondering about Tobias."

Penelope tried to summon any wisp of tact she might possess—her mother often said she was as tactful as a bludgeon—in order to approach what even she knew was a delicate subject—suspecting someone's friend of murder.

Jemima tilted her head to the side and looked at Penelope curiously. "You don't seriously think Tobias did it, do you?"

"Did Tobias and Cissie get along well?" Penelope said, steering clear of Jemima's question.

Jemima stopped with her hand halfway to the glass of white wine the waitress had brought her.

"You really do think Tobias killed Cissie, don't you?"

"Well . . ."

"It's an interesting thought." Jemima took a sip of her chardonnay. "Theirs wasn't exactly what you'd call a match made in heaven." She leaned closer to Penelope and lowered her voice. "Tobias didn't have any money. Apparently the family lost it all at some point. They were living in one of the cottages on the estate after the manor house was sold to the National Trust.

"Tobias resented their loss in status—they kept their titles of course, but he liked the good life. Memberships in the likes of Brooks's and the Turf Club don't come cheap. Nor do bespoke suits from Savile Row." Jemima's diamond ring clinked against her glass as she picked it up.

Or fancy velvet evening jackets, Penelope thought.

"He vowed to marry a rich woman and he succeeded. Cissie's family has pots of money."

"Did they get along? Or did they fight a lot?"

Jemima fiddled with the salt and pepper shakers. "They got along reasonably well. They'd each gotten what they wanted—for Tobias that was money and for Cissie it was the title. I'm sure being Lady Winterbourne gave her a leg up in the fashion business." Jemima shrugged. "At least it didn't hurt."

The waitress arrived with their order. The golden crust on the steak and kidney pie looked delicious, but Penelope was still filled with trepidation about what lurked beneath. She poked at it uncertainly with her fork.

"Of course, Tobias never did get over Rose—Rose Ainsley." Jemima dabbed her lips with her napkin.

Penelope was so startled that her hand jumped and knocked her fork to the floor. She bent to pick it up.

"Tobias and Rose were in love. We all assumed they would get married. But then Cissie came along and things changed. Rose's family didn't have any money, you see." Jemima took a bite of her pie and chewed with relish. "In the end, I guess Cissie's money was too tempting to resist."

The waitress glided by their table with a tray laden with dishes perched on her shoulder. She smoothly slid a clean fork in front of Penelope. Penelope turned to say thank you, but the girl was already making her way through the swinging door into the kitchen.

"We all told Tobias he was making a bargain with the devil, but he didn't want to listen," Jemima said.

Penelope thought back to the night after the ball. She remembered hearing a door open and the sound of someone making their way down the hall. Then there had been the sound of another door opening and closing. Had Rose been sneaking down to Tobias's room now that Cissie was out of the way?

"Do you think it's possible that Rose . . . killed Cissie?" Penelope stuck her fork into her pie.

Jemima cocked an eyebrow. "If I'd been dumped for someone else, just because the other woman had money, I'd be roaring mad," Jemima said coyly. "Wouldn't you?"

P̲enelope decided it was time to get serious about those revision requests waiting on her computer. She couldn't avoid them forever. She'd had a glass of wine at lunch with Jemima, which ought to dull the horror, so this was the perfect time to get cracking.

She got her laptop going and drummed her fingers impatiently as the screen slowly came to life. Now that she'd made up her mind, she was anxious to get going.

She found Bettina's e-mail, opened it up, and began to read.

Darling, this is absolutely wonderful. I can already see this on the bestseller lists. Just a few teensy edits before we put it into production. Parts of the

middle seem to lack tension. Seriously, darling, they
were an absolute snooze fest at times. Can we
tighten those up a bit?

Penelope chewed on a cuticle. She'd been worried about
that herself. At the time, she'd had no idea how to fix it
and she prayed she'd have some sort of epiphany now. She
read on.

I'm afraid the character of Raoul just isn't coming
across the way he should. Really, Pen, what is wrong
with that man? Maybe a hint of backstory would help?

Penelope groaned. She'd had trouble bringing Raoul
into focus during the writing—hopefully she could pull it
off now.

Other than those few tiny things, and some of my
comments on the manuscript itself, I think we're
almost there! I trust you to work your magic and
make this positively shine.

Penelope rubbed her hands over her face. Work her
magic, indeed. There was nothing magic about it—it was
more like pure nose to the grindstone.

But she could do it. She had to do it.

Penelope put her head down and got to work. An hour
later, she thought she'd solved the problem of Raoul—
Bettina had been right—adding in a bit of his backstory
was all that had been needed. She glanced at her watch and
was relieved to see it was time for her book group.

She powered down her laptop and closed the lid with a
sense of satisfaction. She always felt better when she tack-

led a problem headon—the key was to remember that whenever a difficult challenge arose.

Penelope put on her coat, tucked her laptop under her arm, and headed to the Open Book where her book group was meeting. Mabel had set up a cozy spot in the bookstore for them. It was furnished with worn but comfortable chairs that simply invited you to sink into them and relax.

India was the first to arrive. She hung up her coat and smoothed out the wrinkles in her cardigan sweater. Penelope noticed some areas where it had obviously been darned.

India was proud of her aristocratic lineage, although sadly it came with very little money. She lived in a cottage on the Worthington estate that could have used some repairs, but India kept the stiff upper lip ubiquitous to the British and never complained. Keeping up appearances meant everything to her.

"Dreadful business isn't, it?" she said as she nestled into one of the chairs. "I wonder if the police have caught the killer? I don't suppose you've heard anything . . ."

"Sorry, no," Pen said. "Only what's been in the papers."

"*Hrumph*," India said as she settled deeper into her chair.

Violet arrived next, floating in like a wraith, her black wool coat, navy blue skirt, and sweater hanging on her thin frame and looking as if they were still on the hanger and her sparse hair curling around her face.

"What an honor to have your dear husband perform the royal wedding ceremony," India said as she accepted a cup of tea from Figgy, who had arrived with a tea cart laden with cups and saucers and a jam roly-poly on a cake stand.

India's face brightened. "Thank you, dear." She smiled at Figgy.

"Reverend Thatcher must have been right chuffed to

have been chosen to officiate," Figgy said as she cut slices of cake and arranged them on plates. "He did us proud. Was he nervous?" She handed Violet some cake.

Violet sat up straighter and a bit of color actually came into her face.

"He was, rather. But I assured him that he would do just fine. He always does."

"Hello, hello." A fluty voice floated toward them and Gladys appeared around the corner. "I'm here," she said, panting slightly, her face as red as a beet. "I got my brother-in-law to mind the shop while I'm gone, God help us all."

Gladys collapsed into a chair seemingly oblivious to the fact that she was still wearing her butcher's apron with bloodstains all down the front.

Gladys pulled her copy of *Jane Eyre*, the book they were reading, out of the pocket of her apron. Pen noticed that the cover was creased and there was a splotch of grease on it.

"This book is rubbish," Gladys said, stabbing the cover with her index finger.

India looked affronted. "Why do you say that?"

"Jane was a right doormat, wasn't she? Putting up with all that aggro from that so-and-so Mr. Rochester. If I were Jane I would have given him what for."

"I thought he was rather romantic," Violet said with a dreamy look in her eyes. She clutched her copy of *Jane Eyre* to her chest.

India raised an eyebrow. "Romantic? I wouldn't say that. Tormented maybe."

"Anyway," Gladys said, taking a deep breath, "I've got to tell you something. You won't believe who came into the shop." Her smile disappeared and her face hardened. "And I have to say I didn't take to her at all." She set her jaw and straightened her shoulders.

Everyone turned toward her, a variety of curious expressions on their faces.

Finally, India said, "Do tell us, Gladys," in a slightly exasperated tone.

Gladys shot India a sharp look. "I'm getting to it. Let me tell it in my own time, if you don't mind."

"Yes, of course," Penelope said soothingly with a glance at India.

Gladys took a deep breath. "The new detective from the Met came into the shop looking for one of me Cornish pasties this afternoon."

India, Violet, and Figgy exchanged curious looks. All eyes were now trained on Gladys.

It was obvious she relished the attention. She drew herself up straight and assumed the air of an actor about to perform a monologue.

"It seems that the powers that be have decided to call in the Met to investigate the murder at Worthington House." She frowned. "They don't trust our local bobbies to do the job properly."

"Well," India said huffily.

Gladys nodded. "And she's a right stuck-up little miss, too, if I must say so myself. No warmth," she said decisively. "Attractive enough but no warmth, if you know what I mean."

"What did she look like?" Violet said. "One of those stone-faced career women?"

Gladys tilted her head to one side and rubbed her chin.

"Not exactly. She was pretty—blond hair, blue eyes, a fine English complexion. Smartly dressed, too, in one of those pantsuits women seem to fancy these days." Gladys paused. "But she gave me a right chill, she did. A real cold fish."

"Poor Detective Maguire," India said. "What will become of him?"

"He'll be left twiddling his fingers, I should imagine," Gladys said. "But I didn't tell you the whole of it. I overheard the little miss on her cell phone. It seems the police have found the murder weapon that was used to kill that poor woman up at Worthington House."

An audible gasp ran through the group.

"Well, what was it?" India's tone was becoming increasingly waspish.

"It was one of them sticks the toffs play polo with. Seems it had been tossed in that wooded area down by the river. Some young lads found it and were bright enough to realize they should take it to the police." Gladys took a deep breath and pulled down her sweater. "The police are sending it away for . . . Oh, blimey, what's that called again?" She looked around the group.

"I suspect they're sending it for what's called forensic analysis," India said crisply. She was a fan of true crime shows and was proud of her knowledge of police procedure.

A polo mallet, Penelope thought. There was something about a polo mallet she ought to remember, but the memory was tantalizingly out of reach.

They were halfway through their discussion of *Jane Eyre* when Penelope remembered.

"Oh!" she said.

Everyone's head swiveled in her direction.

"Sorry," she waved a hand. "Something just occurred to me. What was that you were saying, Violet?"

Penelope wasn't listening to the answer. She was thinking about the polo mallet and how Worthington had claimed that his had gone missing before the polo game the day before his wedding.

Was that the one that had been used to kill Cissie? And if so, would it implicate Worthington in her death?

Cissie was Worthington's ex-girlfriend. Had there been some sort of unfinished business between them that no one knew about? Or was Cissie really planning to write one of those tell-all memoirs that Charlotte had talked about?

And had that led to her murder?

EIGHT

ᴖᵔᴖ

Penelope, however, didn't believe for one minute that Worthington had killed Cissie. But that didn't mean that the police wouldn't peg him as a suspect now that the polo mallet had been found. Of course they didn't know if it was Worthington's missing one, but Penelope felt the odds were good that that was exactly what it would turn out to be.

Poor Charlotte, Pen thought. She'd been through enough already—the last thing she needed was for her new husband to be suspected of murder. Instead of dealing with all this, she ought to be on her honeymoon right now, basking in the warm sun in the Seychelles.

Penelope thought about Tobias. She remembered a quote from a book by motivational speaker Zig Ziglar that her sister had urged her to read, hoping that it would spur her on to get a "real" career—"The first step to getting what you want is having the courage to get rid of what you don't want."

Was that what Tobias had done? He'd wanted money so he'd dumped Rose and married Cissie. Then, once he had the money, he'd gotten rid of Cissie so he would be free to continue his romance with Rose, his true love.

He had a strong motive, he had the means, and then there was that button found outside the ballroom. Tobias had been looking for something in the garden the morning after the murder. And the distinctive jacket he'd worn to the wedding ball had disappeared from his room.

That gave Penelope an idea. But she didn't want to do it alone—she needed a partner in crime. She went in search of Figgy.

It was nearly five o'clock and Figgy was closing up her tea shop for the night—going through the register and preparing the day's deposit.

"What's up?" she said when she saw Penelope approach. "You look excited about something."

"Not excited maybe, but certainly intrigued." Pen leaned on the counter and helped herself to one of the shortbread cookies Figgy had on a plate next to the cash register. "You know how we couldn't find Tobias's dinner jacket in his room?"

"Yes."

"Let's assume he got rid of it because it might incriminate him. What would he do with it?"

"I don't know. Throw it in the woods or something?"

"I think Tobias is more clever than that. The jacket might be found and he couldn't deny it was his—we all saw him in it." Pen nibbled on the cookie. "No, I think he gave it away to a thrift store or charity shop. There it would all but disappear amid all the other jackets and donated gar-

ments. And whoever buys it will go off who knows where
with it."

Figgy paused with her hand on the till drawer. "There's
an Oxfam shop right by the roundabout at the top of the high
street. Oh!" She clapped a hand to her mouth. "Remember
we saw Tobias speeding off in that sports car of his the
morning after the ball? Maybe that's where he was going!"

"You could be right." Penelope glanced at her watch.
"It's almost five o'clock. I suppose they'll be closing any
minute."

Figgy shook her head. "It's their late night tonight. Let
me finish counting up the change and then we'll go."

The Oxfam shop, like all the other buildings in Chumley, was half-timbered and had a bright green sign
hanging from a pole outside. A display of women's hats, including some very creative fascinators, was in the window.

Inside, garments were neatly displayed on racks or
shelves. A salesclerk with steel gray hair pulled back into a
tidy bun and wearing a plaid kilt and Shetland sweater, was
straightening the dress on one of the mannequins. She
turned around and smiled when she heard Pen and Figgy
come in.

"Can I help you?" she said politely.

"We're looking for the men's section," Pen said, glancing around.

"The back right corner, over there." The woman pointed
in that direction.

They were passing a rack of women's jackets when
Figgy suddenly stopped short.

"Look at this," she said, taking a garment off the hanger

and holding it up. It was a faux fur vest in bright purple. "My favorite color," Figgy said, slipping it on.

"It's so terribly . . . nineteen seventies," Pen said, a smile hovering around her lips. "It reminds me of pictures I've seen of rock groups from that era."

"I know. Isn't it wonderful? It's so Mott the Hoople or Elton John. I have to have it."

Figgy tucked the vest under her arm and followed Pen to the men's section. They began to go through the jackets—most were ordinary—corduroy or wool in solids and plaids.

"Now what?" Figgy said when they came to the end of the rack and hadn't found Tobias's jacket. "Maybe Tobias took it somewhere else?"

"Could be," Pen said. "Why don't we ask the saleslady? Maybe somebody already bought it. She's bound to remember it if it was here."

"Excuse me," Pen said. "We're looking for a men's dinner jacket that someone might have brought in. It's not on the rack and we wondered if it might still be in the back somewhere?"

The woman sighed. "Was it given away by mistake? Or did they leave something important in one of the pockets?" She sighed again. "You won't believe how often that happens."

"Mmmm, not exactly," Pen said. "We only wondered if you've ever seen it."

The woman tilted her head. "Okay," she said uncertainly. "What did it look like?"

"It was a midnight blue burned velvet dinner jacket. Quite distinctive."

"Not your ordinary dinner jacket," Figgy added.

The woman's face cleared. "Of course. I remember it well. It came in only yesterday but we've already sold it," she said with an air of a job well done.

"You don't happen to know who purchased it by any chance?"

Penelope knew it was a long shot but there was no harm in asking.

"As a matter of fact, I do. It was a young man who said he plans to wear it while he's performing. It seems he's in some sort of rock and roll group. He said it would be perfect." The woman's face flushed. "He was quite charming. And quite good-looking, too," she added almost as an afterthought.

"Did he mention the name of the group?" Figgy said.

"Let me see." The woman bit her lip. "It was one of those daft names young people come up with these days." She closed her eyes as she thought. "Now I remember!" Her face brightened. "They're called the Foggy Bottoms." She laughed. "Like I said, some of these names are right daft."

"I've heard worse," Pen said, thinking of a group she'd heard in college named the Flounder March. "Did he say if he was from around here?"

The woman lifted her shoulders and let them drop. "Not in so many words, but I got the impression he knew his way around Chum."

"Thank you," Pen said with sincerity. "You've been really helpful."

The woman flushed again. "I'm glad I could help. Is there anything else I can do for you?"

"I'll take this," Figgy said, putting the purple fur vest on the counter.

The woman smiled at Figgy indulgently and rang up the sale.

"I guess that's that," Figgy said as she pulled away from the curb outside the Oxfam shop. "Fancy a quick drink at the Book and Bottle?"

The Book and Bottle was the Upper Chumley-on-Stoke pub, or, as the residents referred to it, "their local."

The parking lot was barely bigger than a handkerchief, but Figgy managed to squeeze her car into a space between an overbearing Land Rover and a Volvo SUV, a maneuver that had Penelope briefly holding her breath and closing her eyes.

Figgy beeped the car locks and they walked around to the entrance of the Book and Bottle. A sandwich board was propped up on the sidewalk outside, announcing that the Book and Bottle was now featuring live music.

Figgy gestured to the sign. "Looks like the Book and Bottle wants to one-up the competition. Not that there's much completion in Chum."

Pen was about to open the door when she stopped short.

"What did that sign say?" she said, glancing at the sandwich board again. "Look," she cried, pointing to the sign. "The group they're featuring tonight is the Foggy Bottoms. The clerk at Oxfam said she sold Tobias's jacket to a member of that band."

"I guess we're in the right place, then," Figgy said as they walked inside.

All the seats at the bar were taken, but a couple of tables were still available. They chose one and Penelope went up to the bar with their order.

A bored-looking barmaid in a Renaissance style uniform, with a puffed-sleeves, low-cut blouse and a corset-style vest, a micromini skirt, and thigh-high leather boots, appeared.

"Two ciders, please," Pen said. "By the way"—she gestured toward the makeshift stage set up at the back of the pub—"when does the music start?"

"When they're good and ready I should think," she said. "They ought to be on now, the slackers."

Pen carried their drinks back to the table and sat down.

She was taking her first sip when a discordant guitar chord echoed through the pub. She swiveled around in her seat. Foggy Bottoms was slowly assembling onstage.

"I'll be right back," she said to Figgy as she pushed back her chair.

"Good luck," Figgy shouted after her.

Penelope approached the stage. The guitar player was wearing a plaid shirt with the sleeves rolled up—no jacket. The drummer had on a vest over a T-shirt with a saying on it—Penelope couldn't quite see all the words.

She hovered on the fringes of the stage as the guitar player tuned his instrument and the drummer warmed up with random bits on the drums. Finally, two other band members emerged from the storeroom at the back of the pub.

And one of them was wearing Tobias's jacket.

It was unmistakable in both fabric and design. Penelope watched as he crossed the stage and began to fiddle with the microphone, alternately raising and lowering it until it was just right. He leaned forward, tapped it, and said, "Testing, testing, one, two, three."

"Excuse me," Penelope said, raising her voice to be heard above the din in the increasingly crowded pub.

The young man turned around. His eyes were dark blue and fringed with thick black lashes. The blue velvet of the jacket intensified their color.

He smiled at Penelope, revealing strong even teeth. "What can I do for you?" he said amiably, running a hand through his slightly shaggy hair.

Penelope took a deep breath. "Did you purchase your jacket at the local Oxfam?"

A frown clouded the young man's brow. "Yes. What of it?" He stood with his arms crossed over his chest. "The owner want it back or something?"

"No, no, nothing like that." Penelope hastened to reassure him. "I have a rather odd question, I'm afraid."

The young man sat down on the edge of the stage and rested his elbows on his knees.

"Shoot," he said.

"Is . . . is the jacket missing a button by any chance?"

The young man looked startled. "I don't know. I haven't tried to button it, to be honest with you." He looked down at the jacket and fingered the buttonholes. "What do you know?" He looked up at Pen with a surprised expression. "There is a button missing." He frowned. "How did you know that?"

Penelope shook her head. "It's complicated," she said with a smile. "Do you mind if I have a look?"

A strange expression crossed his face and Penelope realized that he thought she was flirting with him! Well, so what. She was far more interested in helping solve Cissie's murder, but he didn't need to know that.

The young man shrugged noncommittally. "Sure. I guess it's okay."

Pen examined the two remaining buttons and wasn't in the least surprised to see they matched the one that the police had found in the garden at Worthington House.

"Thanks," she said. "But I have to warn you that the police might be interested in knowing that. As a matter of fact, I think you'd better take that jacket down to the station so they can have a look. I'm sure they will return it when they are finished with it."

"But why?"

Penelope sighed. "It's possibly related to a murder inquiry."

The young man's startled expression intensified to an almost comical degree. Before he could ask any further questions, Penelope turned around and went back to her seat at the table with Figgy.

"Well?" Figgy said, raising her eyebrows so high they disappeared under her bangs.

"It's Tobias's jacket all right," Pen said as she picked up her glass of cider. "And it's most definitely missing a button. A very unusual button that looks exactly like the one the police found in the garden at Worthington House."

NINE

꿎

Penelope was behind the counter with Mabel, looking through a catalogue, when a woman came in carrying two books in her hands. She was older with gray hair in regimented waves and was wearing a black coat open over a floral-print dress.

Penelope heard Mabel groan and when Pen looked at her, Mabel rolled her eyes and whispered, "It's Cynthia Parfitt again."

Penelope raised her eyebrows but by then Cynthia had reached the counter.

"Good morning, Mrs. Parfitt," Mabel said in a tone of resignation.

"Lovely day, isn't it?" Cynthia smiled and placed the books on the counter.

"What do we have here?" Mabel said, glancing at the titles.

Cynthia tapped one of the books with her finger. "I want

to return these, love. I'm afraid I picked up the wrong titles."

"Again?" Mabel said.

Cynthia didn't look in the least bit embarrassed. She smiled broadly. "I'm afraid so."

Mabel gave her a stern look, but Cynthia either didn't notice or didn't care.

Penelope picked up the books. The spine was cracked on one of them and they both looked rather . . . grubby, she thought.

"I can't give you your money back," Mabel said, filling out a slip. "It will have to be a store credit this time."

"That's fine," Cynthia said, taking the slip from Mabel. "I'll just go find the correct titles, then, shall I?"

"What gives?" Penelope said when Cynthia was out of earshot.

"She's done this several times," Mabel said, watching as Cynthia retreated to the back of the store. "And she's not the only one. Old Mr. Crankshaw does the same thing— always claiming he got the wrong book and bringing it back a week later, clearly having been read."

Penelope frowned. "Can't you refuse to sell them anything?"

"I'm afraid it would cause considerable ill will in the community if I did that. If the books come back too damaged or dirty to sell, I put them on the used bookshelf. Since they're usually new titles, they get snapped up quite quickly."

"You're too kind," Penelope said. She stretched her arms overhead. "I think I'm going to get some writing done if that's okay with you."

"You go on ahead," Mabel said.

Penelope had had an idea for tackling one of the revisions that her editor wanted. It had come to her in the middle of the night and she'd flipped on the light, startling Mrs. Danvers, who had quickly retreated under the bed. She'd scribbled a few words down on the notepad by her bed; and when she'd looked at them this morning, they'd appeared nearly indecipherable, though she'd managed to make out enough to jog her memory.

She tossed her coat over the back of her chair, swung her laptop onto the table, and powered it up. She'd make a few notes now while the idea was still relatively fresh in her mind.

As soon as she'd finished that, Pen gave some thought to the next Open Book newsletter. She'd had the idea to encourage reader involvement by inviting them to make suggestions—in the previous newsletter it had been to recommend books worth reading twice.

Her fingers hovered over the keys as she thought about various possibilities. A lot of the Open Book's customers were avid romance readers—perhaps something to do with that genre?

Finally, Pen had an idea. She would ask them whether they preferred alpha or beta male leads in their books and which romance novel character best embodied their choice.

She began fleshing out an article on various male protagonists in romances—Darcy from *Pride and Prejudice*, Michael Phan in *The Kiss Quotient*, Brandon Birmingham from Kathleen E. Woodiwiss's *The Flame and the Flower*. She finished the piece by inviting readers to send in their choices.

By the time Penelope closed her laptop, Mabel was standing alone behind the counter.

"How was your trip to Oxfam yesterday? Any luck?"

"Yes, as a matter of fact." Pen told her about tracking down Tobias's dinner jacket and confirming that the missing button was the one found by the police.

"Now if we could find someone who saw Tobias go out to the terrace around the time Cissie was killed."

"If anyone at the ball had seen something, I imagine they would have told the police by now." Mabel picked a dead leaf off the philodendron plant she kept on the counter. "But what about someone who wasn't a guest? The butler or maid or the gardener. Although I don't suppose a gardener would be working that late at night."

Penelope felt as if she'd been struck by lightning. She snapped her fingers. "There was a company that put on the fireworks display on the lawn. Perhaps one of the workers saw something."

"Are you going to tell Detective Maguire about finding the missing dinner jacket?" Mabel brushed an errant strand of hair off her forehead and tucked it behind her ear.

"I've invited him for dinner tonight. I'll tell him then. Although with the detective from the Met in charge of the case, I don't know if it will be of any help to him."

Mabel raised her eyebrows. "You're having him to dinner? Sounds like things are getting serious." She smiled.

"We enjoy each other's company," Pen admitted. And that's all she was going to admit to, she thought. Even she wasn't sure exactly what her feelings were.

"What are you making for him? Something typically American?"

"You mean like hot dogs and beans?" Pen said with a laugh. "No, I'm making a good old Yankee beef stew from my grandmother Parish's recipe. I'm going to stop at the Pig in a Poke to get some beef stew meat later."

Mabel glanced at her watch. "You'd better go now then. They often run out of things later in the day."

Penelope slipped on her coat and dashed across the high street to the butcher shop. A large cutout of a pink and smiling pig hung in the window and was depicted on the wooden sign hanging over the door.

Gladys was standing behind the counter, against a backdrop of hanging sides of beef, tying up a package of pork chops for a customer. She handed over the butcher paper–wrapped parcel, rang up the sale, and deposited the pound notes the customer gave her in the till.

She smiled at Penelope as she approached the counter.

"What do you know," Gladys said. "My customer and I were just talking about the Worthington wedding. The duchess looked so beautiful. I saw all the pictures in the *Sun*. Quite a treat to have something like that right in our midst." Her round, apple cheeks were flushed red. The shop was quite warm, and Pen unbuttoned her coat.

Gladys frowned. "But so sad about the murder spoiling the duke and duchess's celebration. Who would have thought something like that would happen?"

The bell over the door tinkled and a woman walked in. She was wearing a plain black coat over a simple dress with a white apron tied around her waist. Penelope recognized her as the maid helping to serve at the Worthington's ball. Pen remembered she'd had a bandage on her hand, but it was gone now.

"Ivy," Gladys said, giving the woman a smile. "What can I get for you today?"

Ivy gave a brief smile in return, showing a gap between her two front teeth. "The duke has a taste for pork tonight," Ivy said. "Cook is making a pork roast stuffed with mushrooms." She snorted. "Waste of a good piece of meat if you ask me. Mother used to serve it roasted on Sundays with a nice gravy and what a treat it was." She put her shopping basket on the counter. "Cook would have come himself, but he's worn out what with all the cooking for the wedding breakfast and the ball, not to mention his knee is bothering him again, so I told him I'd come get it myself."

"That was quite a celebration," Penelope said. "I imagine you're all tired."

Ivy gave her a suspicious look.

"Everything was splendid, including the fireworks. Did the staff put those on?" Penelope said.

Ivy gave her a look that clearly said she thought Penelope was daft.

"Hardly. The duke had to bring in a firm from London to do them. Our little crew here in Chumley weren't good enough, even though they do a fine job of it every Guy Fawkes Day." Ivy sniffed. "But they did have Bert Digby helping out. He's the one that does them here in Chumley."

"Oh?" Pen said. "He's local, then?"

Ivy nodded. "He runs a garage just outside of town. Took it over from his father when old man Digby had that stroke that crippled him."

"I think my MINI could use a tune-up," Pen said nonchalantly. "You don't happen to know the name of the garage, do you?"

Once again Ivy looked at her as if she was daft. "It's called Digby's, of course. What else would it be?"

Ivy turned her back on Pen and began chatting with Gladys. Gladys wrapped up Ivy's pork roast and handed it over.

"I'll put it on the account, shall I?" Gladys said.

"That would be fine," Ivy said as she dropped the package into her shopping basket.

Pen watched as she left the shop and handed the basket to a young man who had been hovering near the door. Together they walked on down the high street. Penelope turned back to Gladys. Gladys shook her head. "She's a hard worker, that Ivy Brown. A bit of a strange one too, if you ask me."

Pen stuck her head into the Open Book to tell Mabel she was going to get some lunch and then headed back to her cottage. Mrs. Danvers was waiting by the door when Pen opened it. She followed Pen into the kitchen, where Penelope put her beef stew meat in the refrigerator and pulled out a container of leftover tikka masala from Kebabs and Curries, which was at the end of the high street near the new Tesco, heated it up in the microwave, and ate it standing over the sink.

She rinsed out the container, slipped her coat back on, and grabbed her car keys from the hook by the back door.

Pen opened the door to her MINI, slung her purse onto the passenger seat, and got in. She started the engine and carefully pulled away from the curb, being sure to check her rear and side mirrors.

She didn't have far to go and managed the mile or so without once straying onto the wrong side of the road—something she was inclined to do when she'd first started driving in Chumley. She mentally patted herself on the back. It looked as if she was finally getting the hang of driving in England.

The parking lot of the Tesco was full with a Vauxhall station wagon jockeying for a space a Ford Gulf was about to vacate when Pen went past, and the rich scent of exotic spices drifted into her car as she came abreast of Kebabs and Curries.

She continued down the high street until the shops disappeared in her rearview mirror and fields stretched out on either side of the road. She hadn't gone far when she spied the rotating sign for Digby's garage.

She pulled into the parking lot and got out. Weeds grew up through the cracks in the concrete forecourt and the smell of gasoline and motor oil hung heavy in the air. The door to one of the garage bays was open and an old model Jaguar was on the lift.

The man standing under the lift was wearing a cap, and his belly strained the front of his grease- and oil-stained overalls. He grabbed a rag from his workbench, wiped his hands and began to walk over toward Penelope's car.

He slapped the MINI on the hood. "Got a problem with her?"

"Not exactly," Pen said.

The man looked at her curiously. "What can I do for you, then?" He scratched the stubble on his chin.

"I understand you helped put on the fireworks at Worthington House the other night."

Digby scowled. "Yeah. I don't know what they needed to call in a London firm for. My guys and I could have done it easy. I guess we aren't posh enough for the Worthingtons."

"I was curious," Pen began somewhat nervously. "Did you happen to see anyone in the gardens or on the terrace while you were setting up?"

Digby took off his hat and scratched his head. "Well, now," he said. "I saw that woman that was murdered step out onto the terrace." He shook his head. "She lit up a pipe and began to smoke it. I don't know what the world is coming to, I honestly don't. Women weren't meant to smoke pipes."

"Anyone else? Did you see anyone else?"

"There was another woman," Digby said. "Pretty thing as far as I could see in the dark."

"What did she look like? Could you tell?"

Digby shrugged his shoulders. He opened his mouth, then shut it. He scratched his chin again, his fingernails rasping against his stubble.

"Like I said, she was pretty. A tiny thing. Put me in mind of a bird."

"So that was it?" Pen said, disappointed.

"Well, there was this bloke in a fancy dinner jacket who came out. I thought maybe he wanted a smoke, too, but he just sort of hovered in the cover of the bushes alongside the terrace. I have to say I did wonder what he was doing. It looked like he was hiding from someone."

Tobias was hiding? Penelope wondered why.

Unless it was because he was waiting for the right moment to hit Cissie over the head with Worthington's polo mallet.

Pen was driving back to the Open Book from Digby's garage when she saw the Jolly Good Grub gourmet shop in the distance. It had been opened by a fellow who had moved to Upper Chumley-on-Stoke from London shortly before Penelope arrived in town. She decided to pop in and pick up some cheeses to serve Maguire when he came for dinner.

She parked the car and stood in front of the shop for a

moment, admiring the wooden sign with *Jolly Good Grub* on it and an artfully drawn wedge of cheese.

A lavish picnic hamper was displayed in the window like a cornucopia with all sorts of delicious-looking goodies spilling out of it—tins of caviar, several wedges of cheese, dried sausages, petits fours, and chocolate truffles.

Pen opened the door and went inside. The aroma in the shop nearly made her swoon.

"Welcome to the Jolly Good Grub," the man behind the counter called out.

He didn't look very old, but the wispy lines under his eyes were a giveaway that he wasn't that young despite his trendy blond haircut and fashionable clothes.

"It's nice to meet someone who is almost as new to Chumley as I am," Pen said as she approached the counter. She frowned. "At least I assume you're not from Chum originally?"

"You're right, darling." He held out his hand. "The name's Grant." He pursed his lips. "I'm on the lam from London actually. Chased out by the critics."

Pen raised her eyebrows.

"Theater critics, darling. I fancied myself treading the boards as the next Laurence Olivier, but alas it was not to be. I've played my last role, I'm afraid. The *London Times* made that quite obvious. After those reviews, I doubt I could get a part in a school play."

"I'm sorry," Pen said.

"Don't be, darling. One must be a realistic. My father was a grocer and to that occupation I have returned although my wares are—how shall I put it—in a class above your frozen bangers and mushy peas and tinned haggis. If those are what you're after, the Tesco is just down the street."

Grant straightened his bow tie. "Now what can I get for you today?"

"I'm looking for some cheese for a cheese plate."

"Right over there, darling." Grant pointed to a case along the wall. "If you can't find it there, you won't find it anywhere. At least not anywhere in Chumley."

Pen went over to the case Grant had indicated and began reading the labels on the cheeses. She was about to select an Irish cheddar with chives when the door to the shop opened and Tobias walked in.

Penelope ducked behind a pyramid of cans of imported olives as Tobias strode to the counter. Grant greeted him with a big smile and reached under the counter. He pulled out a woven picnic hamper, hefted it onto the counter with a grunt, and flipped open the lid. He ran a hand over it like a game show host showing off the grand prize.

"Everything you asked for and everything you could possibly need to provide a most seductive meal for any young lady." Grant waggled his eyebrows at Tobias.

A seductive meal for a young lady? Pen wondered who the young lady was. Tobias hadn't been widowed more than a couple of days—how had he managed to meet someone so quickly? And in a place like Upper Chumley-on-Stoke? Or was Rose the young lady in question?

Pen added up all the facts—Tobias was outside somewhere in the garden when Cissie was murdered. The police had found the button missing from his jacket and Digby had seen him hiding in the bushes. He had a motive as well—rid himself of Cissie, inherit her money, and move on to someone else.

Penelope made a split-second decision to follow him. If he wasn't meeting Rose, she wanted to know who this young woman was. Maybe they'd already known each other for a while and had been in on the murder together?

Pen dropped the block of Irish cheddar back into the case as Tobias headed toward the door, and she followed him outside.

His Jaguar was parked two cars away from hers. Penelope kept her head down as she walked toward her MINI, got in, and started the engine. Tobias pulled away from the curb and she quickly did the same.

She tailed him through town, keeping a safe distance behind him. Traffic was light and she had no trouble keeping up. They went past Digby's garage and out into the country. They were almost to the pub where she'd had lunch with Jemima when Tobias pulled off onto a dirt road that was little more than a track cut through tall grass, giving it the appearance of a jagged scar as it zigzagged up the slight hill.

Penelope waited until Tobias was nearly out of sight before making the turn herself and following him.

She bumped along the rutted track, her teeth clashing together at each jolt, until she saw Tobias's car up ahead. He crested a small hill, pulled up outside a rustic-looking stone building with a large wooden shed alongside it, and stopped the car.

There was nowhere to hide. Pen put the car in reverse and backed down the slight rise far enough to where she hoped her car wasn't immediately visible. She cursed her decision to buy a car in bright red. There had been a dark green MINI on the lot that would have been a lot easier to hide. Of course at the time she hadn't anticipated sneaking around following people, so there was that.

Pen got out of her car and crept toward the house— Tobias had already disappeared inside. When she got closer, she was surprised to see that there was another car pulled around in back of the building. It looked as if Tobias's date had already arrived.

Pen was itching to find out who it was. She hesitated but realized this wouldn't be the first time her curiosity had gotten her into trouble and she reminded herself that somehow she'd always managed to squirm out of it.

She moved closer to the house. The curtains were parted on one of the windows and Penelope slunk toward it, then quickly knelt down so that she wouldn't be visible.

A small sharp pebble dug into her knee and she shifted position trying to get more comfortable on the hard, frozen ground.

She peered through the window, which was surprisingly clean. On closer inspection the building, while rustic, was in good repair. The brief glimpse she'd had of the interior showed a large stone fireplace with the Worthington crest hanging above it and a set of deer antlers on the wall alongside it. The furniture was cozy and comfortable. There was a rack of guns along one wall and several pairs of boots lined up by the back door.

Tobias began walking toward the window and Pen quickly ducked. She banged her head against the sill and bit her lip. She realized she was holding her breath and finally let it out in a rush. She raised herself up slowly and peeked over the edge of the window again.

Tobias had moved away and was busy arranging the contents of the hamper on a low table in front of the fireplace. Pen could see a woman moving off to the side, but she hadn't turned to face the window yet and Penelope couldn't identify her.

She risked rising up a bit higher on her knees and was rewarded with a better view. The woman with Tobias was standing at the island that separated the kitchen from the living area of the room. She was putting two champagne glasses on the counter.

Pen could finally see her face clearly.

It was Rose Ainsley.

TEN

❧✦❧

So Rose and Tobias were a couple again, Penelope thought as she hovered beneath the window. Tobias had dumped her for Cissie—Cissie had a fortune and Rose had nothing—so why would Rose be willing to take him back?

Unless that had been the plan all along—marry Cissie, dispose of her, grab the money, and then marry Rose, who had been the love of his life all along.

Pen risked rising up on her knees again to take another peek in the window. Rose and Tobias were looking very cozy in front of a roaring fire, clinking champagne glasses.

Celebrating their success?

Suddenly Tobias swiveled around in his seat. Had he heard Penelope outside or somehow sensed her presence the way people sometimes do? She ducked down but had she been quick enough? She heard the front door to the shooting lodge open and she froze. If Tobias came around the building, he would find her crouched beneath the window.

Besides it being an incredibly embarrassing position for her to be caught in, there was no telling what Tobias would do. He'd killed once already—what difference would it make if he killed again? You can't hang a man twice, her grandmother Parish always used to say.

Penelope began to inch away from the window. If Tobias was coming from the front door, perhaps she could go in the other direction and make it around the house and into her car before he caught her.

She rounded the corner of the house and paused to listen. Silence. Then she heard a door slam. Tobias had given up and gone inside. Penelope crept back to her position under the window and peered in.

Tobias was on the sofa in front of the fire again, one hand on Rose's knee and the other wrapped around his champagne glass.

Pen felt woozy with relief. She took a couple of deep breaths to steady herself and then began making her way back to her car.

She'd never felt so relieved to be in the driver's seat of her MINI before. Even if the seat was on the wrong side of the car. During her first few weeks in England, she'd opened the wrong door every single time she'd gotten in the car and was just as astonished each time to see that the steering wheel appeared to be missing.

There was no way to turn around on the narrow track, so Penelope stepped on the gas and reversed down the hill, sending pebbles flying in every direction on her descent. She didn't relax completely until she was on the high street and saw the bright red Tesco sign beckoning in the distance.

* * *

Pen stood in front of her closet and examined its contents. It had become a ritual every time she wanted to look nice for a special occasion—or, in this case, a special someone.

She realized that every time she saw Maguire she was wearing her "ordinary" clothes—garments that were warm and comfortable and allowed her to move without being pinched or poked. So far he hadn't objected.

Which meant she really didn't have to worry about it. Not like with her ex-boyfriend Miles, who had been extremely fashion conscious. Penelope still couldn't fathom what he saw in her in the first place. Or, vice versa for that matter.

She finally grabbed a newly washed pair of leggings, a bright red sweater that always cheered her up, and a pair of ballet flats since she was a smidge taller than Maguire and didn't want to increase the disparity.

The air had been slightly humid causing Pen's hair to curl even more exuberantly than normal. She fiddled with it in the mirror and in the end simply pinned it up and out of the way.

She could smell the beef stew simmering on the stove as she descended the stairs to the first floor. She wasn't the most accomplished cook in the world but she could make a mean stew, she knew how to roast a chicken, and she could whip up eggs at least three different ways.

Pen went out to the kitchen where her bright red Dutch oven sat on the burner on the Aga. She lifted the lid and took a deep breath, relishing the scent of the fragrant steam. If it was true that the way to a man's heart was through his stomach, she had it made.

She was putting the finishing touches on the table—dishes lined up perfectly, linen napkins folded just so, and wineglasses sparkling—when the doorbell rang.

Pen felt her heartbeat speed up a bit as she ran to the door. Mrs. Danvers, obviously eager to see who was intruding on their solitude, was right on her heels.

Pen flung open the door. Maguire was standing on the mat, a sheepish expression on his face. He was clutching a wine bottle in one hand and a paper-wrapped bundle of flowers in the other.

He was dressed the way he normally was in jeans, a blue button-down shirt, and a cream-colored cable-knit sweater that looked handmade. Pen was glad she hadn't put on anything too special—it might have made him feel awkward.

"Come in." She led him into the sitting room.

"This is lovely," Maguire said, standing in front of the roaring fire, rubbing his hands together. "It's turned quite bitter out."

"Take the seat by the fire," Pen said. "I'll open the wine."

When Pen came out of the kitchen with two glasses and the opened bottle of wine, she was astonished to see that Mrs. Danvers was curled up next to Maguire. She stared openmouthed at this spectacle.

"What is it?" Maguire said.

"It's just that . . . that Mrs. Danvers doesn't take to anyone. She's usually very standoffish."

Maguire smiled. "I've been told I have a way with animals." He stroked Mrs. Danvers's head and she purred audibly.

Pen put the bottle and glasses down on the table and poured them each some wine. She had already set out a basket of crackers and a plate of cheese. She'd bought some Irish cheddar in Tesco on her way back from following Tobias—she hadn't had the nerve to go back into Jolly

Good Grub. Grant probably thought she was a real nutter, running out the way she had.

Maguire took a sip. "Something certainly smells delicious," he said. He picked up a cracker and added a slice of cheese.

"It's my grandmother Parish's beef stew," Pen said. "I think you'll like it."

"My mother used to make what she euphemistically called lamb stew, but it was more mutton than lamb, and it didn't fool anybody. We all hated it, but we were hungry so we ate it."

Pen rubbed a finger around the rim of her wineglass. "I hate to bring up work, but everyone is wondering since there's been no real news. Has there been any progress in the Worthington House murder?"

The newspapers had taken to calling Cissie's death the "Worthington House murder" and the phrase had stuck—everyone in Chumley was referring to it that way now.

Maguire scowled and rubbed the back of his neck. "Angie Donovan—she's the DCI the Met sent down—isn't exactly known for keeping people in the loop. Short answer—I don't know." He poked at a small hole in the knee of his jeans. "She treats me like I'm the coffee boy." His face was beginning to flush. "Frankly, I don't know how much longer I can keep my cool." He thumped his fist against the couch, sending Mrs. Danvers leaping off in high dudgeon, her tail held stiffly in the air as she trotted off to the kitchen.

"I'm determined to solve the case before she does." Maguire clenched his fists, then forced a laugh. "If I can." He grimaced.

Pen put down her wineglass and turned toward him. She pulled one leg underneath her as she leaned forward.

"I have some information that might be useful."

Maguire looked startled. "Really? What do you mean?" He sounded suspicious.

"You know how you found that button in the garden but couldn't identify the owner?"

"Yes." Maguire scowled, then his expression cleared. "Although, as far as I can tell, Donovan hasn't had any more luck than I have."

"The button came off Tobias Winterbourne's dinner jacket."

Maguire's mouth hung open. "We checked through everyone's clothes. Or at least Constable Cuthbert did. Did he miss it?"

"Not exactly." Penelope decided to amend her story slightly by starting from the end and working backward, thus eliminating the need to admit to the awkward part where she and Figgy went through Tobias's closet.

"We saw a young man wearing Tobias's jacket—he sings in a band called the Foggy Bottoms—"

That elicited a bark of laughter from Maguire.

"They were playing at the Book and Bottle. I asked him where he got the jacket and he said he bought it at the Oxfam shop on the high street. I checked with the clerk there, and she confirmed that she'd sold it to him and that it had recently been brought in."

"But dinner jackets all look the same—black and boring. How did you know it was Tobias's?"

Pen described the jacket. "There weren't any other men in midnight blue burned velvet numbers except Tobias."

Maguire whistled.

Pen held up a hand. "Wait. There's more."

Maguire was listening eagerly now.

Pen explained about following Tobias to Worthington's

shooting lodge and discovering that Tobias had a tryst with
Rose Ainsley.

Now Maguire was frowning.

"I don't like the thought of you putting yourself in danger like that."

"I didn't honestly think it was dangerous," Pen fibbed,
shivering now at the thought of it.

"So Tobias and Rose . . . that certainly gives him a motive for killing his wife."

Pen nodded. "Tobias and Rose were an item, but he
dropped Rose when Cissie came along. Cissie had money
and Rose didn't. Now Tobias inherits his wife's fortune and
is free to marry the woman he really loves."

Maguire sat up straighter. "That's a pretty strong motive.
Of course we questioned all the people that were at the ball,
but they clam up when talking to someone outside their sacred circle. No one mentioned the connection between Tobias
and Rose." He smiled at Pen. "That's incredibly helpful.
Maybe I'll be able to beat Donovan to the punch after all."

He reached for his wineglass. "You know they found the
murder weapon—Worthington's polo mallet." Maguire
frowned. "We sent it to forensics, but the only prints on it
are Worthington's."

"So the killer wore gloves?"

"It looks that way. Unless, of course, Worthington was
the killer."

Penelope whistled—off-key she'd be the first to admit—
as she washed her face and changed into her pajamas—
an old pair of sweatpants and a thermal top she'd bought to
wear the one time Miles had taken her skiing.

The evening with Maguire had gone smoothly, not that Penelope had expected anything different. The beef stew had been tender and well flavored, the conversation had flowed easily, and the whole evening had been relaxed and comfortable. Pen realized that all her interactions with Maguire since they had first met—bumper to bumper on the high street when Pen had veered onto the wrong side of the road—had been that way.

Of course that almost made the evening sound dull, but there'd been a spark of excitement as well—Maguire had lingered over his good night kiss and Pen had quite enjoyed it.

Pen got in bed and pulled up the comforter. The wind had picked up and was battering at the windows as icy sleet tapped against the glass. Pen hugged her knees as she relished the coziness of her warm bed and snug cottage.

She grabbed her phone from the bedside table and began to scroll through her e-mails. She was reading one about a sale on sweaters at Marks and Sparks, as it was known, when the phone rang. She was so startled, she nearly dropped it.

She glanced at the number on the screen and was surprised to see it was her sister, Beryl's. It seemed odd that she would be calling at this hour, but then Pen remembered that it was only early evening back in the States.

"Hello?"

"Pen? Is that you? I'm so glad you're home."

Where else would she be at this hour? Pen wondered, listening to the windows rattling. She shivered.

Her sister's voice sounded odd—strained—almost as if she had been crying.

"I'll be there sometime tomorrow morning," Beryl said.

Penelope stared at the phone in her hand. Surely she hadn't heard correctly. She couldn't possibly have.

"What? We must have a bad connection. I thought you said you'd be here tomorrow morning, which is impossible since you're in Connecticut." She hesitated. "Right?"

"That *is* what I said." Beryl sounded testy. "And I'm not in Connecticut, I'm at Kennedy airport. I'm flying in to Heathrow and I'll be at your place sometime midmorning. I assume there's a train from London."

"Yes," Penelope said hesitantly. "It leaves from King's Cross station."

She was beginning to wonder if she'd missed a text or voice mail from her sister. She must have.

"I didn't know you were coming."

"Neither did I," Beryl snapped.

"Has something happened?"

"I'll tell you when I get there," Beryl said with a sob. "I've got to go. They're calling my flight."

And she ended the call.

Pen was left staring at the phone. What on earth had gotten into Beryl? Her sister never did anything on the spur of the moment—all her activities, her commitments, her social outings were put on her calendar months in advance. She was the only person Pen knew who could tell you exactly what she'd be doing on a specific date six months in the future.

Something must be very wrong. If their mother was ill—at this time of year she'd be in Florida—Beryl would have said and she certainly wouldn't have been flying to England to tell Pen.

It had to be something else. Pen had been getting sleepy but now she was wide-awake. It was so like Beryl to keep her hanging like this.

She turned out the light and rolled onto her side, but sleep eluded her for several hours.

ELEVEN

❧

When Pen woke the next morning, she was convinced she'd dreamed the whole thing. Beryl couldn't possibly be on her way to Upper Chumley-on-Stoke. She'd had very realistic dreams before, but that one certainly took the cake.

She took a quick shower, dressed, and ran a brush through her tangled hair. She was planning to go to the Open Book to do some writing. Those revisions weren't going to wait forever and neither was her editor.

She downed a quick cup of tea and a slice of toast while standing at the kitchen counter, filled Mrs. Danvers's food and water bowls, pulled on her coat, tucked her laptop under her arm, and headed out the door.

Penelope breezed through the Open Book, waving at Mabel, who was surrounded by papers and frowning at her calculator, accepted a freshly baked Chelsea bun from Figgy, and headed for her writing room.

She opened her laptop and brought up her manuscript.
She'd come to view her writing room at the Open Book as
her "sacred space." It was quiet but not lonely—she had a
sense of the life going on in the bookstore right outside her
door—and there were few distractions.

She was bound and determined to tackle the middle of her
manuscript, which Bettina had described as lacking tension.

She pushed her glasses up her nose with her finger and
began reading.

After going through the pages, Penelope realized there
wasn't enough conflict, and conflict was what held the reader's attention. She'd missed a wonderful opportunity for
Raoul and Luna to be speaking at cross-purposes during
their conversation. That ought to add a spark to those pages.

Penelope was halfway through the scene when there was
a knock on the door.

She opened it and found Mabel regarding her with an
apologetic smile. She had her glasses stuck on top of her
head, and there were crumbs on the front of her sweater.
She brushed at them impatiently.

"I hate to interrupt you, but there's a woman here to see
you—a DCI Donovan."

Mabel's raised eyebrows were the only indication of her
curiosity.

"She's the detective they sent down from the Met to help
with the Worthington case."

"She looks like a real piece of work," Mabel said. "Very
buttoned-up and quite impressed with herself, I'd say. Good
luck," Mabel said as Penelope followed her to the front of
the store.

Donovan was standing by the door, her face pinched
with impatience. She was in her thirties, tall and slender,

with blond hair yanked back so tightly into a ponytail that Pen was surprised she could move her eyebrows. Her expression clearly said she meant business.

Donovan glanced at a small notebook in her hand, then looked up.

"Penelope Parish?"

"Yes." Penelope was tempted to add something snide but bit her tongue.

"Is there somewhere we can talk?"

Penelope led her to the back of the store and the sofa and chairs where her book group usually gathered. She was about to sit down when she realized that Donovan had remained standing.

"You attended the wedding ball of the Duke and Duchess of Upper Chumley-on-Stoke, did you not?"

"Yes."

A series of questions followed, which Donovan assured her were being asked of everyone who had been in attendance.

"Strictly routine," Donovan said, but the way she said it made Penelope wonder.

Donovan glanced at her notepad again. "Did you leave the ballroom at any time?"

Penelope wracked her brain. She'd gone to the ladies' room, but she doubted that was what Donovan was after.

She shook her head. "No."

"You didn't go outside to the terrace or the gardens? For a bit of fresh air perhaps? I imagine the ballroom was quite stuffy."

Penelope felt her back stiffen. "No," she said rather tersely.

No wonder Maguire was feeling frustrated with this woman.

"Did you see anyone else leave the room?"

"I've already told Detective Maguire everything I know. Why don't you check with him?"

"I will definitely be doing that," Donovan said. Her lips were clamped together and Pen could see the muscles in her jaw working.

Donovan snapped her notebook shut, dropped it and her pencil into her tote bag, and pulled out a business card. She handed it to Penelope.

"We're asking everyone to stay in the vicinity," she said, almost as an afterthought. "And if you remember anything useful, please let me know immediately." She tapped the card in Pen's hand. "My mobile number is right there."

Penelope was watching as Donovan marched to the front of the store, when her phone suddenly dinged. She pulled it out of her pocket and glanced at it. She had a text. She clicked on it.

It was from Beryl—announcing that she'd landed at Heathrow and would be taking the eleven o'clock train from King's Cross station to Upper Chumley-on-Stoke.

So it hadn't been a dream after all.

She'd been planning to do some more writing, but changed her mind. She'd better head back to her cottage. Pen wasn't a particularly neat person—when the writing was going well she was apt to let the dishes pile up in the sink and toss her discarded clothes on the chair in her bedroom.

Ashlyn, the young woman who came and cleaned once a week, dealt with things like dust bunnies, smudges on the windows, and muddy footprints on the floor, so at least the place was clean.

Penelope was slightly out of breath when she arrived

back at her cottage. She took a moment to greet Mrs. Danvers, who seemed to be in fine spirits, even allowing Pen to scratch under her chin—something she reserved for special occasions.

Pen put her laptop down and glanced around the sitting room. She folded up the throw she kept on the sofa and draped it over the arm in what she hoped was an artful fashion. She straightened the pile of books on the coffee table and put the shoes she'd kicked off the night before by the stairs to be taken up to her bedroom.

The kitchen was next. She wiped down the top of the Aga, which was a bit splattered from last night's stew, and washed up all the dishes from her dinner with Maguire.

Then it was on to her bedroom, where she put her shoes in the closet, hung up her discarded clothes, and made the bed. The spare room was the one she was using as a study. She gathered up her papers and moved them to her room, then she rummaged in the linen closet for a clean set of sheets. She made up the bed, cracked the window a bit to air the room, and piled some clean towels on the dresser. It wasn't the Ritz, but it would have to do.

Penelope was filling Mrs. Danvers's food bowl when the doorbell rang. Mrs. Danvers looked extremely peeved that Pen had been interrupted during such an important task and stalked after her as she headed to the foyer.

Penelope pulled open the door to find her sister standing on the doormat, flanked by two suitcases. Beryl's skin had the pasty look of someone who had just gotten off a long flight and her artfully cut and expensively highlighted blond bob was flattened on the sides. She was wearing a Loden coat, leggings, a tunic-length cashmere sweater, a silk scarf that was slightly askew, and a pair of Everlane shoes that Penelope had seen touted as being a favorite of Angelina Jolie's.

Beryl's whole outfit probably cost more than her entire wardrobe, Pen thought as she held the door wide and grabbed her sister's suitcases.

The girls had always been too different to be especially close. Pen had acquaintances who were best friends with their older siblings but, while she and Beryl shared a family bond, they'd never been comfortable spending a great deal of time together.

Beryl looked Penelope up and down. "You're not still wearing that ratty old sweater, are you? You must have had that since college."

Pen looked at her watch. It hadn't even been five minutes and already Beryl was criticizing her. She took a deep breath and let it out slowly.

Beryl was looking around the sitting room. "Dreadfully cramped, isn't it?" She pursed her lips. "But I suppose it suits you."

"How about a cup of tea?" Pen said brightly, moving toward the kitchen. "You sit and catch your breath while I put the kettle on."

Beryl gave a small smile. "You've gone full-on British, have you?"

"I think you'll be amazed at how restorative a good cup of tea can be," Pen said. "If you want to wash up, the bathroom is at the top of the stairs. You can't miss it."

She pointed toward the staircase and then headed off to the kitchen, trying not to stomp her feet. Once out of sight, she opened her mouth and let out a silent scream, then set about making the tea.

Pen was all smiles as she brought the tea tray into the sitting room. Beryl was perched on the couch, flipping through the autographed copy of *The Fire in My Bosom* that Caroline Davenport had given Penelope.

She tossed the book onto the coffee table. "I didn't think that was your sort of reading material," she said, accepting the cup of tea Pen handed her.

"The author is the new duchess of Upper Chumley-on-Stoke," Pen said, taking the chair opposite the sofa.

Beryl frowned. "I do remember reading something about that. Some sort of scandal?"

Pen took a sip of her tea so she didn't have to answer.

Beryl had put down her cup and was staring vacantly at the far wall. Pen cleared her throat, but Beryl didn't respond.

Pen let the silence lengthen until she couldn't stand it anymore.

"Do you want to tell me what brings you to England?" she said finally in as cheerful a tone as she could muster.

Beryl jumped, as if she'd been startled. She fiddled with the ends of her silk scarf.

"I'm leaving Magnus," she said suddenly.

"What?" Penelope nearly choked on her tea.

Beryl had been a devoted wife from the moment she and Magnus Kent had said "I do"—planning dinner parties to advance his career, spending hours in Pilates classes and at the salon in order to look the part, managing the household so that he could spend his leisure time golfing. What on earth had gone wrong?

"I know it comes as a shock." Beryl twisted the ends of her scarf.

"What happened?" Pen was still in disbelief. "I thought you loved each other."

"We did." Beryl let out a sob. "We do."

"Then what's wrong?"

"Magnus has been . . . Magnus has been arrested."

Pen nearly dropped her teacup. Of all the things she was expecting to hear, that wasn't even on the list.

"Arrested for what? Not paying his parking tickets? For jaywalking?"

As far as she knew Magnus had always been law-abiding in the extreme.

"For . . . for cheating his investors. The feds are calling it a Ponzi scheme."

Since when had Beryl started using terms like *the feds*? Pen wondered. Obviously a lot had been going on while she'd been in England.

"We're going to lose everything," Beryl sobbed. "The lawyers alone are costing a fortune, and if they lose the case, the government will take everything that's left."

Pen didn't know what to say. Here she'd been rehearsing how to deal with things if Beryl said Magnus was having an affair. Or if Beryl herself was having one and had fallen in love with someone else. This, she was completely unprepared for.

"What are you going to do?" Pen said quietly after several minutes.

Beryl held out her hands palms up. "I don't know. I suppose I shall have to get a job assuming I can get a work visa." She gave Pen a pleading look. "In the meantime, can I stay with you for a bit? I can't bear to go back to the States. The press was camped outside the house day and night—it's been a nightmare. I had to trade clothes with my housekeeper to sneak past them. Gina smuggled out my suitcases and her husband drove me to the airport."

Beryl buried her face in her hands.

"The whole time I was waiting for my flight, I was terrified that a reporter would spot me. I hid in the ladies' room until it was time to board." She looked at Pen, her face blotchy with tears. "What's wrong with those people? They're like vultures."

Pen thought of the stories that had been written about Charlotte and she had to agree.

"I've made up the spare room upstairs," Pen said, collecting the tea things and putting them on the tray. "You're welcome to stay as long as you like."

"Thank you." Beryl sighed. "It might be a while until the furor at home dies down. It could be weeks or it could be months."

Penelope gulped. "That's fine," she said without much conviction. "Stay as long as you need to."

"How long are you planning to stay in England?" Beryl said.

"The writer-in-residence position was meant to last a year, but Mabel has hinted that I could extend that if I wanted." Penelope thought of Maguire. She was going to stay as long as possible.

"I hate to be a bother," Beryl said as Pen led her upstairs.

"Nonsense," Pen said. "You're my sister. We have to stick together."

What was she getting herself into? Pen wondered as she opened the door to the guest room.

But she could hardly turn Beryl down in her hour of need. Surely she could cope for a couple of weeks.

A frightening thought occurred to her—what if it took months for things to settle down back in the States? Beryl had said that was possible.

If Beryl was going to be staying with her for that long, Pen feared she might have to resort to taking daily nips from the bottle of Jameson that Mabel kept under the counter at the Open Book.

*   *   *

Beryl was exhausted by her long flight and all the emotions she'd experienced in the past few days. She assured Pen that she would visit the Open Book as soon as she was rested.

Pen packed up her laptop and her notes and headed out the door and down the street. She paused to admire the display in the window of the Icing on the Cake—a delicious-looking Battenberg cake that made her mouth water and a Madeira cake that would be perfect with a cup of tea. Perhaps she'd buy something later—it might cheer Beryl up. Always assuming Beryl wasn't on one of her interminable diets—one week it was the Atkins diet, the next week it was the Mediterranean diet, and the following week something brand-new that some woman's magazine was touting as the answer to everyone's prayers.

Penelope also paused in front of the window of the estate agent's to see if there were any short-term lets on apartments above the shops along the high street. There was one above Pen and Ink Stationers—she would mention it to Beryl if it appeared as if Beryl would be staying for several months.

A horrible thought occurred to Pen as she turned away from the window. Would Beryl have to testify in Magnus's trial? Worse—would they think that Beryl had been in on the scheme? Pen knew her sister and knew that Beryl's main concerns were decorating, arranging dinner parties, securing theater tickets, and maintaining her youthful good looks. She wouldn't know a balance sheet from a bedsheet.

The Open Book was busy as it often was on Saturday mornings and afternoons. Customers browsed the crowded shelves and sprawled, thumbing through books, on the sagging sofas and armchairs.

No one was behind the counter when Pen opened the front door, but as she approached, Mabel popped up, her fluffy white hair trailing across her forehead and a clump of dust clinging to the front of her sweater.

"Howdy," Mabel said when she saw Pen. "How is the newsletter coming, by the way?"

"Almost done with my part. I think you'll like it."

"I know I will." Mabel smiled and the skin around her eyes crinkled. "As soon as it's finished, I'll send it to the designer to put it together and send it out." Mabel drew back and looked at Penelope with narrowed eyes. "What's up? You don't look like yourself."

Pen told her about Beryl's arrival.

"Oh, dear," Mabel said, brushing her hair off her face. "A Ponzi scheme? That doesn't sound good. They've been throwing the book at the chaps running those lately. No pun intended."

"I know," Pen said, her shoulders sagging.

"What are you going to do?" Mabel said.

"I don't know. I looked in the window at the estate agent's—"

Before Pen could finish, her cell phone rang. She excused herself and went into her writing room to answer it. She thought for sure it would be Beryl but was surprised when it turned out to be Charlotte, inviting her to tea later that afternoon.

Pen thanked her but told her that her sister was visiting at the moment and she couldn't leave her. Charlotte responded immediately that Penelope was to bring Beryl along. Charlotte said she had something to discuss with

Pen—something professional—but there was no reason Beryl couldn't be there as well.

For the second time in two days, Pen was left dying of curiosity.

The Duchess of Upper Chumley-on-Stoke," Beryl cried when Pen told her about Charlotte's invitation to tea. "Whatever shall I wear?" She paced back and forth in Pen's tiny sitting room. "The duchess has been praised for her tremendous fashion sense in all the gossip magazines back home. She has only to wear a dress once and it immediately sells out." She bit her knuckle. "I could barely think while I was packing, I was so distressed. I had no idea how long I'd be staying. I just grabbed things willy-nilly off the hanger and stuffed them into the suitcase. I don't think I have a single suitable outfit." She looked at Pen hopefully. "Is there a dress shop in town?"

"There is," Pen said, biting into the apple she'd plucked from the fruit bowl on the kitchen table, "but it's not necessary to buy anything new. Charlotte is utterly charming and utterly without pretension. You look absolutely fine the way you are. I've seen Charlotte in jeans and a sweater at home and running errands in yoga pants and sneakers."

"Are you sure?" Beryl looked down at her outfit, and smoothed out her sweater.

"Absolutely. And if we don't hustle, we'll be late." Pen tossed her apple core into the wastebasket.

Beryl continued to fret during the entire trip, although, truth be told, part of the time it was due to Penelope's rather erratic driving. She really was getting better at remembering to drive on the left-hand side of the street, but she still occasionally made a tiny mistake and drifted over the line in the road.

Beryl gasped when they rounded a bend and Worthington House came into view.

"It's a castle," Beryl exclaimed.

"Yes, it is rather." Pen tried to hide a satisfied smile as she put on her blinker and turned into the long drive leading to the house. She remembered when she had been just as awed as Beryl at the sight.

"When you said Worthington House, I thought you meant—"

"Typical British modesty," Pen said. "Calling it a castle would be nouveau riche and that's one thing the Worthingtons are not." Pen negotiated a bend in the driveway. "The Worthingtons go back centuries. Worthington himself is distantly related to the queen."

"I . . . I had no idea," Beryl said quietly.

Pen parked the car and they walked up the boxwood-bordered flagstone path to the entrance.

The butler who opened the door smiled at Penelope.

"Lovely to see you again, Miss Parish," he said, giving a brisk nod of his head.

Beryl looked at her sister with wide eyes. "He knew you," she whispered as the butler led them down the hall.

Penelope tried not to look too smug but it was nice that for once she was able to impress her sister—something that was a very unusual occurrence indeed.

The butler led them to a small sitting room where Charlotte was waiting for them. The room was cozy and charming with a carved white marble fireplace flanked by bookcases. An overstuffed sofa slipcovered in cream-colored fabric faced the fireplace and was piled with throw pillows in pale pinks and blues. A large vase overflowing with pink and white tulips sat on an end table at Charlotte's elbow.

Charlotte jumped up and greeted Pen with a hug, then turned to Beryl and held out her hand. Beryl appeared to be tongue-tied, and Pen had to stifle a laugh when her sister actually curtsied.

"Charlotte, this is my sister, Beryl Kent."

Pen did notice the look of relief on Beryl's face when she saw that Charlotte was dressed in slim-fitting jeans, a bulky knit white turtleneck sweater, and black suede ankle boots and had her hair up in a bun. Several gold bracelets dangled from her wrist and some impressive diamond studs twinkled in her ears.

"Please, sit down," Charlotte said, taking her place on the sofa and drawing her legs under her. "Our tea will be along any minute."

Charlotte made polite conversation with Beryl, asking her how her flight had been and how she was liking England so far. Beryl's stilted answers were a dead giveaway that she was nervous, but Charlotte did her best to put Beryl at ease.

Finally there was a tap on the door and the butler entered with a tray of tea things, including a tiered platter with an array of sweet and savory delicacies that made Pen's mouth water.

Charlotte poured the tea and handed around the cups. Pen filled her plate with the tiny tea sandwiches—cucumber and cream cheese, chicken salad, and smoked salmon—as well as lemon shortbread, a strawberry tartlet, and a slice of Madeira cake.

Penelope was quite proud of the fact that she now felt completely at ease taking tea with Charlotte—she remembered the first time she'd been invited to the castle, she had been full of nerves, terrified that she would tip over her cup or commit some hideous faux pas.

"You're probably wondering what I wanted to talk to you about," Charlotte said, putting down her cup. She turned to Beryl with a smile. "I do hope you don't mind if we talk shop for a few minutes?"

Beryl's mouth was full of a bite of a chicken salad sandwich, so she shook her head silently.

Charlotte brushed a crumb off her sweater. "I've been asked to put together an anthology of short stories. We want to include multiple genres. I'm providing romance of course, and we hoped you might consider contributing a story with your special Gothic touch."

Pen was surprised. That wasn't what she had been expecting. She thought of the revisions she had yet to tackle and the deadline for her next book.

"How soon would you need the story?"

Charlotte ducked her head. "I'm afraid I'm a bit behind on this project. I got caught up in all the wedding plans." She gave Pen a pleading look. "I would need it in a month, if that's possible."

Penelope gulped. That was going to be tough. But she didn't want to let Charlotte down and, besides, this was a great opportunity to expand her readership.

She was about to answer when Tobias stuck his head in the room.

"Is there any tea, darling?" he said, looking at Charlotte. He rubbed his rather rotund stomach. "I'm positively famished. We had the most vile lunch at the local pub. Their claim to be able to make a decent bangers and mash is vastly overstated."

"I doubt you want to join us," Charlotte said somewhat frostily. "Why don't you go down to the kitchen and ask

Cook to make you something? I'm sure he can pull something tasty together."

"Wonderful idea," Tobias said, winking at Charlotte. "A nice hot cuppa would fit the bill and perhaps some buttered toast with Marmite. That's what Nanny used to make us when we were in the nursery. Believe it or not, I'm feeling a bit nostalgic today."

"Marmite?" Beryl said when Tobias had gone off down the hall, whistling tunelessly under his breath.

Charlotte wrinkled her nose. "It's horrid stuff. Don't let anyone talk you into trying it. It's a food spread made from yeast extract and it tastes abominable." She shivered.

By now even Beryl was beginning to relax and when Charlotte suggested a tour of the castle, they readily agreed.

"Let's start with the great hall," Charlotte said, crumpling up her napkin and tossing it on the tray. "That was the center of life at Worthington House back in medieval times.

"The great hall was used to receive guests as well as for dining," Charlotte said, as they followed her down the corridor that led to the great hall. "And it usually had the largest fireplace in the castle—big enough to roast an ox." Her words echoed in the enormous space as they entered the great hall.

Pen couldn't help but notice the expression of awe on Beryl's face. Worthington House put even the mansions in Newport that Beryl thought were so grand to shame.

The sound of footsteps in back of them startled them and they all spun around together.

The butler was hastening across the great hall, his shoes clattering against the stone. He was obviously in distress and was struggling mightily to maintain the appropriate decorum. The poor man was trying to rush and yet not look as if he was actually rushing—a very difficult feat under the best of circumstances.

Charlotte frowned. "What is it, Royston? Is something wrong? Is Cook complaining that the butcher has delivered the wrong order again?"

Royston shook his head mutely. It took him several moments to catch his breath—his chest was heaving visibly and drops of sweat beaded on his brow.

"It's Lord Winterbourne, your grace," he gasped.

"I believe he was after some tea," Charlotte said. "Was Cook able to sort something out? I hope so."

"I'm afraid it's not that, your grace."

Charlotte frowned again. "Then what is it, Royston?"

"Lord Winterbourne has been taken ill, your grace."

Charlotte gave a small smile and looked at Pen and Beryl. "It must have been the Marmite."

Royston looked confused. He tilted his head inquiringly. "I beg your pardon, your grace? I'm afraid I don't understand."

"Nothing." Charlotte waved a hand. "Forget it. Has someone phoned Dr. O'Connor? I'm sure he'll know what to do."

"I don't know that he can help, your grace." Royston bowed his head.

Charlotte became very still and her face turned white. "What do you mean?"

Royston gulped. "I mean, your grace, that I think Lord Winterbourne . . . well . . . Lord Winterbourne appears to be dead."

TWELVE

❧

Royston led them to the library and stood aside to let them enter. The low table in front of the sofa was set with tea things on a tray—a cup half-full of Earl Grey, a silver teapot, and a plate with the remains of some buttered toast spread with Marmite.

Tobias was sprawled on the floor near the door as if he had been trying to leave the room to get help. He was partially on his side, and his face was visible.

Pen had to stifle a gasp when she saw it. He was nearly unrecognizable—his complexion almost as red as the roses in the vase on the mantel, his eyes and lips swollen to grotesque proportions.

Penelope felt Beryl sway beside her and glanced at her sister in alarm.

Charlotte had obviously noticed as well. "Royston, could you please show Mrs. Kent back to the sitting room?"

Beryl gave Charlotte a grateful look as she followed Royston from the room.

Charlotte dropped to her knees next to Tobias and placed her fingers on his neck.

"I don't find a pulse, I'm afraid." She sat back on her heels. "I can't imagine what happened. Do you suppose it might have been his heart? He did say that the doctor had urged him to take more exercise and to watch his diet."

Penelope noticed that Charlotte's hands were shaking and her lips were trembling.

"It looks like an allergic reaction to me," Penelope said, squatting next to Tobias's body. "We need to call nine-nine-nine."

Now Penelope's hands were shaking as well and her stomach felt as if it had twisted itself inside out.

"I have my cell." Charlotte pulled it from her pocket and began to punch in the numbers. "They're sending someone," she said when she clicked off the call.

"Was Tobias allergic to anything, do you know?" Pen said, looking at Tobias's red face.

"I always ask all our guests about allergies," Charlotte said, playing with the charms on one of her bracelets. "I post a list of any allergies in the kitchen for Cook." She tucked a stray piece of blond hair back into her bun. "I don't remember if Tobias suffered from any." Her voice caught in her throat.

"I think he must have," Penelope said. "This looks like anaphylactic shock. I remember a girl in college who was allergic to cashews and accidentally ate a granola bar that had cashews in it. She went into shock, but fortunately her roommate knew how to use her EpiPen."

Penelope was staring at Tobias's vest—an ornate affair in emerald green metallic paisley—when she spotted a tiny something near the waist. She frowned at it—it looked like a seed of some sort.

"What's that?" she said to Charlotte as she pointed at it.

"It looks like a sesame seed," Charlotte said, peering closer. "Perhaps it's from something he had for lunch?"

Penelope glanced behind her at the tea things on the table.

"That toast looks like plain white bread, so it couldn't have come from that. Are there sesame seeds in Marmite?"

Charlotte shook her head. "No, there aren't."

Pen shrugged. "It's probably nothing."

"What's this I hear about Tobias?" Worthington strode into the room. He was wearing a tweed jacket, jodhpurs, and black riding boots and had a riding helmet tucked under his arm. "I was about to go out to the stables when Royston waylaid me and told me something had happened to Tobias."

Just then Royston knocked on the door and ushered in a stern-looking man with a bushy gray handlebar mustache. He was wearing a suit and carrying a small black bag.

"The medical examiner is here," Royston announced.

Worthington turned to Charlotte. "I'll handle this." He put a hand on her arm. "I hope this hasn't upset you too much? In your condition—"

Pen's ears perked up. Was Charlotte expecting?

"I'm fine," Charlotte said, giving Worthington a weak smile. "But I think I will go sit down."

Penelope followed Charlotte out of the room. She wondered how long before the press picked up on the fact that there was going to be a little Worthington in the near future. The gossip magazines had already been hinting about it—imagining they saw a burgeoning bump in every picture of Charlotte ever since they became a couple.

Beryl was slumped on the sofa in the sitting room when

Penelope and Charlotte got there. Her face was white and the teacup in her hand rattled in its saucer.

"I'm so terribly sorry," Charlotte said, sinking down on the sofa.

"It's not your fault," Pen said. She sat in one of the chairs and absentmindedly stared at the wall.

She was thinking—what if Tobias had been allergic to sesame seeds? And what if someone had purposely mixed some in the Marmite or even in his tea? Charlotte had said that there was a list of guests' allergies posted in the kitchen, so it wasn't likely to have been an accident.

"Do you mind if I go down to the kitchen and check that list of allergies you said is posted there?" Pen said to Charlotte. "I'd like to see whether Tobias might have been allergic to sesame seeds."

Charlotte's expression was blank. "Please. Feel free. Although why he would have been given anything with sesame seeds on it, I can't imagine." She glanced at Beryl. "Would you care for some more tea?"

Beryl shook her head.

Pen slipped from the room and started down the corridor. She thought she remembered where the kitchen was but soon realized she was mistaken. Worthington House was a maze of corridors and rooms upon rooms. She glanced in one—it was an office of sorts with a metal desk, filing cabinets, and an old-fashioned rotary dial telephone.

Finally she found the kitchen. The lights were out, but sun slanted through the tall windows and glinted off the long metal table that ran nearly the length of the room.

Penelope looked around, but she was alone. She tiptoed into the room. A bulletin board was hung on the wall opposite the windows. A draft coming from near the ceiling fluttered the edges of the various pieces of paper stuck on it.

She felt like a thief sneaking into the kitchen but she had Charlotte's permission, although it would still be awkward if someone caught her sneaking around.

She glanced at the bulletin board quickly—various menus were tacked to it along with the odd recipe. In the lower right corner was a list of the house party guests. Pen scanned it—Yvette was allergic to MSG, Ethan had a reaction to shellfish, and Tobias was allergic to—Pen bent closer—sesame seeds!

The sesame seed she'd noticed on his vest would indicate that he'd come in contact with them somewhere. But where? He wouldn't have knowingly ordered a dish prepared with them. And most people with allergies were very careful to question the waitstaff about any food served in restaurants.

Pen thought that anaphylactic shock came on rather quickly. She pulled her cell phone from her pocket and brought up Google. She found a medical website and confirmed that it could be as rapid as five minutes.

If that was the case, then Tobias had to have ingested the seeds just recently at Worthington House.

Pen was about to leave the kitchen when one of the staff entered. She recognized her as Ivy, the woman who had been buying meat at the Pig in a Poke. A man followed her into the room. He was short and stocky with close-cut dark hair and a low forehead. For some reason, he made goose bumps prickle up Penelope's arms. He stood off to the side with his arms folded across his chest.

Ivy's face was expressionless as she regarded Penelope.

"Were you wanting something, madam? A cup of tea perhaps?"

"N-n-no, thank you," Penelope said, giving Ivy what she hoped was an innocent smile. "I'm just leaving." She was about to go when she turned around. "Did you happen to make Lord Winterbourne his tea this afternoon?"

"Lord Winterbourne, miss? No, I'm afraid I did not. Is he wanting some?"

"Er . . . no, not exactly," Pen said. "I suppose it must have been Cook who prepared it, then."

Ivy tilted her head to one side. "I should suppose so, miss."

Penelope dropped Beryl off at the cottage—she was overwhelmed and thought she'd rest—and then headed to the Open Book. She had her book group that afternoon. There was already a book group but they'd become so popular that she'd started a second one—although Pen was never sure whether that was because of her leadership abilities or because of her proximity to gossip from Worthington House.

Laurence Brimble was the first to arrive with his usual military punctuality. Pen didn't know if he'd ever actually served, but he looked like central casting's version of a British colonial guard with his ramrod posture and handlebar mustache.

"Cheerio," he said when he saw Penelope. She half expected him to click his heels. He glanced around and sniffed in disapproval. "Where is everyone?"

"You're the first, Laurence," Penelope said. "You're early."

He glanced at his watch. "So I am. If you call five minutes being early."

Penelope and Brimble were just sitting down when Tracy Meadows rushed in, unbuttoning her coat as she crossed the bookstore.

"Sorry," she said as she unwound her scarf. "The baby-sitter was late—that girl's got the motivation of a slug—but she's good with the baby, so there's that."

Shirley Townsend arrived right after Tracy. She was a big-boned woman wearing dark slacks, a vivid floral blouse, and a chunky statement necklace of large blue beads. She had a red wool coat slung over her arm.

She was slightly out of breath as she approached the group.

"Oh, my," she declared. "Have you heard the news?" She stopped and put a hand to her chest. "My cousin Philippa works at the police station and she told me there was another murder at Worthington House." She paused. "Well, they're not sure it's murder, but someone has died." She finished, panting slightly.

Tracy's eyes widened. "Who is it? Who has died?" She put a hand to her heart. "Not the duke I hope."

"No, no." Shirley shook her head. "It was one of the guests who was there for the wedding—Earl Winterbourne."

Brimble cleared his throat. "Quite some goings-on at Worthington House," he said, looking around. "What's the world coming to?"

"Cor, you'd think the place was cursed," Shirley said, fingering her necklace. "Two murders in as many years. Three, if this recent death turns out to be murder as well. And those last two being a married couple dying one after the other."

"There was a rumor a long time ago that the castle was cursed," Brimble said authoritatively. "The third duke of Upper Chumley-on-Stoke was found murdered in his bed and then the wife of the fifth duke was killed in a riding accident that some say was highly suspicious. It seems she'd been carrying on with the head gardener and many suspect that the duke had had enough of it. He went on to marry again—someone much younger—so it does make you wonder." Brimble smoothed his mustache with his index finger.

"Yes, well . . ." Shirley said.

"I read in one of those magazines they have by the checkout at Tesco that the duchess is in the family way," Tracy said.

"Oh, go on!" Shirley said. "You don't believe everything those magazines print, do you? They're just making it up like they always do."

Tracy laughed. "Well, if the duchess does have a bun in the oven, I'm sure she'll have an easier time of it than I have. Hot and cold running nannies, no doubt."

"You're friends with the duchess," Shirley said, turning to Penelope. "Is that possibly true or is it just another one of those stories those magazines print in hopes that we'll buy them?"

Penelope thought of what Worthington had said—*in your condition*—but she feigned a look of innocence and insisted she had no idea.

Finally Penelope managed to get the book discussion under way. Figgy wheeled over a cart with tea things and a delicious-looking lemon drizzle cake for them to enjoy while the discussion wrapped up.

After the book group was finished and everyone had departed, Figgy joined Penelope, and together they cleaned up the dirty cups and saucers and plates sticky with lemon and sugar. Figgy was scratching at a bit of glaze that had stuck to the table when she paused and looked at Penelope.

"So with Lord Winterbourne dead," she said with her hands on her hips, "that means he isn't likely to have killed his wife. Unless there are two killers running around Worthington House."

"I know," Penelope said, stacking plates on Figgy's cart. "That certainly eliminates him. But why kill him?" She turned and looked at Figgy.

Figgy shrugged. "To silence him? Maybe he saw something that night? Maybe he saw the person who hit Cissie with that polo mallet."

"That's true." Penelope's shoulders slumped. "I was convinced he was the culprit. But you're right. Tobias must have seen something. Or at least the killer thought he had."

Pen picked up a used teacup and placed it on the tray. She gasped and turned toward Figgy.

"Rose left the ballroom, too. Digby, who was helping with the fireworks, saw her." Penelope bit her lower lip. "He didn't know her name of course, but the description fit. She and Tobias must have been having a liaison outside. If Tobias saw something, then maybe she did, too." Pen gasped again. "And if that's the case, that means her life could be in danger as well. If the killer murdered Tobias to keep him from talking, why not kill Rose as well?"

THIRTEEN

❧

Pen thought about it and finally decided that she needed to warn Rose that she might be in danger.

Mabel was counting out the register and had flipped the Open sign on the front door to Closed. Night was falling, and the last shoppers were scurrying past the window of the Open Book, packages in hand, as they hurried home to make their tea.

Beryl had said she was going to rest and Pen felt confident she would be fine for another hour at least. It wasn't going to take her that long to pop over to Worthington House and have a word with Rose.

Penelope felt a surge of emotion as she steered her MINI down the high street past all the shops that had become so familiar to her. She felt at home for one of the first times in her life.

She was stopped at a crosswalk when one of the pedestrians turned and waved to her—it was Violet Thatcher. Pen waved back, feeling a lump gathering in her throat. From being suspicious of Pen upon her arrival—an American intruding on their small, tightly knit community—the residents of Upper Chumley-on-Stoke had come to accept her—or at least tolerate her—a stranger in their midst.

Pen headed away from town, and soon Worthington House came into view, looking majestic perched on the slight rise above the town. She passed the gatehouse and negotiated the long drive to the castle itself.

Penelope parked her car, went up to the front entrance, and rang the bell. After a moment the door was pulled open by Royston. He still looked shaken by the afternoon's events—his lugubrious face appearing even longer than usual, his brow so furrowed it seemed as if it were permanently frozen in that position.

"Good evening, miss." His tone was somber.

"Good evening, Royston. I was hoping to have a word with Miss Rose Ainsley. I believe she's still here?"

"Certainly, miss. I will phone her."

Royston picked up the telephone on the foyer table and dialed a number. His movements were slow and heavy. He spoke briefly, hung up the telephone, and turned to Penelope.

"Miss Ainsley is in her room if you care to come with me."

Penelope followed him down the corridor. Sconces along the walls had been lit and cast pools of light on the jewel-toned Oriental runner. They passed the open door to the bedroom where she and Figgy had stayed. The beds were made, the duvet precisely folded, and the scent of lemon furniture polish drifted out into the hall.

Finally they paused before a closed door at the end of the corridor.

"Here you are, miss," Royston said as he retreated.

Penelope could hear the rustling sounds of Rose moving about inside. She knocked softly.

When Rose opened the door, it was clear she was in distress. Her face was bloated with tears and her eyelids were swollen.

"Rose, I'm so sorry," Pen said as Rose let her into the room. "Tobias's death must be a great shock to you."

A suitcase open on the bed was stuffed every which way with garments.

"You're leaving?" Pen said.

Rose sniffed. "I want to. I don't know. I'm waiting to hear from that detective. I don't know if they'll let me go." She balled up the fabric of her sweater in her hand. "Charlotte said I can stay, but I don't think I can stand it here another minute longer."

She began to cry.

Penelope pulled a tissue from her purse and handed it to her.

"Th-th-thank you." Rose sniffed as she wiped her nose and eyes. "Poor Tobias." She began to wail again. "Who would do something like that?"

She began shredding the tissue. "I never stopped loving him. Never. We were going to get married." She hiccoughed. "He was so unhappy."

"Tobias?" Pen perched on the edge of the bed.

Rose nodded. "He said Cissie didn't care about him at all. He said he thought . . . he thought she was having an affair."

"Oh?" Pen's ears perked up. "Did he say with whom?"

"He didn't know, but he had his suspicions." Rose yanked a dress off the hanger in the closet, wadded it up, and stuffed it into her suitcase. "He wanted to leave her but he couldn't.

She wouldn't give him any money. And it wasn't as if some-one in his position could go out and get a job like some commoner."

"Is that what he said?"

Rose nodded. "Yes. He said it would be unseemly." She fiddled with the handle of her suitcase. "Cissie treated him horribly, but she wouldn't let him leave. She couldn't bear to see him happy with me."

Pen had a sudden thought. She'd assumed that Tobias had killed Cissie to get out of the marriage while keeping her money. But what if Rose had been the one to do the deed? She'd been seen outside near the terrace as well.

As if Rose had read her mind, she said, "And don't think I killed Cissie. I couldn't do something like that." She shud-dered. "I faint at the sight of blood. I'm very sensitive."

A hard look came over her face. "Besides, why don't you ask Yvette what she was doing in the boot room the day Worthington's polo mallet went missing? She had no cause to be in there. I think she has some explaining to do." Her breathing was agitated.

Penelope waited until Rose had calmed down.

"I actually came here to warn you," Pen said.

Rose froze with her hand on her suitcase. "Warn me?"

"Why did someone kill Tobias? What if it was because he saw the killer out on the terrace around the time Cissie was murdered and they killed him to keep him quiet?"

Rose's face turned white and she bit her lower lip so hard a drop of blood pooled around her tooth.

"What if they thought you saw something that night as well?" Penelope said.

"But I didn't . . . we didn't. I'm sure Tobias didn't."

"Did you hear anything?"

Rose hung her head. "No. I'm afraid we were . . . concentrating on each other."

"But I don't suppose the killer would realize that. If they knew you'd been outside . . ."

Rose's hand flew to her throat, and she gasped. "They might try to kill me, too," she whispered.

P en was about to leave Worthington House when she ran into Charlotte.

"Penelope!" Charlotte exclaimed. "I didn't know you were here."

"I stopped by to see Rose," Pen said, eyeing Charlotte.

She didn't look well—she seemed agitated—her hands tugging at the neck of her sweater in an uncharacteristically nervous gesture that Penelope had never seen her make before.

"Is everything okay?"

Charlotte opened her mouth, and Pen had the impression she was about to deny anything was wrong, but then she obviously changed her mind.

"Something has gone missing again and I don't know what to make of it." Charlotte ran her hands through her blond hair, which was loose and cascading past her shoulders. "It can't be the servants—they've been with Arthur forever. Some of them even worked for his father. And nothing's ever gone missing before—not even so much as a farthing, as Arthur always says."

"What is missing? Could it have been misplaced?"

Charlotte shook her head. "It's a Dresden lace figurine of a dancing lady. It belonged to Arthur's mother—it was given to her by a dear friend when she married Arthur's father. It was a favorite of hers, although heaven knows what Arthur thought of it." A ghost of a smile played around Charlotte's lips. "It seems a bit . . . feminine for his tastes—all those crinolines and porcelain lace." She sighed. "Still, the piece is valuable and who knows what is going to go missing next?"

"Do you still have houseguests?" Pen said. "Aside from Rose, of course."

"Yes, there's Jemima and her husband, Ethan, and Tobi—" Charlotte stuttered to a halt. She wiped a hand over her face. "I keep forgetting that poor Tobias is gone. It's almost impossible to take in—like the plot in a terrible novel." She pulled at the neck of her sweater again. "That horrible detective they sent from the Met—Angie Donovan—doesn't want anyone to leave until the case is solved, although she's allowed Yvette to commute to her dress studio in London." Charlotte bit her lip. "I do wish we were dealing with Maguire instead. I'm sure he'd be more reasonable."

She gave her shoulders a small shake as if trying to physically shed her worries.

"I suppose under the circumstances, it's a bit ridiculous to be fretting about a missing figurine even if it is worth several hundred pounds at least."

"I imagine you're right," Pen said as Charlotte walked her to the front door.

Pen said good-bye and went out to her car. As Worthington House retreated in her rearview mirror, she thought that, as grand as it was, she still preferred her cozy little cottage, and she breathed a sigh of relief when she pulled up in front of it.

Beryl was waiting at the door when Penelope walked in.

"Do you know you left the stove on?" she said, pursing her lips in disapproval.

"It's an Aga," Pen said, as she took off her coat. "It's always on."

"What on earth for?" Beryl said, straightening the stack of magazines on Pen's coffee table. "At any rate, I decided to take a walk and get some fresh air. I ended up in your grocery store—Tesco I think it's called—and I bought some things for dinner."

"How lovely." Penelope suddenly realized delicious smells were coming from the kitchen.

"It's nothing special—a simple *poulet à la crème* and a green salad."

Penelope remembered Beryl had once taken a cooking course with Pierre Laurent, the famous French chef and restaurateur.

Beryl patted her stomach. "I must start watching my waistline though—now that I'm going to be single." The last word came out on a sob.

"You're divorcing Magnus?" Pen said.

"Yes. I don't know." Beryl held her hands out, palms up. "What else can I do? If he's going to prison—the lawyers seem to think it would be for a long time—I'll have to get on with my life."

"Come on." Penelope pointed toward the kitchen. "This calls for a glass of wine."

"Do you have any vodka?" Beryl said as she followed Penelope out to the kitchen. "I could do with something a bit stronger than a chardonnay at this point."

"Vodka it is."

The pot sitting on the stove was giving off a delicious

aroma. Pen lifted the lid and let the fragrant steam bathe her face briefly before opening the cupboard and pulling out her bottle of vodka.

She put a few cubes of ice in a glass, poured the liquor over it, and handed it to Beryl. Beryl took a huge sip and then looked at Penelope.

"I'm going to need to get a job," she said more matter-of-factly than Penelope would have expected.

"A job? Yes, I suppose so." Pen had poured herself a glass of wine and she took a sip. She sat down at the table opposite her sister. "What sort of work would you be looking for?"

Beyond modeling, Beryl had never done much of anything unless you could count selling Pampered Chef products at parties attended by her friends.

Penelope was setting the table when several ideas came to mind—two different ideas to be specific—that hatched a third idea.

She'd been thinking about what Rose had said—that Yvette had been seen in the boot room the day Worthington's polo mallet disappeared. Rose might simply have been trying to throw suspicion on Yvette or she might have been telling the truth.

And if Rose was telling the truth, Penelope wanted to learn a little more about Yvette. And Beryl was the key to killing two birds with one stone. Although under the circumstances, that wasn't perhaps the best choice of idiom.

But if Pen played her cards right, she would have an excuse to go to Atelier Classique in London to talk to Yvette and she might—just might—manage to score Beryl a job, assuming Beryl could get a work visa.

*   *   *

Pen already had the coffee on when Beryl appeared in the kitchen the next morning.

"That smells heavenly," Beryl said, pulling her robe closer around her. Her blond hair was tousled and her face creased with sleep. "I guess I'm still jet-lagged. I could have slept all day." She covered her mouth and yawned.

"I thought we'd go to London tomorrow," Pen said, as she poured out two mugs of coffee. She'd taken to drinking tea in the mornings—English breakfast—but in honor of Beryl's visit she'd switched back to coffee.

"You've got to be kidding," Beryl said. "I'm in no mood to go sightseeing. Besides, I've been to London numerous times already with Magnus when he was there on business."

Beryl accepted the mug from Penelope and wrapped her hands around it. She stared pensively at it for a moment.

"Magnus proposed to me in London, did I ever tell you?" She turned toward Penelope. "It was so romantic. He took me out to dinner at this fabulous restaurant—believe it or not I can no longer remember the name and it's long been closed—and I ordered a chocolate lava cake for dessert. When I dug my spoon into it—there it was—a diamond engagement ring." Beryl sniffed and dabbed her eyes. She looked at Penelope, her mouth downturned. "What went wrong?"

Magnus got greedy, Pen thought to herself. And now he had to pay the price. It was unfortunate that it was going to cost Beryl as well. All Beryl had ever tried to be was a good wife.

"We won't be going to London to sightsee," Penelope said. She went to the refrigerator and removed a carton of eggs. She glanced toward the back door, where Mrs. Danvers was curled up in a beam of sunlight coming through the window.

"I need to go to the Atelier Classique on Sloane Street in Belgravia."

Beryl perked up. "Atelier Classique? I love their designs." Beryl's face took on a dreamy expression but then quickly clouded over. "Not that I can afford them now."

"They designed the Duchess of Upper Chumley-on-Stoke's wedding gown."

"Don't tell me you're planning on buying something." Beryl put down her mug with a thud.

"Of course not. We're going there to get you a job. I happen to know someone who works there."

"You can't be serious?" Beryl's mouth hung open. "I'm way too old to model, if that's what you're thinking."

"I'm not thinking anything in particular," Pen admitted as she cracked some eggs into a bowl. "Maybe they need a sales consultant or a stylist. Or even, yes, a model for their in-house fashion shows. You may not be twenty anymore, but you're hardly ancient." She faced Beryl with her hands on her hips. "We'll see what happens when we get there."

Penelope poured the eggs into a pan on the stove. They sizzled and spit momentarily. She grabbed a spoon from a container by the Aga and gave them a stir.

"Today, I thought I'd take you to the Open Book and you can meet the cast of characters I've gotten to know while I've been here. Afterward, we can do a bit of sightseeing and then have lunch. There's a pub that does a very good steak and kidney pie."

Beryl's eyebrows shot up. "Steak and kidney pie?"

Pen nodded. "Trust me. You'll love it."

*   *   *

This is so charming," Beryl said when they were standing in front of the Open Book. "I feel as if I've stepped into a fairy tale. The whole town feels that way."

Penelope felt a rush of pride. "The inside is equally charming," she said as she held the door open for Beryl.

Mabel looked up and smiled when she saw them. "You must be Beryl," she said, as she came out from behind the counter. "Welcome to the Open Book. We've been dying to meet you."

"This is lovely," Beryl said, looking around. "So wonderfully cozy." She turned to Pen. "No wonder you love it."

India came out from behind one of the bookshelves and Pen motioned her over.

"India, this is my sister, Beryl Kent."

"India Culpepper," India said crisply in her posh, upper-class accent. She squinted at Penelope and Beryl. "You two don't look terribly alike," she proclaimed.

"Beryl got our mother's good looks," Penelope said, "while I've always been told I take after my father."

"Quite," India said, fingering her pearls. "How are you getting on?" she said to Beryl.

"It's been a bit overwhelming," Beryl said. "I hadn't expected to visit a castle and meet the Duchess of Upper Chumley-on-Stoke. What an honor. Or to be on the scene of a murder." She shuddered.

"Murder?" Mabel's eyebrows shot up.

Figgy came up to them and held out a plate of shortbread cookies. "Help yourself."

"Tobias Winterbourne appears to have died from anaphylactic shock," Pen said, reaching for a cookie.

"My sainted aunt," Mabel said. "Another murder at Worthington House?"

"We don't know for sure that it's murder. Yet," Penelope said.

"Poor Tobias," Figgy said. "He was a bit of a tosser, but still, that's no reason to murder him."

"I suppose we'll know more soon," Penelope said.

Figgy turned to Beryl. "I'm Figgy. You must be Beryl." She smiled.

"Figgy?" Beryl said. It was clear that she thought she hadn't heard correctly.

Figgy fingered the stud in her ear. "Actually it's Lady Fiona Innes-Goldthorpe, but that's such a mouthful that everyone calls me Figgy."

"How long will you be staying?" India said, peering at Beryl.

Beryl hesitated. "To be honest, I don't know yet."

India nodded briskly. "I hope you enjoy your stay."

"Why don't you show Beryl around?" Mabel called over her shoulder as she headed back to the counter where a customer was waiting.

Pen led Beryl around the shop, pointing out the rather extensive used-book section and the display of royal books she'd put together in honor of Charlotte and Arthur's wedding.

"Very nice," Beryl said. "You're quite creative."

"Thanks."

"It's not very tidy, is it?" Beryl eyed a tottering stack of books waiting to be shelved. "But that's part of its charm." She pointed to one of the armchairs. "That looks comfortable. The perfect place to curl up on a rainy day."

"You must see my writing room," Pen said, leading her across the shop. She opened the door and Beryl peeked in.

"It's tiny but I imagine there are no distractions."

"Exactly." Penelope shut the door again.

"I guess you really are an author," Beryl said with a note of pride in her voice. "I'm sorry I didn't take your writing seriously before." She squeezed Pen's arm. "It's actually quite impressive." She gave a bitter laugh. "Certainly more impressive than marrying a man with money and spending your time going to Pilates classes, arranging flowers, and hosting dinner parties."

Beryl was quiet as they said good-bye and headed out the door. "Everyone seems to be quite fond of you," she said when they were on the sidewalk. "I can see that you've made a life for yourself here."

"Yes," Penelope said in surprise as they headed out. "I guess I have."

Beryl was ready early the next morning. Penelope took that as a good sign—she was excited to go to London—or at least not totally against the idea.

She was dressed for it, too, in a very smart outfit—high-waisted black pants, a black-and-white houndstooth-print silk blouse with a chunky necklace at her throat. Penelope felt decidedly un-chic in her plain black pantsuit and white blouse.

Beryl was quiet on the drive to the train station although she did gasp once or twice. Penelope thought she was overreacting—she was doing a fine job of staying on the left side of the road.

Beryl breathed a very loud sigh of relief when they arrived at the train station parking lot. Penelope thought it sounded sarcastic—if a sigh could be said to be sarcastic.

Beryl paused outside the station. "I feel like I've stepped back in time—or have fallen into a Charles Dickens novel," she said, regarding the small Victorian brick structure. "This is so charming."

"The trains are quite modern though," Penelope said as she purchased their tickets.

"I'm almost disappointed," Beryl said, fastening the buttons on her coat.

The day had dawned bright and cloudless, but the wind had a sharp edge to it as they stood on the platform waiting for the train.

Finally a whistle sounded in the distance and the train slowly chugged around the bend, rattling as it went over the switches.

The train came to a halt and Penelope and Beryl boarded and found seats. The carriage was warm and they unbuttoned their coats and settled in.

They didn't say much on the trip—Beryl spent most of the time staring out the window. Penelope could imagine how she felt—being betrayed by Magnus and having her life change overnight. She said a prayer that their trip to London would be successful.

Penelope noticed that Beryl perked up as soon as the train pulled into King's Cross station. The station was humming with activity and sunlight streamed through the arched glass-paneled ceiling. The hands on the large old-fashioned clock suspended next to the platform appeared to be working and read ten o'clock—a far cry from the clock at the Chumley train station that had been stuck at six o'clock for longer than anyone could remember.

Penelope had checked a map before their arrival in London. "We can take the Tube to Sloane Street from here," she said as they joined the crowd heading toward the exit.

"We'll have to walk a bit when we get off, but it's a lovely day if a bit chilly."

"A brisk walk will warm us up," Beryl said, buttoning her coat.

Beryl's attitude had definitely changed, Penelope noted as they made their way through the crowd to the tube station. Even if things with Atelier Classique didn't work out, this had been a good idea.

They caught the Tube and exited at Sloane Square Station. As they turned onto Sloane Street, the shops became fancier and fancier—Prada, Tom Ford, Chanel, and other high-end retailers. The women they passed on the sidewalk, laden with glossy shopping bags, were all increasingly elegantly dressed and coiffed.

Beryl appeared to be drinking it all in, pausing occasionally to examine an outfit in one of the windows. She was obviously in her element. She stopped in front of one display and pointed to the mannequin.

"Isn't that dress fabulous?" she said to Penelope. She put her hand on the door handle. "I have to try it on."

Suddenly Beryl's shoulders drooped. "I forgot. Those days are over." She dashed a hand across her eyes and lifted her chin. "I shall have to make the best of, it as Grandma Parish always used to say."

Finally they came to Atelier Classique. A vivid emerald strapless gown with a small bustle and a train was featured in the window. They went inside, where the walls were covered in rose moiré silk and all the mirrors were gilt framed.

A saleslady, dressed all in black, glided over toward them.

Penelope felt more than a little out of her element but she forced herself to stand up straight.

"We're here to see Yvette Boucher," she said to the saleslady with as much confidence as she could muster.

The saleslady raised an eyebrow. "Madame Boucher is on the second floor." She cocked her head toward the back of the store. "The elevator is in the rear."

The elevator, which could barely hold both Penelope and Beryl, reminded Penelope of a gilded birdcage. She pushed the button for the second floor, and the car jerked into motion, moving incredibly slowly to the next level.

The doors opened onto an airy workshop with large windows and a high ceiling. Several dress forms were scattered around, and bolts of brightly colored fabrics leaned against the walls.

A young woman was sitting at a drafting table, sketching, her lower lip caught between her teeth.

"Hello?" Penelope said and the young woman jumped.

"Sorry, I didn't mean to startle you."

"That's okay." She got up and walked toward Pen and Beryl. "I guess I was lost in what I was doing. Are you here for a fitting?"

"No. We're looking for Yvette Boucher. The saleslady thought she would be here."

"She's in a meeting." The woman glanced at her watch. "She should be out in ten minutes or so if you'd like to wait."

They took off their coats and Beryl began wandering around the workroom, peering at the sketches pinned to the wall and fingering some of the fabrics.

"I hope we're not keeping you," Pen said to the woman. "Are you very busy?"

The woman shook her head. "Not terribly. It was a huge rush, but now that the wedding is over—you may have heard we did the gown for the new duchess of Upper

Chumley-on-Stoke—things have quieted down." She stuck out her hand. "I'm Olivia, by the way."

"Penelope." Pen shook her hand. "I was actually at the wedding of the duke and duchess. The gown was beautiful. Lady Winterbourne did an amazing job with the design. And of course Charlotte Davenport looked beautiful in it."

Olivia frowned. "Lady Winterbourne? Of course, she owns Atelier Classique."

Olivia paused.

Penelope suspected there was a "but" coming and she was right.

"But . . . she doesn't have anything to do with the designing. Yvette Boucher and her people create all the designs sold at Atelier Classique."

"So Lady Winterbourne didn't design the Duchess of Upper Chumley-on-Stoke's wedding gown? Not at all?"

Olivia shook her head vigorously. "No. That was all Yvette and her team." She ducked her head. "I'm proud to say that I'm a member of her team."

Penelope thought back to the night before Charlotte's wedding to Worthington. She remembered the look Yvette had given Cissie when Cissie had mentioned "her team." That must have infuriated Yvette, who was being treated like nothing more than a seamstress when in fact she was a very talented designer.

And Rose had seen Yvette in the boot room where Worthington's missing polo mallet should have been.

Had Yvette taken it? And used it to bash Cissie Winterbourne over the head until she was dead?

Penelope heard the elevator doors open and a hint of perfume wafted toward them. Olivia scurried back to her drafting table and Pen turned around to see Yvette headed their way. Yvette looked momentarily startled to see

Penelope, but then her face resumed its usual closed and unreadable look.

"It's Penelope, isn't it?" Yvette said smoothly, eyeing Penelope's pantsuit.

Penelope introduced Beryl and noticed Yvette smiled approvingly at Beryl's more stylish outfit.

"Can I help you with something?" Yvette said, tilting her head to one side as she regarded Penelope.

"My sister"—Pen pointed at Beryl—"is looking for a job. She has experience as a model and I thought of you and that perhaps . . ." Penelope's voice trailed off under Yvette's icy glare.

Yvette spun around and looked Beryl up and down, her eyes narrowed appraisingly.

"You're the perfect size," she said finally. "I am starting a new collection for the more mature woman and will need someone to fit the clothes on as well as model them in the salesroom." She glanced at her watch. "I have appointments all afternoon, but if you come back tomorrow, we can talk about the details. I'll need to sponsor you for a work visa, so there will be applications to fill out."

"That's wonderful, Beryl." Pen smiled at her sister. She turned to Yvette. "Olivia told me that you're the one who actually designed Charlotte Davenport's wedding gown," Pen said. "I'm sorry that you didn't get credit for it. That must hurt."

Yvette's face froze. Pen noticed her chest rise and fall as she exhaled sharply.

"It's business. It's not unusual. I didn't expect anything else. The name Lady Winterbourne carries a bit more weight than mine, I'm afraid."

But Penelope wasn't so sure. She had the feeling that Yvette had actually been quite hurt. She could imagine how she'd feel if she wrote a book and they put someone else's name on it. Surely Cissie could have admitted Yvette's contribution to the design of the gown to her circle of friends at least.

It wouldn't have harmed anything and in the end, its omission might have been fatal to Cissie.

FOURTEEN

❧

"I didn't realize I'd become a mature woman," Beryl said as the train was pulling out of King's Cross station on their way home. She gazed out the window, her arms crossed over her chest.

Penelope thought she sounded slightly miffed and had to suppress a smile.

"I suppose it depends on how you define *mature*." She squeezed her sister's arm. "But you have a job. Isn't that fantastic?"

Beryl smiled. "Yes. It's a huge relief. The commute will be a bear, but there should be a lot of men on the train so it will be the perfect opportunity to meet someone." She pursed her lips. "Of course, now that I'm *mature*, I may have to settle for someone older—someone who's balding with a large paunch."

Penelope thought of her brother-in-law's thick head of

dark hair and muscular physique honed by weekends spent playing tennis and taking seventy-five-mile bike rides.

"I don't see why you should have to settle," Pen said decisively. "You're still a very attractive woman. But don't you think you should give yourself some time to adjust? To be on your own and to find yourself, as they say?"

"I don't want to find myself," Beryl said, her expression set. "Oh, Pen," she cried suddenly, "I'm not independent like you are. I don't know how to do . . . things. Other than plan dinner parties and make socially acceptable small talk. I haven't balanced a checkbook in years and years."

"It's like riding a bike—it will come back to you, don't worry."

Beryl sighed. "I don't know. . . ."

"Listen, Beryl, you've got me. If you need help with something, I'll be here."

Beryl looked doubtful. "I don't know," she said again.

P en's cell phone was ringing when they walked into the cottage. Mrs. Danvers looked highly insulted when Penelope gave her a peremptory pat and then proceeded to take the call. The cat stalked off and sat in the corner, occasionally glaring over her shoulder at Penelope.

Penelope was surprised to hear Maguire's voice on the other end of the line, asking if she'd care to join him for a quick dinner at the Book and Bottle. Penelope looked at Beryl and hesitated.

Beryl flapped a hand at her and mouthed, *Go on*.

"Are you sure you don't mind?" Penelope said when she'd hung up.

"Not in the least. I'll have leftovers from last night and

then probably go to bed early. I'm exhausted. And I'll have to be up early tomorrow to catch the train to London."

Penelope flew up the stairs to her bedroom, jettisoned her pantsuit, and slipped into a more comfortable pair of leggings and a bright purple sweater. She yanked a brush through her hair and headed back downstairs.

Beryl looked at her disapprovingly. "I thought perhaps this was a date but with you looking like that . . ."

"We're friends," Penelope said. "Besides, he's seen me before—he knows what I look like."

Beryl raised an eyebrow but didn't say anything further.

Pen grabbed her coat and slipped it on. She planned to walk to the Book and Bottle in order to avoid having to introduce Maguire to Beryl. She wasn't ready for that. They were still feeling their way with each other—no need to throw family into the mix.

Before Beryl could make any more comments, Penelope was out the door and walking briskly toward the Book and Bottle.

The door to the pub swung open as Penelope was approaching and the sound of convivial conversation floated out into the night air along with the smell of beer and fried food.

Maguire was waiting for her by the entrance. He leaned over and gave Penelope a brief kiss. She could feel the chill coming off him and his lips were cold. He must have just arrived.

The pub was fairly uncrowded with a couple of open stools at the bar and a choice of tables. The chatter of voices was punctuated by the sound of the fruit machine pinging in the background and the clink of glasses and rattle of cutlery.

"How is this?" Maguire said, leading them to a somewhat secluded table.

He pulled out Penelope's chair, then leaned over with his hands on the table. "What would you like to have? I'll run up to the bar and we can have our drinks while we're waiting for our order."

Penelope glanced at the blackboard on the wall, but she already knew what she wanted.

"I'll have a cider, please, and the bangers and mash."

Maguire smiled. "Coming right up."

Penelope watched as he walked toward the bar. He had a confident way of moving—it wasn't a swagger—there was nothing boastful about it—but it was purposeful and assured.

She pretended to be studying her phone as he walked back toward their table, drinks in hand. She hoped he hadn't noticed her watching him.

"Here we go." He placed the drinks on the table and took the seat opposite Penelope.

Penelope took a sip of her cider. "I didn't tell you," she began, "my sister is staying with me at the moment."

Maguire looked up. "Oh?"

"She wanted to escape from a big brouhaha over in the States. It seems my brother-in-law was involved in some sort of Ponzi scheme. The press has been camping out on the doorstep night and day. She couldn't stand it anymore."

"I can hardly blame her. I know how vicious those tabloids can be." He scrubbed his hands over his face.

"Rough day?" Penelope said, leaning forward with her elbows on the table.

"Kind of." He exhaled sharply. "It's that DCI the Met sent down—Angie Donovan. I feel like she's reduced me to a police constable. Next thing you know, she'll have me out directing traffic on the high street." He smiled. "I did score some points, though, for alerting her to the missing button from Tobias's jacket. That was right brilliant of you, I have to say."

The warmth in his eyes made Penelope's face flush.

"Have they done the autopsy on Tobias yet? Did they discover what killed him? Frankly, it looked like anaphylactic shock to me."

Maguire nodded. "It was. You were spot-on." He took a sip of his lager and ran a hand over his face again. "But that puts paid to the idea that Tobias is our killer. He's turned into a victim."

"I think he might have seen something while he was out in the garden."

"That makes sense to me," Maguire said. "But the DCI seems to think the two murders are unrelated."

"What?" Penelope paused with her glass halfway to her mouth.

Maguire nodded. "Personally I think she's got hold of the wrong end of the stick. Two murders so close together and in the same place?" He shook his head. "They've got to be related." He shook his head. "If only they'd let me handle this case."

He glanced over toward the bar. "Looks like our food is ready. I'll be back in a tick."

Moments later Maguire returned with two plates of bangers and mash. The aroma of the food drifted toward Penelope and she realized she was quite hungry. She and Beryl had done a lot of walking while in London, having added a bit of sightseeing to their visit.

She picked up her fork and then put it down again.

"Do you remember interviewing an Yvette Boucher after the murder? Petite, dark hair, French?"

"Yes." Maguire forked up a bit of his mashed potatoes.

"I've discovered she might have a motive for killing Cissie Winterbourne."

"Oh? You're turning into quite the detective," Maguire teased.

"Is that a polite way of saying I'm nosy?"

Maguire threw back his head and laughed. "You said it, not me."

"Fair enough." Penelope smiled. "I found out something interesting today." She sliced off a piece of her sausage. "Yvette worked for Cissie at the design studio Cissie owned—Atelier Classique. They designed Charlotte Davenport's wedding gown."

Maguire raised an eyebrow.

"It's quite a big deal actually," Pen hastened to explain. "It was a huge drama beforehand—all the tabloids and even some American magazines were dying to find out who was going to design the dress and what it was going to look like. Whoever the designer was, was going to become a household name overnight."

Penelope took a sip of her cider. "Cissie claimed to have been the one to design the gown, but in reality it was Yvette who did all the work. I got the sense that she was quite put out about Cissie's taking credit for it. It could have been a real boon to Yvette's reputation if it had been known that she was the designer."

"'Quite put out'?" Maguire said, dabbing some mustard on his sausage. "You'd have to have a pretty twisted mind to let that goad you into committing murder." He was quiet for a moment. "Still, I have to say I've seen people kill for a lot less."

Penelope was thinking. "Maybe that was the proverbial

straw that broke the camel's back? Maybe there's something else? Something worse?"

"Could be. Or it could be the opposite. Did Yvette have anything to gain by Cissie's death?"

Penelope shrugged. "I don't know."

But she vowed she was going to find out.

Penelope saw Beryl off on the train the next morning. Her sister looked as smart as always and had seemed excited although she did confess to having had an attack of nerves while getting ready.

Penelope stood on the platform and watched until the train began to chug out of the station. She waved to her sister and when Beryl's carriage disappeared from view, headed to her car.

Mabel was in the window of the Open Book, rearranging the display, when Penelope arrived.

"Hand me that book over there, would you?" Mabel said when Penelope walked in.

Pen held up a volume. "This?"

"Yes," Mabel said. "That's the new Deborah Crombie. It just came in."

Mabel moved another book out of the way and positioned the new one on top of the stack in the display. She backed out of the window and brushed some dust from her sweater.

"Hang on," Pen said. She plucked a dust bunny from Mabel's fuzzy white hair.

Penelope noticed Figgy walking toward them.

"Good morning," Figgy said.

Penelope turned and opened her mouth to say good morning but the words didn't come out. She stared wide-eyed at Figgy.

Figgy looked as if she had been scrubbed clean. The extra earrings that normally adorned her earlobes were missing; there was no ring in her nose; her hair was no longer spiked with gel but smoothed into a glossy helmet; and her clothes . . . well, her clothes were ordinary—like an outfit off a mannequin at Marks and Spencer and not the haphazard assortment of garments Figgy normally wore that looked as if she'd pulled them from her closet blind-folded.

"What gives?" Pen said, still in shock.

Figgy made a face. "I'm meeting Derek's parents tonight for the first time for dinner. He's picking me up as soon as we close."

"Didn't want them meeting your real self, eh?" Mabel said, leaning her elbows on the counter.

Figgy looked at the floor. "I was afraid they wouldn't approve of the real me," she said quietly.

Mabel came out from behind the counter and put an arm around Figgy's shoulders.

"Don't be daft. They're going to love you—the real you."

"I hope so," Figgy said so quietly Penelope almost couldn't hear her.

Penelope was standing behind the counter—she'd taken over for Mabel who wanted to run a few quick errands—when an older man came into the shop. Penelope thought he looked like everyone's idea of the typical Brit-ish professor—trench coat hanging open, tweed blazer, rumpled shirt and slacks, and an unlit pipe clenched in his teeth.

"Good morning," Penelope said and smiled.

The man pulled off his hat, leaving his thin white hair standing out around his head like a halo.

He took the pipe out of his mouth, waved it in front of Penelope, and grunted. "Do you have any books on World War Two?" He glanced around him and stuck his pipe back in his mouth, clamping down on it with yellowing teeth.

Penelope thought of all the books they carried on World War II and tried not to sigh. "Is there any specific aspect of the war you're interested in?" She started to come out from behind the desk. "D-Day or the Battle of the Bulge or the role of the RAF?"

The man frowned. "Something on the lives of ordinary people at the time perhaps. Surviving during the Blitz and all that."

"I think we can help you," Penelope said, heading for the stacks. "We have a couple of books you might find interesting." She crouched down beside one of the shelves and pulled out several volumes. "Perhaps you'd like to glance through these?" She held up one of the books. "*The Longest Night: The Bombing of London on May 10, 1941* is excellent."

She carried the stack over to one of the armchairs and placed them on the side table.

"Thank you," the man said before putting his pipe back in his mouth.

The scent of a woodsy tobacco mixed with a cherry aroma wafted off him. Penelope found it oddly soothing.

As she walked away she had a sudden thought that nearly stopped her in her tracks. She remembered the night of the Worthingtons' ball when Jemima had come over to speak to Penelope before the fireworks. Penelope remembered quite distinctly that the smell of tobacco smoke had clung to Jemima's hair. Penelope was quite certain that Jemima didn't smoke. But Cissie did—she had gone out to the terrace to light her pipe.

Had Jemima joined her on the terrace? And had Jemima been the one to murder her?

FIFTEEN

꠷

"S he could be one of those closet smokers," Mabel said
when Pen told her about Jemima smelling of smoke,
which potentially put her out on the terrace where Cissie
was killed. "The type who are ashamed of the habit and
hide it from everyone."

Pen felt slightly deflated. "I wonder if Charlotte knows.
She may have caught Jemima sneaking out for a cigarette
at one time or another. Besides, it's hard to hide the smell."

"It's possible." Mabel picked up a catalogue from the
counter. "I suppose you could ask her."

Penelope nodded.

"What do you think of this?" Mabel said, turning the
catalogue around to face Penelope. She pointed to a photograph of some board games. "I'm thinking of expanding
our inventory and carrying a few impulse items—those
things people pick up on their way to the cash register."

"That's a great idea. Perfect for a birthday gift or something for Christmas."

Mabel took the catalogue and thumbed through it. "I was thinking about some leather-bound journals as well. What do you think of these?"

Penelope glanced at the catalogue. "Lovely. I'm sure they'd sell well."

"We can set up a table over there," Mabel said pointing to a spot in the store. "For these gift items." She turned to Pen. "What do you think about calendars at the end of the year? They'd make great Christmas gifts, don't you think?"

"What are you two cooking up?" Figgy said, wandering over with a plate piled with shortbread cookies.

"Just what I needed," Pen said. "Suddenly I'm starving."

"Why don't you nip out and get yourself a proper lunch?" Mabel said sternly. "Some fish-and-chips or a takeout curry. You can't exist on cookies alone no matter how delicious they are." She smiled at Figgy.

"I thought I'd stop by Worthington House and see if Charlotte is in."

"Following up on your hunch?" Mabel's eyes had a twinkle in them.

"Maybe," Pen said rather enigmatically.

Penelope approached Worthington House with a level of confidence she hadn't felt on her very first visit. Things had certainly changed. But she still felt a sense of awe as the castle came into view and almost had to pinch herself to be sure she wasn't dreaming.

Royston opened the door when Penelope rang. He gave a slight bow and ushered Penelope in.

Penelope asked if Charlotte was in and Royston nodded affirmatively. He picked up the telephone and dialed.

"Her grace is in her office," he said. "I will show you the way."

Although Pen had been to Charlotte's office numerous times, she was still grateful for Royston's lead as they wound their way down the numerous corridors.

Royston stopped in front of a closed door, opened it with a flourish, and announced, "Penelope Parish is here, your grace."

Charlotte was behind her desk, her laptop open on top and some scribbled notes by her elbow. She was casually dressed in black leggings and a black turtleneck that emphasized the pallor of her face. Penelope noticed there were dark circles under her eyes.

"Please sit down," Charlotte said, motioning toward a chair.

"I hope I'm not interrupting. . . ."

Charlotte smiled. "Not at all. I'm due for a break. I've been working for hours. I'm afraid I'm a bit behind and need to do some catching up." She massaged her forehead with her fingers. "How is your writing coming?"

"I'm deep in revisions at the moment," Penelope said. "I'm quite pleased with how they're going. So far at any rate." She laughed.

"I know what you mean." Charlotte leaned back in her chair. "Would you care for some tea?" She glanced at her watch. "Goodness, it's almost lunchtime. I could see what Cook has in store for us today if you'd like." She put a hand on her stomach. "I'm afraid I haven't had much of an appetite these days."

"Thank you, but I just have a quick question and then I'll let you get back to work."

Charlotte cocked her head.

"Is Jemima Dougal a smoker?"

Charlotte looked surprised. "No, why? She has asthma I believe—I've seen her using an inhaler so I doubt she'd take up smoking."

"Because the night Cissie Winterbourne was killed, I noticed that at one point during the evening, I smelled smoke on her hair."

"Could it have been from the bonfire?"

Penelope shook her head. "It was before the bonfire had been lit. And it was definitely smoke—tobacco smoke."

Charlotte shook her head in disbelief. "You're not saying that you think Jemima killed Cissie? Why would she?"

"I don't know," Penelope admitted. "Something from their past?"

Charlotte tilted her head. "That could be. All the same people run in these circles and have known each other since they were in diapers, and Jemima went to the Oakwood School for Girls with Cissie."

"So it's perfectly possible there could be some ancient history between them."

Charlotte shrugged. "I suppose so. But why would Jemima kill Cissie now? Why wait all this time?"

"I don't know. Maybe something stirred things up again? An old grudge perhaps?"

Charlotte picked up her pencil and began tapping it against the desk.

"That could be. But if that's the case, I'm afraid I have no idea what it is."

"That's all I wanted to know," Pen said, starting to get up. "I'll let you get back to work."

She declined Charlotte's offer to fetch Royston to escort her and began traversing Worthington House's maze of corridors herself. She was passing the library door, which was open, when a movement caught her eye.

Jemima had her back to Penelope and was standing next to a small side table. Penelope watched as she snaked out a hand, picked up an ornate Fabergé egg, and slipped it into her pocket.

Penelope didn't know what to do. Should she tell Charlotte that Jemima was the one who had been stealing things? Penelope thought back to the wedding and the time she'd caught Jemima in the drawing room. Jemima had been startled—as if she'd been caught in something. Had she been about to pocket something then?

Charlotte deserved to know, Penelope decided, and she headed back the way she had come. She knocked on the door to Charlotte's office, but there was no answer. She cautiously opened the door and peeked in, but the room was empty.

She'd phone Charlotte later. She could hardly wander all over Worthington House looking for her.

She decided she'd check in with Mabel and make sure that everything at the Open Book was okay and let her know that she was going to be a bit longer. She had an idea and she was puzzling over just how to pull it off.

Penelope turned onto the high street and headed out of Chumley and into the countryside where open fields bordered the road on either side. It wasn't long before she saw the white sign with the gold crest that read *Oakwood School for Girls*. She turned onto the nearly quarter-mile-long drive that led to a large campus dotted with Gothic Revival–style buildings.

Charlotte had said that Jemima and Cissie had both been students there. Penelope hoped to find someone that might have known them and might remember something from their past that would have pushed Jemima to murder all these years later.

Penelope drove down the circular drive leading to the impressive stone building that housed the administrative offices and parked her car. She pulled a notebook and pencil from her tote bag and got out. She crossed her fingers— she hoped her plan was going to work.

Pen pushed open the large carved wooden door of the administration building. The foyer's marble floor was inlaid with gold tiles outlining the school crest. The walls were covered in rich wood paneling that gleamed in the light of the chandeliers that lit the hallway.

Two girls were coming toward Penelope, whispering to each other, their books tucked under their arms. They were wearing the Oakwood School uniform of plaid skirt, white blouse, and dark gray blazer with the school crest on the pocket.

Pen approached them, plastering a smile on her face much like a dog wags its tail to show it's friendly.

"Can either of you girls help me?"

They both stopped and stared at Penelope wordlessly, the blonde twirling her long hair around her finger.

"I'm from *Tatler*," Penelope said, brandishing her notebook and pen. "It's a magazine. Have you heard of it?"

They stared at her blankly. Finally, the brunette said, "I think my mum reads it."

"I'm looking to speak to someone who's been at the Oakwood School for around twenty years or so. Maybe one of the teachers . . . ?"

The girls looked at each other.

"You'd want to speak to T. Rex, then," the blonde said and giggled.

"Did you say T. Rex?" Penelope said. She had to have misheard. Parents sometimes gave their children unusual names but . . . T. Rex?

The girl giggled again. "Yes. Actually, her name is Tina Resse and she's worked here for absolutely ages. She's positively ancient."

"Where can I find miss, uh, Resse?"

The blonde pointed to a door with a plaque with *Maribel Northcott, Headmistress* on it. "She's Miss Northcott's assistant. Miss Northcott is the headmistress. T. Rex sits right outside her office."

Penelope smiled again. "Thank you."

She was relieved that the girls had shown a singular lack of curiosity as to what a reporter from *Tatler* was doing at the school. She hoped all would go as smoothly with Ms. Resse.

The door the girls had indicated was open, and Penelope knocked softly on the doorjamb before walking inside. It was a fairly large office with high arched windows, two desks, and a row of filing cabinets along one wall.

One desk was in front of a closed door with a small nameplate that read *M. Northcott.* The other desk was pushed into a corner. Two women sat at the desks and it was obvious which one Tina Resse was.

She had the bigger desk situated directly in front of the headmistress's door. The desk was very tidy—papers aligned, stapler, tape dispenser, and pencil sharpener all in a neat row. Tina was the picture of efficiency in her stark navy pantsuit with her thick dark hair sprayed into submission in a short bob that ended awkwardly just above her earlobes.

A younger girl sat at the other desk, her long mouse-brown hair brushing her waist and her desk piled with papers and folders.

Tina looked up sharply when she heard Penelope's knock.

"May I help you?" She started to stand up.

"I don't mean to be a bother," Penelope said, "but I'm looking for a Miss Resse."

"That would be me."

"Wonderful," Penelope gushed. "One of the students directed me to you—she said you'd been working at the school for quite a while."

"More than twenty years," Tina said with a note of pride in her voice. "Miss Northcott always says she wouldn't know what to do without me. Mrs. Gregor said the same when she was head and I worked for her. I started right after finishing secretarial school."

Tina was turning out to be quite chatty and Penelope breathed a sigh of relief. Hopefully that would make her job easier.

"I'm Penelope Hargreaves," Penelope said, deciding not to give her real name. "I'm freelancing for the *Tatler*. I don't know if you're familiar with it. . . ."

"Of course I am." Tina beamed. "I've been reading it for years—all that delicious royal gossip." Her face colored slightly. "It's my one indulgence."

"Wonderful," Penelope said, holding up her notebook and pencil. "You may have heard about the recent wedding of the Duke of Upper Chumley-on-Stoke and Miss Charlotte Davenport?"

"Of course," Tina said as if she couldn't imagine that anyone might not have. "I've followed every story." She picked up a mug that was sitting on her desk. Charlotte and Worthington were pictured in profile on the front. "I even treated myself to this and a set of tea towels. I'll never use them, of course—I'm going to frame them and hang them in my sitting room along with the ones from the wedding of the Duke and Duchess of Cambridge."

The girl at the other desk had turned around and was sitting with her arms folded on the back of her chair, a look of awe on her face.

"Go, on," she said. "You're really from *Tatler*?"

Was her cover about to be blown? Penelope wondered. But the girl simply introduced herself as Wanda.

"I'm doing a story on some of the guests who were at the wedding," Penelope plunged on, trying to keep her voice from squeaking and betraying her nervousness. "I understand two of the ladies in attendance were students at the Oakwood School—Cissie Winterbourne—I believe she was Cissie Emmott at the time—and Jemima Dougal. I'm afraid I don't know her maiden name."

"That would be Jemima Kirby you're meaning." Tina straightened the already straight collar on her blouse. "She and Cissie Emmott were thick as thieves when they were girls here. Although they could be competitive as well. I remember the time Jemima made the winning goal in our game against St. Mary's—Cissie threw down her hockey stick and stomped off the pitch. And Cissie didn't speak to Jemima for three weeks after Jemima was elected head girl. Cissie felt she deserved the position herself."

Tina reached out and moved her stapler a quarter of an inch to the right.

"They made up eventually. They could never stand to be apart. But that's the way it is with girls, isn't it?" She looked at Penelope.

"I suppose so," Pen said.

"Such a shame about Cissie, wasn't it?" Tina shuddered.

"Murder isn't something you expect at a royal wedding." She shook her head. "Poor Jemima. She must have been devastated. Were they still close, do you know?"

"I don't know," Pen admitted although *devastated* wasn't the word she would have used to describe Jemima's reaction to Cissie's murder.

"Of course, even best friends are going to lead separate lives as adults. It's not like being at school, is it?" Tina said. She waved a hand. "Marriage and children become your focus."

Wanda cleared her throat. "Didn't you tell me something about that girl Jemima Kirby?" she said, brushing her hair back from her shoulders.

Tina looked alarmed. "I don't think that's something we should—"

But Wanda was already continuing. "I remember you said she had some sort of disease. I don't remember what you said it was called but it had to do with people compulsively taking things." She looked at Tina, her eyebrows raised.

Tina let out an exasperated breath. "It's not a disease— it's a mental illness. It's called kleptomania."

Penelope was so startled she nearly dropped her notebook. "Jemima Kirby suffered from kleptomania?" she said.

A host of emotions passed across Tina's face and she plucked nervously at the collar of her blouse.

"I really shouldn't talk about it."

Penelope made a great show of putting her notebook and pencil in her tote bag.

"Off the record," she said.

Tina hesitated but only for a second. "It was like this. Things were going missing from the girls' rooms—little things—like someone's Alice band or a picture frame or a keepsake like a stuffed animal. The girls complained to Mrs. Gregor but she put it down to carelessness. She was always on at the girls about straightening their rooms. It was no wonder they couldn't find their things, she used to say." Tina clucked her tongue.

"But then more expensive things started to go missing— a gold locket, a silver-backed brush, a wallet. That's when Mrs. Gregor began to take the girls' complaints more seriously." Tina pursed her lips. "I, myself thought there was something to it right from the start."

Tina shifted in her chair. "Mrs. Gregor asked the girls to come to her in the strictest confidence if they knew something or suspected someone. Not long after, Cissie Emmott appeared, wanting to see Mrs. Gregor, and shortly after that, Jemima Kirby was sent for."

There was a rustling sound from behind the closed door and a look of panic crossed Tina's face. Penelope held her breath but the door remained closed.

"Of course, Jemima's parents were summoned immediately and it was arranged for her to see a counselor. It seems her parents were going through a difficult divorce and it was unsettling the poor girl, as I'm sure you can imagine," Tina said in a lowered voice.

Penelope's parents had divorced and she hadn't resorted to stealing things, she thought. But perhaps it had been more of a shock to Jemima—being away at a boarding school, she might not have seen the writing on the wall so to speak.

There was another louder noise from behind the closed door to the headmistress's office, and Penelope hastily thanked Tina, said good-bye to her and Wanda, and began to leave.

Her stomach rumbled as she was walking to her car and

she realized she hadn't had anything to eat. On the other hand, she certainly had enough food for thought. From what Tina had said, Cissie had clearly resented her friend Jemima's successes. Penelope knew the type—there'd been a girl like that in her class in high school—she expected all the accolades to come to her and resented it when they didn't.

It also seemed likely that Cissie knew about or had discovered Jemima's stealing and had told the headmistress. Did she consider it appropriate revenge for the times Jemima had stolen the spotlight from her?

Had history repeated itself? Had Cissie caught Jemima red-handed, lifting one of the items missing from Worthington House? And had Cissie threatened to spill the beans on Jemima and the only way for Jemima to stop her had been to kill her?

Had Jemima recently acquired something that Cissie wanted or thought should be hers? And had that led to a deadly conclusion?

SIXTEEN

࿐

That smells delicious," Mabel said, pointing to the bag in Penelope's hand.

Penelope held the bag up—a splotch of grease was beginning to bleed through on the front.

"I was starving so I picked up some fish-and-chips from the Chumley Chippie. I have enough to share if you'd like?"

"No, thanks." Mabel patted her stomach. "My waistbands are getting a bit tight. I'm on a slimming regimen at the moment."

Penelope thanked her lucky stars that she still didn't have to worry about her weight at least.

She took her feast into her writing room, spread it out on the table, and opened her laptop. She scrolled through her e-mail as she munched her chips and picked at her battered haddock.

She thought about working on her revisions but wasn't

in the mood—although after reading an e-mail from her editor, she realized she needed to get into the mood *tout de suite*, as the French would say.

> Darling Pen, I do hope you aren't finding those revisions too odious. Any idea when they'll be done? Everyone is so excited about your latest and of course the powers that be hope it will make them pots of money. I know that once you shore up that middle, we'll have a huge hit on our hands. Cheerio, Bettina

Penelope somewhat reluctantly pulled up her manuscript and got out her revision notes, but her mind kept wandering.

What might Jemima have had that Cissie wanted—if that was, indeed, what had driven Jemima to murder?

Charlotte had been right—people like Cissie and Jemima and Tobias kept to the members of their own exalted circle and it was nearly impossible to break in or gain their confidence. She was sure that plenty went on behind the scenes that no one knew about—not even the reporters and photographers prying into their lives from a distance with their cameras and long lenses.

Still, they did manage to uncover plenty of secrets and scandals. And that gave Penelope an idea. Perhaps she'd find a nugget of some sort in the society magazines and scandal rags—something that would hint at what might have gone on between Jemima and Cissie.

She closed her laptop, bundled up the wrappings from her lunch and stuffed them into the bag, and tossed them in the trash.

Mabel was on the telephone, arguing with a publisher whose shipment of books had arrived damaged. Penelope straightened the books on display as she waited.

"How was your lunch?" Mabel said after she hung up the telephone.

"Great. No wonder the British like fish-and-chips so much," Pen said. "You don't by any chance happen to have a collection of society and gossip magazines, do you?"

Penelope seriously doubted that Mabel would—Mabel was about as down-to-earth as they came—but people had hidden depths, so she figured it wouldn't hurt to ask.

Mabel raised an eyebrow. "What on earth do you want those for?"

Penelope explained her idea.

"You'll be wanting to talk to India, then. She collects *Tatler* and *Hello!* and all those others along with that royal commemorative tat she so adores."

As a distant relative of the Duke of Upper-Chumley-on-Stoke, India had inherited a small cottage on the Worthington estate. Penelope had been there once and she hoped she would remember how to find it.

At the time, she'd been shocked at the state of disrepair of the cottage as well as the obvious signs of India's straitened circumstances. She'd talked to Mabel and Mabel had promised to put a bug in Worthington's ear.

Even as she approached the cottage from a distance, Penelope could see that the roof had recently been repaired; the window frames had been painted; and the bushes, which had been wildly overgrown, had been trimmed and tidied. Obviously, Mabel's word to Worthington had borne fruit.

India, when she answered the door, was wearing her usual English gentlewoman's outfit of wool skirt, twinset, and a strand of yellowing pearls.

India's broad smile, quickly suppressed, indicated her pleasure at having a visitor. Penelope knew she lived alone and had no close relatives. The Open Book was her refuge when she became too lonely to stay at home.

India's tiny sitting room, with its beamed ceiling and wavy-paned windows set in thick stone walls, was comfortably toasty. Sitting in pride of place in front of the sofa was a brand-new flat-screen television replacing the old model that had been there the last time Pen had visited.

India must have noticed her looking at it. "I came into some money from a relative I quite frankly didn't even know I had. One day a check arrived from a solicitor's office in London along with a letter saying that I had been left a bit of money. I was that surprised."

Penelope smiled to herself. Obviously Mabel's word to Worthington had done a world of good.

India clutched at her pearls. "I know it's quite an indulgence—a new television when the old one worked just fine most of the time—but I do enjoy my programs. At my age, there isn't all that much to look forward to, you know."

"I'm glad you treated yourself," Penelope said.

"How about a cup of tea, my dear? I can have the kettle on in a jiff."

"That sounds wonderful. Can I help?"

India pointed to the sofa. "You sit and put your feet up. It won't take me a minute."

India came bustling back moments later with a tray set

with cups and saucers, a teapot in a hand-knitted cozy, and a plate of McVitie's digestive biscuits. She put the tray on the coffee table and set about pouring the tea.

Penelope accepted a cup along with a biscuit. She'd become rather fond of this ritual of afternoon tea. It slowed the pace of the day down just enough to allow one to catch one's breath.

"It's so lovely of you to visit me," India said, nibbling the edge of her biscuit.

Penelope felt guilt wash over her knowing that she was there with an ulterior motive.

"I'm actually hoping you can help me," Pen said.

India became as attentive as a bird keeping its eye on a worm. Her eyes glowed and she clasped her hands together.

"Don't tell me you're doing your detecting again," she said. "It was the talk of Chumley last year when you tracked down Regina's killer."

It was more like Regina's killer had tracked *her* down, Penelope thought. She shuddered at the memory.

"I am trying to locate some information," Penelope admitted. "Mabel thought you had a collection of gossip magazines—you know, the ones that write stories about the royals and other aristocrats and people in the news."

"I certainly do," India said, setting down her teacup. "I have albums of clippings as well, although sadly some of the newsprint is beginning to turn yellow and quite brittle." Her hand trembled slightly as she reached for her cup. "Believe it or not, I even have clippings from the newspapers of Prince Charles's investiture as the Prince of Wales."

Penelope did her best to look impressed. She cleared her throat.

"Do you have anything more recent? I'm looking for

stories about Cissie—about Lady Winterbourne—and that crowd."

India looked slightly insulted. "Of course I do. I have all the back issues of *Tatler* from when I first subscribed and also any of the issues of *Hello!* and *OK!* that cover the royal family and the nobility. I pick them up at the library's used-book sale for pennies." She hesitated. "Would you like to see them?"

"Yes, if it's not too much trouble."

India put her hands on her knees and pushed herself to a standing position. "I'll go get them, shall I?"

She disappeared into another room and returned moments later with a stack of magazines in her arms.

"I've brought the ones that are most likely to have what you're looking for." She grunted as she put the pile on the floor near Penelope.

"This is marvelous," Pen said, picking up the first magazine—a *Tatler* from several years ago. She began thumbing through it.

Cissie Winterbourne, or the Loo Paper Princess, as the tabloids referred to her, featured frequently in the pages of the magazine, but there was nothing that particularly stood out to Penelope.

She started in on an issue of *Hello!*, whose coverage was a bit more gossipy—stories intimating that Kate and Wills weren't speaking to each other, or they weren't speaking to the queen, or one or the other of them wanted a divorce. There were plenty of blurry photos shot from a distance with lurid captions underneath.

Cissie wasn't absent from these pages either, although she mostly appeared in photographs, dressed to the nines, at some charity function or other. Several times articles included pictures of her when she was younger and dating

Worthington with headlines like The Queen Drove Them Apart or Who Cheated First?

Penelope shuddered. She was certainly glad she wasn't famous. Even writing a bestselling novel had hardly made her a household name worthy of salacious coverage in the tabloids.

She picked up another magazine and came upon a collage of photos of Cissie, including one when she was quite young—barely out of her teens—Penelope thought. She was standing at the foot of a rather grand staircase dressed in a dark blue ball gown. Penelope assumed the man standing next to her was her father—partially bald and rather portly with a double chin and wire-rimmed glasses. Standing off to the side was a young girl, approximately Cissie's age, in a pair of dark slacks and a rather worn-looking sweater. There was a look of wistful longing in her eyes although her mouth was stretched into a smile showing a gap between her two front teeth.

Penelope flipped through a few more magazines. This wasn't getting her anywhere, she thought. She was about to give up when she turned a page and came upon a large photo of Cissie dressed in a short cocktail dress and sky-high heels. She was in a clutch, as Pen's grandmother would have said, with a man who was nuzzling her neck. Penelope thought he looked vaguely familiar.

She read the caption—*Cissie Emmott, the Loo Paper Princess, and Lord Ethan Dougal caught in some steamy PDA.*

Penelope let the magazine drop into her lap.

"Is everything okay, dear?" India said, lowering her own magazine and peering at Penelope over the tops of her reading glasses.

Penelope smiled. "Yes. Fine." She gathered the magazines into a pile. "I must get going."

"You're welcome to stay as long as you like," India said hopefully.

"Thank you. I do appreciate your showing me these magazines. Let me help you put them away."

"It's no bother, dear. Did you find what you were looking for?"

"Yes," Penelope said.

She certainly did find what she was looking for, she thought, as India stood at the door and waved good-bye.

That magazine photograph had made it quite clear that Cissie and Ethan Dougal were once a couple. Cissie had obviously been in search of a title to go with her money, and Ethan had one.

Had Jemima come along and swept Ethan away? And had Cissie waited for the right moment to exact her revenge, which had finally arrived when things began to go missing from Worthington House? Had Cissie threatened to embarrass Jemima by revealing her kleptomania as she had once done back in their school days?

The smell of curry wafted out of the cottage when Penelope opened her door. She dumped her bag in the foyer, hung up her coat, and followed her nose out to the kitchen.

Beryl had set the table for two and had even placed a vase of flowers in the center.

"What are those delicious smells?" Pen asked as she opened the refrigerator and took out a bottle of white wine.

"I picked up some chicken biryani from Kebabs and Curries on my way back from the train station," Beryl said, reaching out to straighten one of the napkins. "The taxi driver was most accommodating."

"Who did you have," Pen said pouring two glasses of pinot grigio, "Mad Max, who is about one hundred years old and drives twenty miles under the speed limit, or Dashing Dennis, who flirts with all his passengers via the rear-view mirror?"

"Definitely Dashing Dennis," Beryl said, her mouth quirking into a smile. "And here I thought it was me, but now you say he's that attentive to all the girls."

"Fortunately, he's harmless." Penelope pulled out a chair and sat down. "How was your day?"

Beryl's face brightened. "As the British would say, it was quite brilliant. You should have seen some of the clothes I got to model. Dreamy!" Beryl rolled her eyes heavenward. "Yvette is working on a new spring collection that's going to be beautiful."

"She certainly did a marvelous job on Charlotte's wedding dress."

Beryl opened the takeout bag, and the scent of curry intensified in the kitchen.

"Do you have some dishes for the chicken and rice?" she asked Penelope.

Penelope got two bowls out of the cupboard. She wasn't about to confess to Beryl that she normally ate her takeout right from the containers.

Beryl emptied the contents of the containers into the dishes and put them on the table. Penelope carried their wineglasses over and set them beside their places.

"What is Yvette like to work for?" Pen said as she dished up some chicken biryani. "She seems very . . . reserved."

Beryl cocked her head, her fork suspended in the air.

"She is rather reserved, but everyone likes her. Apparently she's very fair and also quite encouraging of the younger designers." Beryl rolled her eyes. "But you should have heard what the staff had to say about Cissie Winterbourne."

"Oh?" Penelope speared a piece of chicken with her fork. "Wasn't she well liked?"

"I should say she wasn't," Beryl said. She pointed her fork at Penelope. "You already know she took credit for designing Charlotte's dress, but apparently she took credit for everyone's designs. One of the young girls—Francine—wanted to see if she could make a go of it on her own. It's not an easy business, you know, but she had a backer who was interested in investing in her. Cissie managed to quash the whole thing! Yvette said she tried to reason with Cissie—she seems to be very protective of the staff—but Cissie was determined that if Francine left the studio, she would never work in fashion again." Beryl lowered her voice. "According to Yvette, Cissie thought Francine was making eyes at Tobias." She put her fork down. "Everyone said Cissie could be very vindictive. Francine quit and apparently Cissie made good on her threat. One of the girls heard that Francine was working at Harrods selling lingerie."

Beryl picked up her fork again and pushed her food around on her plate. "Cissie did do one good thing, though."

"What's that?" Pen said around a mouthful of rice.

"She left Atelier Classique to Yvette."

"What?" Penelope started to cough and choke.

Beryl looked at her in alarm. "Do you want some water?"

Penelope waved a hand and dabbed at her eyes, which had begun to tear.

"I'm fine, thanks." Penelope took a deep breath. "Cissie left the studio to Yvette?"

"Yes."

If that didn't give Yvette a perfect motive for murder, then Penelope didn't know what did.

SEVENTEEN

❦

Figgy was wiping down the tables in the Open Book's tea shop when Penelope breezed in the next morning.

She'd gone full-on Figgy again with all her earrings in place, her hair gelled into its usual spikes, and an outfit that could best be described as bohemian chic. Still, she didn't look like the usual Figgy to Penelope. Something was missing—the glow that usually emanated from her.

"Is everything okay?" Pen asked, putting her laptop down on one of the tables.

"No," Figgy said and burst into tears.

Pen put her arm around her friend's shoulders. "What's wrong?"

"Nothing. It's only that—" And she burst into tears again.

"Did you and Derek have a fight?" Pen tightened her arm around Figgy.

"Not exactly," Figgy said and sniffed loudly. She rummaged in her pocket, pulled out a tissue, and blew her nose.

"I'm out of guesses, Fig; tell me what's wrong, okay? Maybe I can help."

"No one can help," Figgy said and hiccoughed.

"Did you have dinner with Derek's parents last night? Did something go wrong?"

"Not wrong exactly," Figgy said, swiping at her eyes with the crumpled tissue. "I don't think his parents liked me," she said finally.

"Not like you? How could they not like you? Everybody likes you," Pen said. "What makes you think they didn't like you? Did they say something to Derek?"

Figgy shook her head. "No. They didn't say anything. That's the problem. They hardly spoke at all. It was awful," she said, beginning to cry again. She sniffed loudly. "Derek said that was due to cultural differences. He said they're always quiet. They're very reserved people."

"But—but . . ." Pen sputtered. "That doesn't mean they didn't like you."

"That's what Derek said."

"So why don't you believe him, then?"

Figgy shrugged. "I don't know. It's just a feeling I have." She shuddered. "It was as if I'd walked into a freezer the minute I sat down—they seemed that cold to me."

"I suspect it was just your imagination."

"I don't know." Figgy blew her nose again. "Derek and I are thinking of eloping. Because I can't imagine a wedding with his parents and my parents and all the tension that would create. Maybe we'll run away to Scotland or have the captain of the Dover ferry marry us."

Somehow that sounded more like Figgy's style to Penelope. She couldn't picture her friend in a white wedding gown and long veil traipsing down the aisle for a traditional ceremony.

Penelope went back to work and was putting some books back on their shelves when the bell over the front door jingled and a harassed-looking woman came in. Her parka was open and she was wearing a sweatshirt, jeans, and a pair of green rubber Wellingtons although it wasn't raining out and hadn't for several days. A young girl, who Penelope guessed to be about three years old, was hanging on to her arm.

"Can I help you find something?" Penelope asked as the woman approached her.

"Yes," the woman said, sighing, tugging the young girl by the arm. "I'm looking for a book."

Well, you've come to the right place, Penelope thought to herself.

The little girl's face was sticky with something, and she was wearing purple floral-print corduroy pants and a red-and-white-striped top.

The woman shrugged. "She insisted on picking out her own clothes today," she said apologetically. She flashed a smile at her daughter.

Penelope smiled. "I remember having an argument with my mother over why I couldn't wear a pair of leggings and a swimsuit top to kindergarten."

The woman laughed. She looked relieved. She gestured toward her boots.

"Of course I couldn't find any of my shoes this morning. Our Matilda does like to hide them, don't you, pet?" She patted the little girl on the head.

"What sort of book are you looking for?"

"It's for my book club." The woman laughed. "Although I think we should call it the wine club because we do more drinking than reading. Anyway, I can't remember the title exactly, but I know it had the word *all* in it." She snapped her fingers. "Oh, and there was a picture on the front and I think the cover was blue."

That ought to narrow it down to a couple thousand books, Penelope thought.

She smiled again. "Do you remember what sort of book it was? Women's fiction perhaps or suspense?"

The little girl was now poking her mother in the stomach with her index finger. The woman grabbed the girl's hand and held it.

"Dunno, I'm afraid. It was the sort of book that a book club would read."

Penelope took a deep breath, held it for a second, and then let it out. She pushed her glasses up her nose with her index finger.

She was mentally going through every title she could think of that had the word *all* in it.

"Was it *All the Missing Girls*?" she said, taking a stab at it. "Or perhaps *All the Ways We Said Good-bye?*"

She thought of *All Quiet on the Western Front* but doubted that was the sort of title a women's book club would choose.

The woman shook her head. "It had a blue cover," she said again.

Penelope was running out of ideas when the woman suddenly shouted.

"There," she said pointing to a display. "That's it. *All the Light We Cannot See.*"

Penelope breathed a sigh of relief, grabbed a copy of the book, and carried it up to the front counter.

"Is there anything else you're looking for?" she said to the woman.

She shook her head and reached into her purse for her wallet.

Mabel rang up the sale, slipped the book into a paper bag, and handed it to the woman.

"What was that all about?" Mabel said when the door had closed in back of the woman and her child. "You look a bit shirty."

"I'm okay. That woman was looking for a book and couldn't remember the title. All she knew was that it had a blue cover with a picture on it and the word *all* was in the title."

Mabel laughed. "Welcome to bookselling. I can't tell you how many times that's happened since I started the Open Book. It's right annoying, isn't it? As if we were mind readers." She used the edge of her sleeve to wipe some crumbs off the counter. "Or when they get the title wrong. I had a young girl come in looking for a book she'd been assigned to read. Got the title all wrong—said it was something like *For Whom the Doorbell Rings*. Fortunately I was able to decode that." She tapped her head. "One of the times when my MI6 training came in handy."

Penelope laughed. "I suppose she meant *For Whom the Bell Tolls*. Still . . ." She shook her head. "No point in getting exasperated, I suppose.

"I'm off to shelve those new books that came in," Pen said, heading toward the stacks where a carton of books sat at the end of one of the rows. She was halfway there when she had a sudden thought—she'd never called Charlotte to tell her about Jemima.

She tried out different ways to break the news to Charlotte in her head as she shelved some books. No matter how you cut it, it was bound to be awkward and she wasn't looking forward to it. But as her grandmother always said, the Parishes didn't shirk their duty.

As she was placing the last book on the proper shelf, she had a thought. What if she spoke to Jemima first? She might be able to convince her to return the objects that she'd stolen, and then maybe it wouldn't be necessary to talk to Charlotte after all.

Penelope had butterflies in her stomach as she headed toward Worthington House again. How was she going to confront Jemima about her kleptomania without offending her? She had to be realistic, Penelope thought—no matter how delicately she put it, Jemima was bound to be upset. Just so long as she didn't become wildly upset.

The sun had disappeared behind the clouds that had slowly rolled in, turning the scene gray and dreary. Worthington House loomed in the distance. Penelope could picture an enemy army advancing on the castle and storming the ramparts under cover of dark and surprising the unsuspecting people inside.

She shivered. Her upcoming task was turning her gloomy. She took a deep breath as she pulled the MINI into a parking spot and got out.

She felt like Marie Antoinette going to the guillotine as she headed toward the front door. Her hand shook slightly as she rang the bell. Its sonorous notes sounded inside and moments later Royston opened the door.

"Is Lady Dougal in?" Penelope asked as she stepped over the threshold. She was secretly hoping the answer would be *no*. Then she could retreat to the safety and warmth of the Open Book.

"Yes, Miss Parish. I will ring her."

Moments later, Royston was leading her to a small sitting room where a cozy fire was burning in the grate. A painting of sheep grazing in a field hung over the mantel. That's how she felt, Penelope thought—like a sheep being led to the slaughter.

Jemima was sitting in an armchair, reading. She put the book down when Royston announced Penelope.

Jemima's eyes narrowed as she looked at Penelope. Did she suspect what Penelope's mission was? Penelope smiled to put her at ease, but she could feel her mouth trembling slightly at the corners.

"Hello," Jemima said, her voice so cold Penelope nearly shivered despite the crackling warmth of the fire. "I know why you're here. You've been spying on me, I hear. You visited my old school and talked to Tina Resse. She called me."

The sentence hung in the air as Jemima reached for the teacup on the low table beside her and took a sip, studying Penelope intently over the rim.

Penelope didn't know what to say.

"So now you know my little secret." Jemima put down her cup. "I'm a kleptomaniac. Tina confessed to having let the cat out of the bag."

"I didn't mean to pry," Penelope said, clasping her hands. "But I saw you take that Fabergé egg from the drawing room and I wondered. . . ."

"I imagine you've run to Charlotte to tell her," Jemima said, a sneer twisting her face.

Penelope sat up a bit straighter, lifted her chin, and cleared her throat.

"Actually, no, I haven't. I wanted to give you a chance to return the items—the snuffbox is particularly dear to Charlotte and her husband. If you give everything back, there will be no need for me to say anything. Charlotte need never know."

Jemima looked off into the distance. "It's not as if I need those things," she said. "I can't help it. The doctor says it's a mental illness." Jemima gave a bitter laugh. "As if that's supposed to make me feel better." She clenched the arms of the chair. "He said it's a lack of some chemical in the brain—I can never remember what it's called."

Penelope was very quiet and as still as she could manage. It was almost as if Jemima was talking to herself.

"I've tried to stop but I can't. The tension builds and builds until I can't stand it anymore and afterward . . . such blessed relief. But it comes at a price. Afterward also comes the shame and self-loathing and I promise myself I'll never do it again. At least until the next time."

Her smile was tinged with sadness.

"You said you don't actually need or want the things you take. What do you do with them?" Penelope said, leaning forward slightly.

Jemima shrugged. "I donate them or if they're worthless— it's not the value of the item that attracts me—I stash them somewhere—somewhere where Ethan won't find them. He'd divorce me if he knew." She looked down at her hands, which were knitted together in her lap.

"You went out on the terrace where Cissie was killed," Penelope said. No point in tiptoeing around, she decided.

Jemima's head shot up. "How do you know that?"

"I smelled smoke on your hair. Charlotte assured me you're not a smoker. But Cissie was—she went out on the terrace to smoke her pipe. Why did you go out there? What did you want to talk to her about?"

"I don't suppose you'd believe me if I said I merely wanted to have a friendly chin-wag with a friend." Jemima laughed. "Cissie had threatened to tell Charlotte about the thefts. I went out there to beg her not to. I think it gave her a sense of power having that to hold over me. Cissie could be cruel sometimes."

"Don't you think Cissie was trying to pay you back?"

"What . . . what do you mean?" Jemima's hand went to her throat.

"According to Tina Resse, Cissie couldn't stand it if someone else got something that she felt was rightfully hers."

Jemima's face had turned white. "I don't know. . . ." She stiffened her shoulders. "I don't have to answer your questions." She started to stand up.

"I'm not asking you a question—just speculating. I think Cissie was in love with your husband—I found some pictures in an old magazine of the two of them together."

Jemima opened her mouth but then closed it again. She had sunk back in her chair.

"I think you came along and Ethan fell in love with you. He broke up with Cissie—maybe he had already even proposed to her—and married you instead."

"It wasn't my fault. I never intended for us to fall in love."

"But you did. And that angered Cissie—you took something she wanted. She certainly waited a long time to get her revenge," Penelope said. "But then what is that saying—revenge is a dish best served cold?"

"But Cissie was alive when I left her, I swear," Jemima said, her eyes glittering with tears. She put a hand on her heart. "Cissie and I may have had our differences over the years but we were friends—have been ever since we were at school together."

Penelope was quiet.

"You have to believe me," Jemima said. "Tobias must

have seen me—" She stopped abruptly and grasped the fabric of her skirt. "Poor Tobias. He shouldn't have died like that. But surely Rose can verify that Cissie was alive when I went back inside." Jemima's expression changed to one of censure. "Rose and Tobias were out there, snogging like teenagers. It's a miracle that Cissie didn't see them."

A surprised look came over Jemima's face. "Maybe she did see them. And that's why Tobias had to kill her." She raised an eyebrow. "I wonder if Cissie knew . . . about Tobias and Rose? I suppose she did. Cissie always seemed to know everything."

"But Tobias is now dead. Who killed him? The murders have to be related."

Jemima's shoulders sagged. "That's true." She straightened up. "But I didn't kill her, I assure you. Or him." She began to get up. "Now if you'll excuse me, I've somewhere I need to be."

EIGHTEEN

❧❧

Penelope followed Jemima down the hall and to the right. She thought she remembered her way to the front door but instead found herself in the wing where the guest rooms were. She was about to turn around and retrace her steps when she heard someone in the room that had been Tobias's.

She peeked through the open door. A maid was packing Tobias's things into his suitcase. Penelope recognized her as Ivy—the maid she'd met in the Pig in a Poke and who she'd talked to in the kitchen.

As Penelope watched, Ivy closed the lid, picked it up, and headed toward the door. Penelope quickly stepped out of the way.

"Excuse me, miss," Ivy said as she walked past Penelope.

Penelope hesitated for a second but as soon as Ivy disappeared around the corner, she stepped into the room. She didn't know what she was looking for—something—anything—that might be a clue to Tobias's murder.

The armoire door hung open; it was empty but for a lone handkerchief with Tobias's initials embroidered on it forgotten on the floor.

Penelope glanced around the room, but there wasn't much to see. A small, elegant desk was placed under the window. She walked over and opened the drawer. Stationery with a gold crest and *Worthington House* in script at the top was lined up neatly alongside a stack of envelopes and some pens.

Pen closed the drawer and glanced in the wastebasket next to the desk. It was empty but for a crumpled piece of paper. She retrieved the paper and smoothed it out.

It was cheap, ordinary stock—the kind that came in a pad. A note was scrawled on it with numerous cross outs that suggested it was the draft of a letter.

Tobias's handwriting was large and sprawling but Penelope was able to read the note easily enough.

Dear Rose,

I fear we must break things off. Cissie knows about us and has given me an ultimatum. If I don't end our affair, she will divorce me. I am afraid I signed a prenuptial agreement that would leave me with a mere pittance. You know I couldn't bear being poor so I am sure you will understand.

Yours faithfully,

Now that was interesting, Penelope thought—Tobias was breaking it off with Rose. She assumed that he had copied the final version of this note onto a piece of the Worthington House stationery. Did he slip it under Rose's door during the night?

Penelope left the room and retraced her steps to the front door.

If Tobias did give Rose that note, it would change everything. Maybe Rose killed Cissie, thinking that would clear the way for her and Tobias to be together. But then Tobias broke up with her and furious, she turned around and killed him, too.

She was at Worthington House when Tobias was poisoned. She'd known him for years, so it was quite possible that she knew about his allergy to sesame seeds.

Was Rose capable of killing? Penelope had no idea. But she was determined to find out.

Penelope spent the afternoon in her writing room at the Open Book, struggling with her revisions. She glanced at the date on her computer and shuddered. She'd probably get another e-mail from Bettina any minute now asking where they were. The cover was done, the blurb written, and the book was already up for preorders at all of the on-line bookstores.

Penelope had to deliver . . . or else.

Two hours later she stretched her arms over her head and yawned. She'd managed to come up with a plot twist that she hoped improved the lag in the middle of the manuscript. She was pleased with it—she'd have to wait to see what Bettina thought.

Mabel was talking to a customer when Penelope emerged from her writing room. When he turned slightly toward her,

Penelope realized it was Laurence Brimble. She was surprised to see that Mabel's face was quite pink and she didn't object when Brimble moved closer to her. It looked as if they were having an intimate conversation.

Was Brimble flirting with Mabel? Penelope wondered. Mabel didn't look unhappy about it. As a matter of fact, she was glowing in a way Penelope had never seen before.

She caught Figgy's eye from across the room and Figgy gestured toward the couple with a nod of her head, then winked.

So Figgy had noticed it, too. How interesting, Penelope thought. Obviously it was never too late for romance.

Penelope was on her way home from the Open Book when the car in front of her stopped to let someone cross the street. It was the same woman and little girl who had been in the Open Book earlier. They had just started across when the child yanked her hand from her mother's and bent to pick up something she had spotted in the road. Penelope couldn't see what it was exactly, but she thought it might be a coin that had attracted the little girl's attention.

Suddenly someone tapped on Penelope's window. She jumped. It was Maguire. She rolled the window down.

"Sorry, I didn't mean to scare you," Maguire said, smiling. "I wondered if you'd like to come for a pint at the Book and Bottle?"

In her head Penelope ran through all the things she ought to do—she ought to pick up something for dinner; she ought to get back to the cottage because her sister was probably home by now; she ought to feed Mrs. Danvers who would be waiting for dinner even though her bowl was still most likely full.

"Yes," she said finally. "I'd love to."

Maguire saluted and stepped away, and Penelope continued down the high street until she came to the Book and Bottle. She pulled into the drive and around to the parking lot. She had to wait while someone maneuvered out of a tight space, and Maguire was already standing by the front door when she came around the side of the building. He broke into a grin when he saw her.

"Pleasure to see you," he said, kissing her on the cheek.

The Book and Bottle wasn't terribly full. A couple of men in worn jeans and work boots sat at the counter, nursing pints and having their tea of steak and kidney pie or Welsh rarebit.

Maguire led Penelope to a booth and waited until she sat down before sliding onto the bench opposite her.

"What will you have?"

"A cider, please." Penelope had grown quite fond of the British alcoholic cider.

"I'll be right back."

The barmaid wasn't busy and she quickly filled a glass with cider and pulled a pint for Maguire. He carried the drinks back to the table and sat down with a sigh.

"Is DCI Donovan still getting you down?" Penelope said after Maguire had had a sip of his beer.

Maguire ran a hand through his hair, leaving it slightly rumpled—a look Penelope found rather endearing.

"I'm stuck with her until the case is solved. My only consolation is that she's put up at the Thorn and Thistle just south of Chumley and it's well-known that the rooms are cramped and the whole place smells of damp." He grinned.

"Is she any closer to solving the case?"

"I don't think so." He laughed. "Not that she'd admit it. I'm taking a perverse pleasure in watching her struggle." He frowned. "Is that really terrible of me?"

"Not at all. It's perfectly understandable."

"Something interesting did turn up." Maguire tapped his fingers on the table. "I'm mates with one of the men on the SOCO team. We worked together when I was in Leeds. He said they examined the remains of the bonfire after it had cooled down and found a piece of cloth among the ashes."

Penelope sat up straighter and leaned her arms on the table. "So someone tried to burn something?"

"Righto. They were quite successful—all that was found was this little scrap of fabric. The edges were charred and it was difficult to make out the exact color but it didn't look as if the cloth had a pattern on it."

"Why would someone want to burn a piece of cloth? I can understand burning paper—documents or letters or the like—things that someone might want to keep confidential." Penelope pushed her glasses up her nose. She had a sudden thought. "Maybe the killer did it. Maybe the killer got blood on a piece of their clothing when they killed Cissie and had to dispose of it, so they threw it on the bonfire."

"That was my first thought, too. But wouldn't someone have noticed if they'd appeared without their shirt or pants?"

Penelope giggled at the image that that brought to mind. "True. But if they were staying at Worthington House, they might have snuck back to their room and changed." Penelope tried to imagine that scenario. "On the other hand, everyone was in formal wear and it would have looked odd if a woman had suddenly reappeared in a different dress."

Maguire tilted his hand. "Would it have even been noticed, do you think? There was a lot of champagne flowing—enough to dull people's observation powers I should imagine."

Penelope shook her head. "Women would notice. We pay attention to those sorts of things."

"But what about a man? Other than Winterbourne's rather unusual dinner jacket, they all looked somewhat alike. Easy enough to substitute one for the other."

"That would mean someone brought two sets of dinner clothes with him. He would have had to plan it in advance. There were no formal events scheduled for the wedding other than that ball."

Maguire scratched his chin. "True. And it looks as if the murder was more a matter of opportunity." He tapped an index finger against his glass. "The fabric has been sent to forensics, so hopefully they will be able to tell us more." He grinned. "My mate has promised to give me the results the minute they get them. That'll give me a jump on Donovan who won't get them until they've put together their report. Not much of a jump, but I'll take whatever I can get. I need to show them I'm not just a bumbling country copper and that I've got what it takes to do the big jobs and not only break-ins and petty thefts."

"You're still hoping to beat her to the punch, then?"

Maguire reached out and put his hand over Penelope's. He grinned. "You bet."

Penelope left the Book and Bottle on a bit of a cloud. Maguire had walked her to her car, his arm tight around her shoulder, and had given her a lingering kiss as they stood next to her MINI. It was all Penelope could do to keep her mind on driving on the correct side of the street, and she felt relief wash over her when her cottage came into view.

She was acting like a schoolgirl, she chided herself as she hung up her coat and bent to pet Mrs. Danvers, who sniffed her suspiciously as if detecting some alien aroma. Time to come down to earth, she thought. She liked Maguire and he obviously liked her. She'd had plenty of relationships that had started out like that and had subsequently fizzled to nothing. It was too soon to get excited.

But she found herself humming as she walked out to the kitchen. She expected to see Beryl sitting at the table, sipping a glass of wine and flipping through a magazine, but the room was empty.

Penelope was making herself a cup of tea when she heard the front door open and Beryl call out.

"Hello. I'm back."

Penelope walked out to the foyer, her cup in hand. Beryl had brought in a whiff of fresh cold air with her, and her cheeks were rosy and her eyes glowing.

"You look like you've had a good day," Pen said, cradling her mug.

"I have," Beryl said as she unwound her scarf. "Let me get a glass of wine, and I'll tell you all about it."

They went out to the kitchen, where Beryl got a bottle of white wine from the refrigerator and two glasses from the cupboard.

"You have to join me," she said, filling both glasses and carrying them to the table. She motioned to Penelope to leave her tea.

"Are we celebrating?" Pen said, raising her eyebrows.

"Sort of." Beryl slid into a seat. "Nothing's been confirmed yet, of course, but just the possibility is very exciting."

"Come on," Pen urged. "Out with it."

Beryl gave a rather coy smile and ran her finger around the rim of her glass.

"I had a drink with a modeling agent after work at this delightful little wine bar—terribly chic and wonderfully edgy. It felt so good to be back in a sophisticated milieu."

Penelope took a sip of her wine. She was beginning to wonder if Beryl was ever going to get to the point.

"Nothing's certain yet." Beryl held up a hand, palm out as if she was stopping traffic. "But . . . the agent thinks I'd be perfect for this new campaign Molton Brown soap is launching." Beryl made a face. "It's aimed at the *mature* woman—meaning anyone over thirty, which is why the agent thought I had a shot at it."

"So what's next?" Penelope wasn't sure how these modeling gigs worked.

Beryl put a hand on Penelope's arm. "This is the best part—it's a print campaign but they are doing some television advertising as well, and I would be considered for both."

Penelope was glad to see her sister so excited. She hoped she wouldn't be disappointed. If this campaign was as big as Beryl made it sound, there was bound to be a lot of competition.

"When will you know?"

"Who knows?" She shrugged. "This meeting was strictly preliminary. I'll have to have some current pictures done for my comp card. . . ." Beryl looked at Penelope. "A comp card is like a business card for models and actors," she explained.

Penelope nodded. "That's very exciting."

"It is, isn't it?" Beryl looked down. She traced the pattern of the wood grain of the table with her finger. "I thought I was no longer capable of taking care of myself—that I was totally dependent on Magnus." She looked up at Penelope and Penelope noticed her eyes were filled with tears. "I thought my life was over when Magnus was arrested."

A coy expression slowly dawned on Beryl's face. "Speaking of men—what about that man of yours? You haven't told me anything about him. I haven't even met him. I'm dying of curiosity."

Penelope shrugged. "There's not much to tell . . . yet." She decided it would be prudent to change the subject. "You know that murder I told you about at Worthington House—well, two murders actually?"

"Yes." Beryl shivered. "Is the place haunted?"

"No, I don't think so."

"It will be now." Beryl laughed.

Penelope gave her a stern look. "The police found a scrap of fabric in the ashes from the bonfire that was lit that night."

"A bonfire," Beryl said, getting up to refill her wineglass. "They really went allout, didn't they?"

"There were fireworks, too."

"That puts a simple champagne toast to shame." Beryl laughed. "So what's this about finding a bit of material?" she said, taking a seat again. She leaned back in her chair and stretched out her legs.

"It's been sent to forensics, but in the meantime I'm trying to figure out what someone might have tossed on the fire to burn."

"A piece of clothing, don't you think? I mean, if it was cloth, what else could it be?"

"That's what I thought. But who burns an item of clothing? No, I think the killer got blood on something they were wearing and tossed it into the flames to get rid of it."

"How gruesome." Beryl shuddered.

"But what I can't figure out is what it could have been. The men were in dinner clothes and the ladies were in gowns. If they'd stripped down and tossed something on the fire, it would have been noticed."

"Maybe it was something they didn't really need, like a shawl? Or perhaps a scarf of some sort?"

"That could be," Penelope said, as she got up to begin dinner.

Something was niggling at her mind but she couldn't quite grasp the thought. She had the feeling it was important. Perhaps it would come to her later.

The next morning Penelope set out early for the Open Book. She wanted to get started on her revisions right away. Bettina had sent another e-mail, asking her how things were going. Penelope knew that the subtext was actually *When am I going to see the finished manuscript?*

Beryl had left on an early train to London, flushed with excitement about the day ahead. She had an appointment with a hairdresser and was having pictures taken for her comp card that afternoon.

The Closed sign was still on the door when Penelope reached the Open Book. She unlocked the door and went inside.

The lights in the store weren't on and the sales floor was in shadows, but the lights were on in the Teapot where

Mabel and Figgy were sitting at a table, sipping cups of tea. Figgy had an old-fashioned-looking apron tied around her waist, making her look a bit like a milkmaid.

"You're early," Mabel said when Penelope approached them.

"Let me pour you a cup of tea." Figgy reached for the teapot. "There are some hot buttered crumpets if you're hungry." She gestured toward a plate on the table.

Penelope helped herself to a crumpet. Butter dribbled down her chin as she ate it and she quickly grabbed a napkin.

"These are delicious." Pen reached for another, then hesitated. "I'd better be careful or I'm going to gain weight."

Mabel looked at her with one eyebrow raised. "You? Gain weight? I don't believe it. Besides, you could stand to put on another stone."

Pen took a sip of her tea. "You and Laurence Brimble seemed to be getting along very well yesterday," she said to Mabel.

Figgy poked Mabel on the arm. "I do believe he fancies you."

Mabel fumbled with her teacup and it clanged against the saucer. Her face had a pinkish tinge to it. She laughed. "Better late than never, I guess."

"He seems like a nice man," Pen said.

"A bit stiff." Figgy frowned. "That military posture and all."

"He's quite charming when you get to know him. He's just shy." Mabel brushed some crumbs off the front of her sweater. "He's an amateur photographer as it turns out and so was my father. I dabble in it myself. My father enjoyed teaching me." She looked down at her hands. "He's not Oliver—I'll never forget him—but we enjoy each other's company." Mabel paused dramatically. "And . . . he's taking me to dinner at Pierre's tomorrow night."

"Look at you," Figgy said. "Sounds like you two are becoming an item."

"Yes. You'll soon see our picture in *Tatler* no doubt." Mabel laughed.

"I talked to Detective Maguire yesterday," Pen said. She noticed Mabel and Figgy glance at each other with raised eyebrows but decided to ignore them. "He said they found a piece of cloth in the remains of the bonfire at Worthington House. It seems someone tried to burn something."

"How odd," Figgy said, picking up some crumbs from her plate with her finger. "Why would someone do that?"

"Don't you think it was probably the killer? They might have gotten blood on their clothes and needed to destroy them," Mabel said.

"That was my original thought," Pen said. "But they could hardly walk around with no shirt or pants."

"They'd have to hide in the shrubbery." Figgy giggled and reached into her pocket for a tissue.

As Penelope watched her, she had a sudden idea. It was so startling she nearly leapt from her chair. She actually banged her knee against the table.

Mabel looked at her in concern. "Are you okay?"

"Yes. Fine—sorry."

Penelope now knew what the killer had thrown on the fire.

She was positive of it.

NINETEEN

꒫꒷

Penelope could barely focus on her revisions. She had to keep going back over what she had done. She couldn't stop thinking about the idea that had suddenly come to her while she was having tea with Mabel and Figgy.

She ought to call Maguire and tell him. Penelope grabbed her purse and pulled out her cell phone.

"Detective Maguire, please," she said when the call was answered.

"He's not here at the moment. Gone off to a funeral in Leeds, he has. Going to be a pallbearer for a mate."

"I'm sorry," Pen said, clutching her phone between her ear and her shoulder as she closed up her laptop.

"Tragedy," the man continued. "Shot trying to apprehend a robber."

"I'm sorry," Pen said again. The man was certainly chatty. "Can you ask him to call me?" She gave him her number and hung up.

*   *   *

I'm running an errand," Pen said as she waved to Mabel and headed out the door of the Open Book.

She was planning to pick up something special from the Jolly Good Grub to take home for dinner. Surely by now Grant had forgotten about her earlier rather awkward visit.

The weather was fine and she turned up her collar and pulled on her gloves as she headed down the high street. She passed the newsstand where stacks of newspapers were bundled up outside the front door. She glanced at the headline of the *Daily Mail* as she went by.

Did Worthington Kill His Ex-Girlfriend Cissie Emmott? was splashed across the front page in bold black letters.

Poor Charlotte, Penelope thought. Now that the tabloids had gotten hold of the story, they would be hounded. Penelope didn't doubt Worthington's innocence even though his polo mallet was the weapon and his were the only prints found on it, but she could easily imagine how the press would use that information against him.

Penelope waited for a break in traffic to cross the street—not that there was ever that much traffic in Upper Chumley-on-Stoke—but there were some elderly drivers who could be quite the menace behind the wheel. She'd nearly been hit at least once, so she had learned to be extra careful.

She was passing the Knit Wit Shop when she had a very odd sensation. The back of her neck prickled and the hair stood up. She tried to identify the strange feeling and realized that she had the impression she was being followed.

She ducked into the doorway of Pen and Ink Stationers and peered around the edge. The only person coming toward her on the sidewalk was a teenaged girl in a short skirt, thigh-high boots, and a fake fur jacket. She passed the doorway to the stationer's without even giving it a glance.

Her nerves were getting the better of her, Penelope decided as she continued down the street toward the Jolly Good Grub, but try as she might, she couldn't shake the feeling that someone had been following her.

Stalking her. The thought nearly brought her up short in her tracks. Why would someone be stalking her? Had she touched a nerve—the killer's nerve?

Penelope was relieved when she reached the door to the Jolly Good Grub. She glanced behind her one more time, but there was no sign of anyone following her.

She must have imagined it.

S everal hours later Penelope was still thinking about the idea she'd had earlier that morning about the piece of cloth found in the ashes of the bonfire. She wished Maguire had been at the station. He would have known what to do.

As Penelope was leaving the Jolly Good Grub, bulging shopping bag in hand, she decided the only thing to do was to go back to Worthington House and follow up on her hunch.

She rang Mabel at the bookstore to let her know she wouldn't be back until later that afternoon, then headed home to pick up her car and put her groceries in the refrigerator.

Mrs. Danvers was curled up in a sunbeam when Penelope got back to her cottage. She looked up briefly as if to acknowledge Penelope's presence, then put her head back down and closed her eyes against the beam of light coming through the window.

Penelope put her shopping on the kitchen table and began to unpack the bag. She planned to make a simple meal out of all the treats she bought—cheeses, pâté, smoked sausage, and some crusty bread.

She put everything in the refrigerator, checked that Mrs. Danvers's bowls were both full, fished her keys out of her purse, and headed out the door.

She had no idea what she was going to say when she got to Worthington House. What would Royston think if she said she wanted to go down to the kitchen? Perhaps she could say she had something important to tell the cook? Or, perhaps she could say she'd left something in the . . . drawing room but head to the kitchen instead?

Penelope felt her stomach knot as she headed up the drive to Worthington House. She parked the car and with a sense of dread, rang the bell.

Royston was his usual calm, imperturbable self and didn't bat an eyelash when Penelope announced she needed to go to the kitchen to talk to the cook.

"Certainly, Miss Parish," Royston said with a slight nod of his head. "Do you know the way or shall I guide you?"

"I can manage, thank you," Penelope said as she stepped into the foyer, silently thanking the British for their traditional reserve. Of course Royston wouldn't be so forward as to ask why on earth Penelope wanted to talk to the cook.

Royston nodded his head again and Penelope headed toward the kitchen. Soft strains of classical music came from behind one of the closed doors and the low murmur of voices from behind another. She had no idea what she'd say if she encountered Charlotte or Worthington himself and she was relieved when she rounded the corner to the kitchen without having bumped into anyone.

A symphony of aromas emanated from the kitchen. The cook was lifting a large piece of iridescent pink salmon out of a pan of poaching liquid. He placed it on a platter that had been decorated with fresh green parsley. Penelope watched as he took roasted asparagus from the oven, arranged the stalks on another platter, and drizzled them with melted butter.

Penelope's mouth began to water. The cook transferred the platters of salmon and asparagus to the large ornate silver serving tray sitting on the kitchen table. Ivy and a young woman, whose hair was shaved up the sides, were seated at the table, peeling carrots and turnips presumably for the staff's more modest dinner. The young man Penelope had seen with Ivy in town was leaning against the counter nursing a cup of tea. He leaned over and said something to Ivy and Ivy laughed.

Penelope looked at Ivy and had the distinct feeling that she was missing something, but she couldn't quite put her finger on what it was.

No one seemed to notice Penelope as they bustled about carrying out their various duties.

A footman appeared, picked up the silver tray, and carried it out of the kitchen. Ivy stood up, wiped her hands on her apron, and disappeared through a swinging door on the other side of the kitchen. The fellow who had been leaning against the counter followed close behind her, still clutching his mug of tea.

The cook pulled a handkerchief from his pocket, swiped at his sweating brow, and left through the same door.

The young woman sitting at the table looked up, a half-peeled carrot in her hand.

She frowned and looked up at Penelope.

"Who was that young man?" Penelope said. "He looks familiar," she said, crossing her fingers.

"Him?" The woman jerked a thumb toward the door. "That's Ivy's cousin. Floyd's his name.

"Another quick question if you don't mind?"

The young woman looked wary but she nodded.

"Have you had any aprons go missing?" Penelope laughed to show that she knew that must seem like an absurd question.

"Oh, you're from the police, then?" the woman said, putting down the carrot. "We've had them around several times already asking their questions." She snorted. "Who would want to go nicking aprons?" She shook her head. "Certainly not me. I guess you never know about people, do you?"

Penelope nodded. "But did anyone complain that aprons were missing? Or that they couldn't find theirs?"

"Not that I know of. And, believe me, if there was something to complain about, this lot would. Some people." She shook her head.

"Do you know if any of the staff went outside during the wedding ball?"

The woman picked up the carrot again and finished peeling it. She cut it into sections and dropped it into the metal bowl in front of her.

"I wasn't working that night, more's the pity. I would have liked to have seen all of them fancy dresses. They're quite something, aren't they?" She shook her head. "I was down with a cold and was tucked up at home in bed with a mustard plaster on my chest."

"Is there anyone who worked in the kitchen that night who might know?" Penelope gave what she hoped was a winning smile. "It's important."

"Let me see." She put a finger on her chin. "There's Bridget Sullivan. She's done no end of talking about the ball. Trying to rub it in, if you know what I mean."

"Is she here? Is there any chance I could speak to her?" Pen mentally crossed her fingers.

"Sure. She's in the pantry, polishing silver. His grace is hosting a dinner party tonight. A bunch of fancy people down from London, no doubt."

The young woman got up from the table and pushed the swinging door open.

"Bridget?" Pen could hear her yelling.

Moments later the door opened again and Bridget appeared. She was wearing a plain bib apron over a simple blue uniform. Her hair was as red as the carrots in the bowl on the table and her face was covered in so many freckles that in places they almost blended together.

She glanced at Penelope with a guarded look in her eyes. "Lucy said you wanted to see me?"

Penelope gave her a reassuring smile. "Just a quick question if you don't mind."

Bridget looked at Penelope suspiciously. "Go on then."

"Did you happen to notice if any of the staff went outside the night of the Worthingtons' wedding ball?"

Bridget's eyebrows drew together. "There was Ivy that was taken faint on account of the heat, if that's what you mean. She stepped outside for some air. It was that hot in the kitchen what with the ovens going full blast and all the burners on."

"Was she outside long?"

"I didn't exactly look at my watch, did I? I'd say a good twenty minutes. I was about to go out and look for her when she finally came back in."

"How did she seem?"

Bridget tilted her head to one side. "Seem? What do you mean?"

"Was she nervous or excited or worried?"

"I don't know about that. She seemed the same as always to me. Ivy tends to keep to herself."

"Did she have her apron on?" Pen said.

Bridget looked startled. "Her apron? I can't say I noticed one way or the other. Why?"

Penelope was quite certain it was an apron that had been thrown on the bonfire the night of the ball. It was the one thing that the killer could have burned that wouldn't have been likely to be noticed if it was missing.

Penelope's head was swimming. It was possible that one of the guests had snuck into the kitchen, borrowed one of the aprons, and then gone out to the terrace to murder Cissie, afterward throwing the bloodstained garment on the bonfire.

But it was also quite possible that one of the staff had done it. The question was why. How did any of them even know Cissie well enough to compel them to murder her?

As Pen drove away from Worthington House, she thought about what she'd learned. According to Bridget, Ivy had gone outside the evening of the ball, claiming she felt faint. Had she really felt ill or had she gone out to murder Cissie?

But what reason would she have had for killing her? As far as Pen knew, Cissie and Ivy didn't even know each other.

She sighed. She wished Maguire was back from Leeds—surely he'd be able to puzzle this out.

As Penelope was heading back to town, the elusive thought that she'd been trying to grasp as she'd been watching Ivy peel carrots finally came to her. She turned the car around and headed back toward the Worthington estate.

*   *   *

Worthington House soon came into view, but Penelope continued driving, headed beyond it to India's little stone cottage.

She hoped she'd find India at home. She knew India did her shopping on the high street and frequently visited the Open Book, but Penelope didn't think she normally did much of anything else.

Pen parked her MINI in front of the cottage and got out. The rosebushes that bordered the path to India's front door had been cut back for the winter and the branches on the trees were bare and skeletal.

Pen rapped on the door and waited. A minute or two went by. She stuffed her hands in her pockets, sorry that she hadn't taken the time to put on her gloves.

Finally the door opened a crack and India peered out. When she saw it was Penelope she pulled the door wider.

"Come in," she said, obviously pleased to have a visitor. "The day has turned quite brisk, hasn't it? I'm sure you could do with a cup of tea. Come sit down and warm yourself by the fire and I'll put the kettle on."

Penelope really didn't want a cup of tea, but it was the Brits' way of showing hospitality and it would have been rude to refuse.

She fidgeted impatiently while she waited for India to appear with the tea. She hoped her idea would pan out— she thought it would, or at least she hoped it would— although doubts were beginning to creep into her mind.

Finally India appeared with the cups and saucers and plate of biscuits rattling on the tray in her hands. She put the tray down on the table.

"Will you pour?" India said to Penelope. "My hands are

a bit shaky today. It's nothing serious the doctor says—some kind of tremor that comes and goes."

Penelope poured out two cups of tea and handed one to India.

"I have another favor to ask of you," she said as she stirred sugar into her tea. "Do you think I could look at those magazines of yours again?"

"Of course. Let me get them for you."

India stood up with a grunt, putting a hand to the small of her back. She smoothed down her pleated plaid skirt and left the room.

Penelope listened to the crackling and spitting of the fire and the ticking of the clock on the mantel as she tried to remember whether the article she was looking for had been in *Hello!* or *OK!* magazine. She was fairly certain it hadn't been in *Tatler.* She sighed. She would just have to go through the issues again until she found what she was looking for.

India reappeared with the stack of magazines in her arms. She placed them on the floor in front of Penelope.

"Are you doing some more investigating, dear?" she said as she resumed her seat.

Penelope hesitated. "Sort of. I have a theory that I want to check out."

India clucked her tongue. "You do realize it could be dangerous. Remember what happened last time. You gave us a terrible fright." India smiled and the creases around her eyes crinkled. "We've grown quite fond of you." She put her hand over Penelope's.

"Whatever information I find is going straight to Detective Maguire," Penelope reassured her.

India frowned. "Is that dreadful young woman still investigating? The DCI sent from the Met? Quite insufferable, I must say."

"She is. But Detective Maguire is doing his own investigation."

Penelope began flipping through the first issue of *OK!*. She turned the last page but still hadn't found what she was looking for.

"Perhaps I can help?" India said, putting down her teacup and reaching for a magazine.

"I'm looking for an article they did on Cissie Winterbourne. There wasn't much text—it was mostly a collage of photographs of her at various times in her life."

"I think I know the article you mean," India said, slipping on her reading glasses. She began flipping through the magazine in her lap.

They went through the stack in silence, the only sound the rustling of pages or the clink of cups in saucers.

"Is this it?" India said suddenly, handing a copy of *Hello!* to Penelope.

Penelope glanced at the pictures. "Yes!" She held out her hand for the magazine. There was the picture she'd been looking for—Cissie as a young girl in a ball gown standing with her father in front of a sweeping staircase. Penelope looked closer at it. Her heart was beating faster with excitement. It was just as she remembered—the young girl off to the side was smiling—and showing a wide gap between her two front teeth.

Just like the Worthingtons' maid Ivy.

Penelope could barely contain her excitement as she drove away from India's cottage. She had the issue of *Hello!* on the seat beside her, having promised India that she would return it as soon as she was done with it.

India had probed—subtly of course—and Penelope knew her curiosity had been piqued, but she didn't want to share what she'd discovered just yet—it might, after all, amount to absolutely nothing.

If that was Ivy in the picture with Cissie, then it was obvious they must know each other, even if it had been far in the past. Penelope thought back to the night of the Worthington's prewedding dinner and the sharp words Cissie had spoken to someone behind Penelope—*I have no idea who you are.* Had she been speaking to Ivy?

But why would Cissie deny knowing her? She must have recognized her.

Penelope glanced at her watch. She ought to be in time to catch Tina Resse at the Oakwood School. Hopefully she would be as forthcoming as she had been on Penelope's previous visit.

Tina was at her desk when Penelope arrived at the school. She was dressed in a rather severe-looking pantsuit again—a dark gray one this time. She smiled when she saw Penelope hesitating in the doorway.

"So you're back," she said, starting to stand up.

"Please don't get up," Penelope said, stepping farther into the office. She glanced at the other desk, but Wanda wasn't there.

"How can I help you?" Tina said with brisk efficiency.

"I'm wondering if you can identify a girl in this photograph from *Hello!*."

Penelope had the magazine, open to the relevant page, tucked under her arm. She placed it on Tina's desk and pointed toward the photograph of Cissie with her father.

Tina slipped on a pair of reading glasses and glanced at the picture.

"Well, that's Cissie Emmott, of course. And that's her

father. I remember him from our annual Parents' Day. He never missed a one. He was that proud of his daughter."

"Do you have any idea who the other girl in the photograph is? The one with the gap between her two front teeth."

Tina frowned and a tiny wrinkle appeared between her eyebrows.

"I'm afraid I don't recognize her. I don't believe she was ever a pupil here at the Oakwood School for Girls." Tina handed the magazine back to Penelope. "But I know who would know. Cissie's old nanny still lives here in Chumley. She might be able to help you."

"You don't happen to remember her name or her address by any chance?" Penelope held her breath waiting for Tina to answer.

Tina frowned. "I'm afraid I don't." She snapped her fingers. "But Greta Danbury might. She's our German teacher and, if I'm not mistaken, she lives near Cissie's former nanny." Tina craned her neck and looked at the clock on the wall. "Her class is ending in three minutes. If you don't mind waiting here, I'll go and get her as soon as the bell rings."

"Thank you." Pen breathed a sigh of relief.

She could hear Tina's pumps tapping against the marble floor as she walked away down the hall. She pulled out Wanda's empty desk chair and sat down. She suddenly realized she hadn't had any lunch and was beginning to feel a bit light-headed.

She glanced at Wanda's desk. An ordinary black frame held a photograph of Wanda kneeling on the ground, the ends of her long hair nearly brushing her ankles and her arm around a shaggy Saint Bernard.

A copy of the local paper sat on top of a pile of file folders. Penelope picked it up and began to scan the front page.

She was beginning to wonder if Tina was ever coming back when she reappeared with a piece of paper in her hand.

"Greta remembered Cissie's nanny. They were neighbors until Greta married and moved away." She handed Penelope the paper. "Her name is Alice Thurston. And here's her address."

"Thank you." Penelope took the paper and stood up, pushing Wanda's chair back into place.

Penelope glanced at the paper. Alice didn't live too far away. She'd check in with Mabel and then go pay her a visit. But first she was going to get something to eat.

The aroma of fish-and-chips and hot oil drifted out the door of the Chumley Chippie when Penelope opened it. It was a bit late in the day for lunch, but there were still a few people scattered among the tables.

"Can I help you, love?" the bored-looking clerk behind the counter said without looking up from his newspaper.

"The pollack, please, and a side of chips."

"Sorry, love, we ran out of pollack an hour ago. Would the plaice do you?"

"Sure." Penelope had no idea what the difference was between the two types of fish, but at this point she was starving and ready to eat anything.

She watched as the fellow behind the counter lowered the plaice into a vat of oil that sizzled and spit and bubbled up around the fish. He then filled a wire basket with potatoes and plunged it into the oil. The chips immediately crackled and spat, slowly turning golden brown.

She dug some bills out of her wallet, paid for her meal, and took her tray over to a vacant table. A young man was sitting at the next table over facing her. He looked familiar, but Penelope couldn't immediately place him.

He had slightly shaggy hair, and even from a distance Penelope could see that his eyes were a deep, vivid blue. He looked up from his plate of fish-and-chips and smiled at Penelope. She was surprised when he got up from his seat and began to walk toward her.

As he got closer, Penelope realized he was the lead singer for the Foggy Bottoms—and the young man who had purchased Tobias's blue velvet dinner jacket at the Ox-fam shop in town.

"This is a bit of good luck," he said when he reached Penelope's table. "We met at the Book and Bottle. Do you remember? I was singing with my group, the Foggy Bottoms, and you asked me about my jacket."

"Yes, of course. I do remember," Pen said. "You did an excellent cover of 'Here Comes the Sun.' I really enjoyed it."

The young man dipped his head shyly. "The name's Sean, by the way." He stuck his hand in his pocket and jingled the coins in it nervously. "I was hoping I'd run into you again—the odds are good in a town as small as Chumley." He thrust his hand in his other pocket and pulled out a photograph. "I thought I ought to give you this. I found it in that jacket I bought at Oxfam—the one you were asking about the other day. I thought perhaps the owner might want it back." He handed the picture to Penelope.

She looked at it quickly. It was a photo of Tobias with his arms around a woman with long blond hair. She was clearly young—Penelope doubted she was much older than her early twenties—and very pretty. And it was obvious from the pose that Tobias was more than just a casual acquaintance. Penelope glanced at the date stamp on the picture—it was taken quite recently.

Sean tapped the photograph in Pen's hand. "Can you see that that gets back to the owner?"

Penelope didn't have the heart to tell him that the owner—Tobias—was dead.

"The police came and took the jacket, by the way," Sean said as he turned to leave. "But they've promised to return it when they're done with it. I've become quite fond of it." He grinned.

Penelope studied the photograph again. If Rose had gotten wind of the fact that Tobias had taken up with someone else, how devastating that would be, especially if she had killed Cissie so that she and Tobias could be together. If Tobias had sent that letter Pen found in his wastebasket, Rose would have known it was over. But perhaps she had convinced herself that she could get Tobias back?

Was it really Tobias that Rose was interested in or was it the money she knew he would inherit from Cissie? And had her anger at the thought of losing out on a fortune eventually turned to murderous rage?

TWENTY

❧✦☙

Penelope got in her car and started the MINI's engine. The smell of fish-and-chips clung to her clothes and she rolled the window down a crack. She'd already rung Mabel to let her know she might not be coming back to the Open Book that afternoon. There had been a note of curiosity in Mabel's voice but Penelope had promised to fill her in on everything later.

Penelope drove down the high street, which soon dwindled to a country lane. The grass in the fields on either side of the road was scrubby and brown, and parts of the fence along the footpath had come down. In the distance, Penelope spotted a rambler with a walking stick and a man wearing a Barbour jacket who was heading in the opposite direction, his border collie sprinting ahead of him.

Penelope's mind was wandering when her car suddenly began pulling hard to the left. She tightened her grip on the steering wheel, but the MINI continued veering toward the side of the road. Suddenly the front left side of the car dipped, the engine slowed, and she coasted to a stop with an ominous scraping sound. The road had little shoulder to speak of, but she managed to pull slightly off to the side and onto the grass.

Her palms were sweating as she opened the door and got out. She circled the car and soon discovered what the trouble was—her front left tire was totally flat. How on earth had that happened? Penelope wasn't particularly knowledgeable about cars, but the tires had been fine when she left India's cottage.

She reached into the car and grabbed her cell phone off the console. She was about to ring Digby's garage when she saw a car coming toward her. The driver was slowing and eventually pulled over alongside Penelope's car. He rolled down the window and stuck his head out.

"Trouble?" It was Maguire.

"Yes!" Pen said. "My tire seems to have gone flat."

Maguire pulled off the road as far as he could and got out. He walked over to Penelope's car and squatted down to examine the damage to her tire. He poked and prodded the tire and finally looked up with his face creased with concern.

"Your tire's been slashed."

"What!" Penelope felt the blood drain from her face. "Who would do something like that?"

"I don't know," Maguire admitted. "We don't have a lot of vandalism in Chumley—mostly kids' pranks like the occasional trampled flower bed or broken lawn ornament— so I can't imagine who would have done this. It takes a bit of strength to slash a tire like that." He raised an eyebrow. "And a knife."

He stood up and gestured toward Penelope's trunk. "Got a spare?"

Penelope bit her lip. "I don't know," she admitted.

"Let's take a look." Maguire opened the trunk and Penelope was glad to see a spare tire nestled in the space. "I'll have this fixed for you in a tick." He leveled his gaze at Penelope. "But what I'd like to know is why did someone choose to slash your tire. Were you singled out or was it random?"

Penelope thought about all the questions she'd been going around asking. Was it possible someone was trying to warn her off investigating? "I don't know."

Maguire jacked up the car, removed the ruined tire, and tossed it in the trunk. He quickly put on the spare tire, checking to make extra sure all the lug nuts were tightened. Finally, he stood up and brushed some dirt off his pants.

"That should do the trick until you can get to the garage."

The phrase *knight in shining armor* flashed through Penelope's mind.

"You're a lifesaver," she said.

"Glad to be of service." Maguire tipped an imaginary hat.

Penelope was about to tell him about her theory that the cloth found in the ashes of the bonfire must have come from an apron when loud, strident honking startled them both.

A large van was stopped in the lane and the driver was glaring at them. The lane was narrow and so was the shoulder of the road and with Penelope and Maguire's cars stopped side by side, there wasn't enough room for him to pass.

"Be careful, please," Maguire said as he ran to his car. "Sorry, mate," he called over his shoulder to the van driver as he hopped in and started the engine.

Penelope's hands were still shaking a bit as she turned the key in the ignition and released the brake. The thought that someone might have slashed her tire on purpose was frightening enough to make her consider dropping the entire investigation, dumping everything in Maguire's lap, and going back to minding her own business, writing her book, and working at the Open Book.

As Penelope drove along, the scenery, with its open spaces and wide vistas, soothed her nerves and the tension in her shoulders began to ease. Surely there would be no harm in paying Alice Thurston a call.

Alice Thurston's cottage was not unlike Penelope's, although it was set down a dirt drive in the middle of a field with sheep grazing in the distance on the sparse grass.

Penelope pulled up in front of it, parked her car, and walked to the front door. The brass knocker was highly polished, and she noticed starched white curtains hanging in the windows on either side.

A tall, elegant woman in gray flannel slacks and a blue cashmere turtleneck answered the door. She had black hair threaded with silver strands that was swept back from her high forehead and twisted into a bun at the nape of her neck.

"Yes?" she said when she saw Penelope.

"I'm looking for Alice Thurston?" Penelope said.

"You've found her." She kept her hand on the doorknob. "Are you selling something?"

"No," Penelope hastened to reassure her. "I wanted to ask you a few questions, if you don't mind . . . about Cissie Emmott. I believe you were her nanny at one time."

"Yes. Yes, I was—for Cissie and her little brother. Dreadful news about the murder." She drew back a bit. "You're not with one of those horrid tabloids, are you?"

"No. I'm . . . I'm a friend of Cissie's," Pen said. That was stretching the truth a bit. Okay, rather a lot actually.

"You might as well come in." Alice held the door wider.

The door opened directly into a small sitting room where the walls were lined with bookshelves. Some of the books were obviously old classics although the spines of the more colorful dust jackets suggested a collection of contemporary fiction as well.

"What did you say your name was?" Alice said as she motioned toward a comfortable-looking armchair covered in worn chintz.

"Penelope Parish."

"Like the author of *Lady of the Moors*?"

Penelope was taken aback. Despite her having written a bestseller, the people that recognized her name were still few and far between.

"Yes. That's me, actually."

"Delightful book. I enjoyed it tremendously," Alice said, moving toward the door. "Would you like some tea—that great British panacea?"

By the time she was done with this, Penelope thought, she was going to be awash with tea.

"Or would you care for something stronger? I have a lovely single malt Scotch with a delightful peaty aroma." Alice laughed. "Surely the sun is over the yardarm somewhere. Although that expression has come to be interpreted as *after five o'clock* when sailors, who originated the expression, were actually referring to eleven in the morning."

Penelope had never been a fan of hard liquor. "Thank you, but I'd better not."

"Tea it is, then," Alice said as she swept from the room.

Penelope found her eyes drawn to the books. She never could pass a bookshelf without checking out the titles.

Alice came back into the room with a tray of cups and saucers and a teapot.

She gestured toward the books on the wall. "You're probably wondering how I ended up taking a job as a nanny." She put the tray down on a low table and began pouring. "I read English at university—specifically the romantic poets. I was working on a biography of William Blake when my husband died in a car accident. I needed to support myself so I got a job as a nanny. Studying poetry doesn't exactly give you a lot of marketable skills."

Penelope accepted the teacup Alice held out and took a sip. Lapsang souchong, she thought. It had a slightly smoky taste—probably like Alice's favorite Scotch.

"So what did you want to know about Cissie Emmott?" Alice said. "Have you known her long?"

"Not terribly long, no."

"Are there any suspects? Have you heard?"

"Not yet. At least not that I know of. But that's one reason why I'm here. I've been doing a little digging and—"

"You're playing amateur sleuth?" Alice clapped her hands together. "Like Miss Marple? What fun."

Penelope felt her face get hot. "Sort of." She cleared her throat. "I'm wondering about a woman named Ivy Brown and if she had any relation to Cissie."

"Ivy? Of course. She was the daughter of Gemma, the upstairs maid, who was a particular favorite of Mrs. Emmott's."

"Were Cissie and Ivy . . . friendly?" Pen finished her tea and put her cup down.

Alice leaned back in her seat and crossed her legs. She pursed her lips.

"Friendly? I don't know that I would call them friends. But Ivy did live with the Emmotts." She raised one eyebrow. "A highly unusual circumstance but, as I said, Gemma was a favorite of Mrs. Emmott's."

"Did Cissie and Ivy do things together? Play together when they were young or hang out with the same crowd?"

"When they were small, yes, they did play together—games with other children like what's the time, Mr. Wolf and red letter. I remember that Cissie would become quite upset if she wasn't the victor and eventually the other children learned to let her win. I found that quite alarming—that's no way to build character—but when I mentioned my observations to Mr. Emmott, he didn't want to hear about it. Cissie was the apple of his eye."

Alice crossed her arms over her chest. "I didn't pursue it because eventually Cissie was sent off to board at the Oakwood School for Girls and I was confident that the headmistress would soon sort things out."

"What about Ivy? Where did she go to school?"

"The local primary school, of course."

"Did that cause friction between Cissie and Ivy?"

"Obviously Ivy understood her position. The Emmotts were very good to her, but there are limits. She left secondary school at sixteen with her GCSE—what we used to call the O level—and went to work."

"That must have caused some resentment on Ivy's part? It would only be natural."

Alice's glance slipped away from Penelope and focused on the window beyond. She appeared to be debating something. Finally she spoke.

"It wasn't that that caused Ivy's resentment." She fiddled with the silver chain around her neck.

Penelope waited silently, nearly holding her breath. She had the feeling she was about to grasp the thread that would unravel the entire mystery.

Alice let out a sigh, her shoulders rising up and down with the exhalation.

"It happened when they were both around seventeen. Cissie was home from school for October half term and Ivy was still living with her while she worked at a nearby factory. Cissie had taken up with a local boy during the summer holidays. Her father didn't approve—in his eyes, the young man wasn't good enough for his daughter. Besides, Cissie was still young and, well, you know how youngsters can get up to things."

Penelope nodded.

"Cissie's father forbade her to go out with him, but of course they continued to see each other. Cissie went back to school after the summer holidays and we all thought that would put an end to it, but the young man convinced Cissie to come out with him when she was home at half term. It seems he'd gotten hold of some spirits—gin I believe—and had gotten Cissie drunk. Mr. Emmott was beside himself when Cissie got home—he'd been frantic when he discovered she wasn't in her room."

Alice picked up her teacup, but then obviously realizing it was empty, put it back down.

"Cissie and her father had quite a set-to when she finally came in, clearly inebriated. He told her she was grounded for the rest of the term. Cissie went wild—calling her father all sorts of names—names a young lady her age shouldn't have even known—and eventually went storming off to her room, slamming every door she could on the way."

Penelope was wondering how Ivy fit into this scenario but she trusted that Alice would get to that eventually.

"What no one knew at the time was that Cissie crept downstairs after everyone had finally gone back to bed, and slashed a Turner landscape that was the pride of her father's collection."

Penelope's eyes widened. A Turner painting was irreplaceable.

"The thing was," Alice continued, "Cissie didn't take responsibility for defacing the painting—she blamed it on Ivy. Said she saw her do it."

"But why would Ivy—"

Alice held up a hand. "Cissie made the case that Ivy resented her—that Ivy was jealous that Cissie was continuing her education at a boarding school—she was going for her A levels—while Ivy had to go out and work." Alice massaged the bridge of her nose. "I knew the truth—I'd seen Cissie sneaking back into the kitchen with the knife—but Mr. Emmott wouldn't believe me. He couldn't accept the fact that his daughter had ruined his most prized possession. To him that would mean that she really didn't care about *him*."

"What happened to Ivy?"

Alice looked down at her hands resting in her lap. "Mr. Emmott refused to have her in the house anymore in spite of Mrs. Emmott's tears and pleading. Ivy was sent to live with an aunt—a cruel woman living a hard life on a farm up north. She made Ivy work for her room and board and resented every crumb she had to give her. Ivy stayed until she was able to scrape together enough to buy a bus ticket back to Chumley—that's when she got the job at Worthington House. She's worked there ever since as far as I know."

"That's really helpful," Penelope said, picking up her purse and preparing to leave.

"You said you hadn't known Cissie long," Alice said, putting the teacups back on the tray. "She had a tendency to turn on everyone eventually—even her good friends. Ultimately they always forgave her. She would make it up to them with little presents or favors—until the next time. Her father had spoiled her, I'm afraid."

"Did Ivy ever forgive Cissie?" Penelope said, getting up from her chair.

Alice reached out and put a hand on Penelope's arm. "You don't really think Ivy had anything to do with Cissie's death, do you? I'm certain she wasn't capable of murdering someone. She was a good girl—kind and thoughtful."

Alice might be certain that Ivy didn't have it in her to kill, Penelope thought as she thanked Alice and said goodbye, but then the police didn't originally suspect Ted Bundy either, who could, by all accounts, be quite charming.

Ivy certainly had good reason to resent Cissie aside from Cissie's wealth and privilege. Who knew what kind of life Ivy might have had if she hadn't been sent away to live with her aunt? She might have married and had a family.

Cissie certainly owed Ivy a lot, but had she paid that debt with her life?

TWENTY-ONE

❧

The sun was beginning to set when Penelope reached the Chumley high street. She was passing the Upper Chumley-on-Stoke Apothecary when a thought occurred to her. She turned the MINI around and headed back down the high street.

There was no parking in front of the apothecary, so Penelope left the car in the Tesco lot and began to walk back down the street. She had to fight off a sense of foreboding as she walked out of the pools of light cast by the streetlamps and into the shadows. The feeling that someone had been stalking her and then her tire being slashed had stirred up a fear in her that she couldn't shake.

She was relieved when she finally reached the gourmet shop and the cheerful light that shone onto the sidewalk.

She crossed the street and paused briefly in front of the Sweet Tooth and the mouthwatering display of candies in the window. Maybe she'd pick up a treat for herself and Beryl. But first the apothecary.

The apothecary had been in the same building for longer than anyone could determine. Penelope opened the door and stepped inside. The wooden floor creaked and groaned as she walked across it, and a faint medicinal smell hung in the air. The maze of glass shelves behind the counter had been there since the shop opened. It was easy to imagine a gentleman in knee breeches or a woman in a gown with a bustle asking for a poultice to draw out an infection or some arsenic for a case of asthma.

Standing behind the counter was the pharmacist—or chemist, as Penelope had come to learn they were called in Britain—a petite Asian woman with long, silky hair. A short line of people was waiting for their prescriptions, which the chemist filled with brisk efficiency.

Penelope wandered around the store in the meantime. She picked up some face cream, which Beryl told her she really ought to be using lest she be in danger of becoming a wrinkled prune by her thirtieth birthday.

Finally everyone in the line in front of the counter had been taken care of and Pen approached the chemist, who was doing something on her computer.

"Can I help you?" she said. Her long glossy bangs swept across her forehead as she looked up at Penelope's approach.

She had a name badge pinned to the front of her white coat, but Penelope couldn't quite read it.

"I have a rather odd question," Penelope said, cringing slightly inside.

You would think she'd be used to asking people odd questions by now, she thought as she felt her stomach clench.

The chemist tilted her head and raised her eyebrows.

Penelope cleared her throat and gulped. "Has anyone come in recently—within the last two weeks—looking for some cream or ointment to put on a burn?"

"What a curious question," the chemist said. "But, yes, as a matter of fact, someone did. She had a nasty burn on the back of her hand—she said she got it when she was taking a baking sheet of biscuits out of the oven. It was causing her some discomfort. I recommended Acriflex Cream for her."

"You don't happen to remember what she looked like, do you?"

The chemist tilted her head to one side and put a finger on her chin.

"She was quite ordinary, and I'm afraid I don't remember much else about her. We do get a fair amount of customers in a day. I was more concerned with examining the burn on her hand. She did say she worked at Worthington House and that I was to put it on their account."

Penelope tried not to grin at this news. She thanked the chemist, paid for her face cream, and left the apothecary.

Her theory was confirmed, she thought as she walked back toward Tesco and her car. Ivy had told the staff in the kitchen the night of the ball that she felt faint and needed to get some air. No one paid much attention when she went outside. What they didn't know was that she'd most likely stolen Worthington's polo mallet with the intention of using it to kill Cissie. She had gone out to the terrace, committed the murder, and had then thrown her blood-spattered apron on the bonfire, hoping to destroy the evidence.

What she hadn't counted on was burning her hand when she got too close to the sparks. And she'd lied to the chemist about how she got the burn—if she'd gotten it pulling a baking sheet out of the oven without a mitt, the burn would have been on her palm and not the back of her hand.

S omeone slashed your tires?" Beryl's voice went up an octave when Penelope told her what had happened. She stared at Penelope, a bottle of wine in one hand and a corkscrew in the other. "Why would someone do that? You might have been hurt . . . or, worse, killed."

Penelope was sitting in her kitchen, which was filled with the tantalizing aroma coming from a pot of chili simmering on the stove.

Beryl opened the wine and poured some out. Her hand shook and the bottle clanged against one of the glasses. "Do you think someone slashed them because you've been going around poking your nose into an investigation that's best left to the police?"

Beryl stood with her hands on her hips and gave Penelope a stern look. Penelope was surprised she'd been able to restrain herself from wagging her finger.

"It's possible." Penelope took a sip of her wine. She felt the liquid trace a warm path down her throat, and her shoulders began to relax. "It's also possible that it was simply a teenage prank. You know how kids are—they don't always realize how dangerous these things can be."

Penelope got up and peered into the pot of chili on the stove, inhaling the spicy aroma. "How was your day?" she said to Beryl, hoping to change the subject.

"Good. I got my photographs taken and what I saw of them looked great." She drummed her fingers on the table. "Now to wait and see about that big Molton Brown soap promotion. The agent told me they are looking at several people, but that they planned to use more than one model so he's quite hopeful."

"That's great." Penelope got place mats and napkins out of the cupboard.

"I'm thinking of getting a little place in London if I do get the job." Beryl took silverware out of the drawer and began setting the table. "That commute is exhausting and so far I haven't met any eligible men. They're all married, gay, or way too young. Perhaps I'll have better luck in the city."

"Aren't apartments terribly expensive?" Penelope felt her stomach growl as Beryl brought the steaming pot of chili over to the table and placed it on a trivet.

Beryl plunged a serving spoon into the pot. "Yvette has a friend who's going to Mozambique for a few months and would be willing to sublet her place for a very reasonable amount."

Penelope didn't know how she felt about Beryl staying in London. On the one hand, it would be nice to have her sister nearby; on the other hand, Beryl was bossy and thought nothing of intruding on Penelope's life. Penelope had rather been enjoying the freedom to do what she wanted without worrying about what Beryl would think or say.

They were about to start eating when the doorbell rang. Penelope tossed her napkin on the table and pushed back her chair. The legs scraped against the stone floor and Mrs. Danvers looked up from where she was napping with an irritated expression.

"Who could that be?" Beryl called to Penelope as Penelope headed toward the front door.

Penelope opened the door a crack and peeked out. She was surprised to see Maguire standing on the doorstep. She was also secretly pleased.

He brought the scent of cold, fresh air in with him as he stepped into the foyer.

"I wanted to make sure you got home okay," he said, running a hand over the slight stubble on his chin. "That spare should hold up for a bit, but you'd best get a new tire as soon as possible."

Penelope heard footsteps and Beryl appeared behind her. She sighed—she was going to have to explain Maguire's presence. The police generally didn't stop by the houses of everyone who had had a flat tire to see how they were doing.

"Beryl, this is Detective Brody Maguire." She turned to Maguire. "This is my sister, Beryl Kent."

Penelope noticed Beryl giving Maguire the once-over. She must have approved of what she saw. "Won't you join us for dinner?" she said in a slightly breathy voice. "There's plenty and we were just about to sit down."

"I don't want to be a bother." Maguire exchanged a glance with Penelope as they walked through the sitting room.

"It's no bother at all." Beryl stopped short and put a hand on Maguire's arm. "I do hope you like chili."

"I love it. I visited a distant cousin in Texas once—he married an American and now he's a professor of microbiology at the University of Texas at Austin. I couldn't get enough chili while I was there."

"Good." Beryl linked her arm through Maguire's and led him out to the kitchen. "Why don't you sit there." She pointed to an empty spot at the table. "I'll get you a plate."

Penelope was beginning to feel like a third wheel. She reminded herself that if Beryl did get an apartment in London, she'd be an hour away.

Beryl dished out the chili and they all began to eat. She

pointed her spoon at Maguire. "You need to tell Pen to stop investigating those murders at Worthington House." She gave Penelope a stern look. "She said someone slashed her tire today—she could have been hurt—or, worse, killed."

Maguire looked up from his bowl. "She's actually been a great help in the investigation." He smiled at Penelope.

So there, Beryl, Penelope thought.

"But I do worry about her," Maguire continued. "Maybe it would be best if you leave any further investigating to me, okay?" He winked at Penelope.

She looked down at her plate to hide the smile that was hovering around her lips.

"You know that piece of cloth that was found in the bonfire?" Pen said. "I think I know what it was. I tried calling you to tell you, but you were off in Leeds."

Maguire startled and dropped his spoon into his dish.

"How did you . . . What do you think it was?" He looked at Penelope in disbelief.

"An apron," Penelope said somewhat triumphantly. "It's the one thing a person could take off without anyone noticing. It's not as if it's a pair of pants or a shirt. And it would provide protection from any . . . any blood."

Penelope noticed Beryl shudder and turn white.

Maguire inhaled sharply. He picked up his spoon. "I think you could be right. It makes sense."

"I talked to some of the kitchen staff at Worthington House and one of them, Ivy Brown, went outside during the ball. She claimed to be feeling faint."

Maguire's head snapped up. "She did? Did anyone notice if her apron was missing when she returned?"

Penelope made a sad face. "Unfortunately, no. I imagine they were all run off their feet dealing with a party of that size." Penelope pushed her plate away. "I did notice something when they were serving the food though. Ivy had a bandage on her hand."

Maguire shrugged his shoulders. "That could be anything. She worked in the kitchen—perhaps the knife slipped."

Penelope felt a bit like a conjurer pulling a rabbit out of a hat. "It could have been, but it wasn't. I checked with the chemist at the apothecary and she said Ivy came in looking for a cream or ointment to put on a burn on her hand."

Maguire whistled. "Now that's very interesting. Presumably she burned her hand when she tossed the apron onto the bonfire?" He leaned back in his chair and stretched his legs out. "But there's no motive. Did she even know Cissie or Tobias Winterbourne?"

"She did know Cissie. And I imagine she was afraid that Tobias might have caught a glimpse of her while he was waiting in the bushes for Rose."

Penelope explained about her visit to Cissie's former nanny, Alice, and the story Alice had told her about Cissie blaming Ivy for the ruined Turner painting.

"But why wait until now to get her revenge?" Maguire tapped an index finger against his wineglass. "Surely Ivy had let bygones be bygones long ago."

"I think I have the answer to that, too." Penelope put her elbows on the table and leaned closer. "It happened at dinner the night before Charlotte and Worthington's wedding. I heard Cissie talking to someone. Her tone was very dismissive and condescending. She said something like 'I'm afraid I don't know who you are.'"

"How rude," Beryl said, spooning up the last bit of her chili.

Maguire pinched the bridge of his nose. "And she was speaking to Ivy?"

"I don't know—not for sure, at any rate. I had my back to

them." Pen held her hands out palms up. "But it fits, doesn't it? After growing up with Cissie and after what Cissie did to Ivy, she turns around and pretends not to know her."

"Could be." Maguire pushed back his chair. "I'll have a crack at interviewing this Ivy Brown first thing tomorrow."

"What about the DCI from the Met?" Pen said, getting up.

Maguire gave a broad smile. "Donovan doesn't need to know." He turned to Penelope and put his hands on her shoulders. "Do be careful, okay? Let me take it from here?"

"Sure," Penelope said.

She hoped her voice carried the right note of conviction.

TWENTY-TWO

❧❧❧

Penelope spent a restless night going over and over the information she'd gathered so far about the Worthington House murders. Had she done the wrong thing in telling Maguire about Ivy? He said he was going to interview her. But what if she was innocent? It would no doubt be distressing and it would be Penelope's fault.

Maybe Rose was the killer after all and she had sent Maguire on a wild-goose chase. Or the killer could have even been Jemima. She had no alibi and she had a motive.

The tabloids were full of lurid headlines insinuating that Worthington had killed his ex-girlfriend. Some were even hinting that Charlotte had done it. Penelope didn't believe it for a minute, but what if she was wrong?

She rolled over and pulled the blankets up to her ears. Mrs. Danvers was at the foot of the bed and this maneuver obviously disturbed her, because she glared at Penelope, jumped off, and went to curl up on the rug.

* * *

Y ou look terrible," Beryl said when Penelope appeared
in the kitchen the next morning.

Beryl was sitting at the kitchen table, nursing a cup of
coffee—Penelope hadn't yet been able to get her to trade
her morning java for a cup of tea.

Beryl looked as put together as ever even though she was
still in her bathrobe and hadn't yet done her hair or makeup.

Penelope looked down at herself. She'd scrambled into
some clothes, pulling them willy-nilly from the closet. At
least she was comfortable, she thought, as she rummaged
in the cupboard for a mug.

She heated the kettle, warmed her mug with the hot water, added the tea bag, and took it and her laptop out to the
sitting room.

She was going to finish those revisions if it was the last
thing she did.

Penelope pulled up her manuscript and was soon en-
grossed in her work.

An hour later she hit Send and immediately wished she
could get the e-mail back. She should have read it over one
more time—made sure there weren't any repeated words,
missing motivation, lack of conflict. She rubbed her forehead. Maybe she should have scrapped the whole thing and
started over.

Surely her first bestseller had been a fluke and this one
was going to be a bust. Whatever made her think she could
write a book? Who was she kidding?

She looked up when she heard footsteps. Beryl was
standing in front of her with a worried look on her face. She
was dressed for London in a smart-looking suit.

"Whatever is the matter?" Beryl said. "Is something wrong?"

"I've just sent off my revised manuscript," Penelope said glumly.

"Isn't that cause for celebration? It's a bit early in the morning, but I can pick up a bottle of champagne on my way back tonight."

"Thanks." Penelope smiled briefly. "I'm just afraid the whole thing is a horrible mess."

"I'm quite sure that's not the case," Beryl said as they got into Penelope's car for the drive to the train station.

"I'll see you tonight," Beryl said as Penelope pulled up in front of the station. She got out of the car and turned to go but then paused. "Oh, and do cheer up. I'm sure everything is going to be fine."

Penelope parked her car in front of the Open Book, got out, and gave it a last look before pulling open the front door to the bookstore. Last time, someone had slashed her tire—would there be a next time and would the damage escalate? She sighed and stepped inside.

Mabel smiled at her from behind the counter where she was sorting through the day's mail.

Penelope nodded, gave her a quick smile, and then retreated to her writing room to work on a piece for the store newsletter. She was putting her Gothic literature studies to good use by doing an article on some of the more famous Gothic novels like du Maurier's *Rebecca*, Shelley's *Frankenstein*, and Walpole's *Castle of Otranto*. Mabel planned to do a display of the novels mentioned in Penelope's article.

After an hour she yawned, stretched, and stood up. She hit Save and closed her laptop. She was having trouble concentrating. She couldn't stop thinking about Maguire's interview with Ivy and wondering how it had gone—and wondering whether she had done the right thing in the first place by telling him about Ivy's past. If Ivy turned out to be innocent . . .

Penelope sighed and went out into the salesroom. Being around books always cheered her up—the sight of all the colorful covers, the smell of the pages, and the feel of the glossy jackets never failed to lift her mood.

Mabel came out from behind the front counter. "You're awfully quiet this morning," she said. "Is everything okay?"

"Yes." Penelope shook her head. "No." She cracked the knuckles of her right hand. "I'm not sure I did the right thing."

She told Mabel about Ivy and that Maguire planned to interview her that morning.

"What if Ivy is innocent, and now I've put her through all this?"

Mabel smiled at Penelope. "That's what the police do—interview people—often even innocent people." She squeezed Penelope's shoulder. "You did the right thing—you passed on the information for Maguire to handle." She laughed. "I much prefer that to your doing the investigating yourself. I don't want to think about the last time you put on your Sherlock Holmes deerstalker and nearly got yourself killed."

Penelope felt slightly better. By the time she'd helped a few customers find a book, she'd forgotten all about Ivy and Maguire's interview.

Around noon, Penelope realized she'd forgotten to take the meat out of the freezer that she'd planned to cook for dinner that night. She told Mabel she'd be back in an hour—her fiction writing group was meeting that afternoon—and went out to her car.

Mrs. Danvers seemed pleased to see Penelope, and Penelope spent a couple of minutes scratching her back and under her chin. Her fur was warm from the sun. What a life, Penelope thought—lazing in the sun all day.

She ate a bowl of leftover chili for lunch, spent a couple of minutes tidying up the kitchen, checked Mrs. Danvers's food and water, and then headed back out to her car.

She was unlocking the MINI's door when she sensed someone coming up in back of her. She spun around and was surprised to see Ivy's cousin Floyd approaching her. His arm was at his side and he appeared to be holding something.

The sun glinted off the object in his hand and Penelope realized it was a knife. She opened her mouth to scream, but no sound came out. Her legs refused to move and she felt paralyzed. What did Floyd want with her?

Floyd came up to her and held the knife to her back. Penelope could feel the pressure of the point through her coat. She sniffed back the tears that were threatening to engulf her and tried to think.

Should she attempt to outrun him? He looked to be fairly fit—he would probably overtake her before she reached the more populated section of the high street.

Maybe he was after money? Penelope tried to remember how much cash she had on her. Unfortunately she wasn't sure. Unlike Beryl, who arranged her bills according to denomination and always knew exactly how much cash she had at any given time, Penelope was far more casual, stuffing her money into her purse, her pockets, and sometimes even her wallet without thinking about it.

"Get in the car," Floyd growled in a low, menacing voice that sent chills down Penelope's spine.

Penelope fumbled with the door handle, and he increased the pressure of the knife against her back. She imagined she could feel the sharp prick of the tip and she shivered.

Finally, Penelope got the door open and slid into the driver's seat. Floyd trotted around the car toward the passenger side. If she could start the car and pull away from the curb before he got the door open, she could get away and head to the police station, pull up outside, and run in yelling for help. She pictured Maguire coming out of his office and taking her in his arms where she would be safe and secure. . . .

Penelope fumbled with her key, attempting to insert it in the ignition. Her hands were shaking and she dropped it on the floor. She groaned. The passenger door opened as she was bending over, attempting to retrieve the key, and the slightly funky odor of Floyd's clothes and the musky scent of his aftershave filled the car.

"Drive," he said, pointing to the ignition.

By now Penelope had retrieved the key from the floor of the car. She stabbed at the ignition several times before finally inserting the key successfully. She turned it and the engine sprang to life with a soft purr.

She pulled away from the curb and headed down the high street.

"Where are we going?" She turned her head to look at Floyd.

"Just drive," he said again, pointing forward.

Desperation washed over Penelope as they passed the Tesco and Kebabs and Curries, and eventually even Digby's garage was in her rearview mirror and they were headed into more open country.

Her steering was jerky and more than once she veered onto the wrong side of the road.

"Be careful," Floyd barked at her. "Are you trying to get us killed?"

Just you, Penelope thought to herself as she pulled back onto the correct side.

She continued to weave back and forth across her lane, her hands slick with sweat and unsteady on the wheel. If only a policeman were around, surely she'd be pulled over and saved from whatever fate awaited her.

Was Floyd planning on killing her? Had Ivy sent him to do it? She realized now that he must have been the one to slash her tire. She thought about the time she felt as if someone had been stalking her as she walked down the high street. Had that actually been Floyd following her?

"Turn there." Floyd pointed to what was little more than a dirt path heading up a slope before disappearing beyond the hill. Penelope recognized it as the route that she'd taken when she'd followed Tobias to Worthington's shooting lodge. Was that where Floyd was taking her?

Penelope began to shiver uncontrollably, the chattering of her teeth audible in the car as they jolted over the ruts and furrows in the path.

Soon Worthington's shooting lodge came into view. The doors to the large shed next to it were wide open. Two cars were parked in the makeshift driveway—a late model Mercedes that looked familiar to Penelope and a boxy utilitarian-looking Land Rover that had dried mud on the bumpers and the front grill and dings in the paint.

"Pull in there." Floyd pointed to the shed.

The shed was empty and the MINI fit handily. Penelope turned off the engine and waited, her hands still clutching the steering wheel.

"Get out," Floyd commanded.

Penelope opened her door. She couldn't open it all the way without hitting the wall, and had to shimmy out of the driver's seat.

Floyd motioned for her to follow him out of the shed.

He began walking toward the front door of the shooting lodge.

Penelope hesitated. Should she run? She looked around. There was nowhere to hide. She scanned the landscape, but there were no ramblers about or people walking their dogs.

Floyd must have sensed her hesitation because he spun around and in a second he was at her side, the knife pressed against the back of her neck this time. Penelope felt the coolness of the steel blade against her skin.

Her legs began to buckle and Floyd grabbed her arm to steady her. They were nearing the door when Penelope tripped over a bit of uneven ground and fell to her knees. Floyd yanked her to her feet and shoved her toward the lodge.

He took a set of keys from his pocket, inserted one in the lock, and pushed open the door.

Ivy was waiting inside by the stone fireplace.

"You sent that policeman to interview me," she said, glaring at Penelope.

"I didn't," Penelope said. "He was just doing his job."

She really hadn't, Penelope tried to convince herself. It had been Maguire's decision.

"You had to poke your nose in where it didn't belong, didn't you?" Ivy said, her lip curling. "Now you're going to have to pay the price."

"Like Cissie paid the price?" Penelope said, lifting her chin.

"I don't know anything about that," Ivy said, crossing her arms over her chest.

"But you killed her," Penelope said. "Didn't you?"

"No. I killed her." The voice came from behind Penelope. She spun around and came face-to-face with Jemima Dougal.

"What?"

Penelope looked from Jemima to Ivy and then back again. Her head was spinning. She'd gotten it all wrong. She tried to think it through—it was like trying to unravel a tangled thread.

"You said you went out on the terrace to talk to Cissie—to beg her not to tell Charlotte that you'd stolen the things that had disappeared. But you'd gone out there to kill her."

Jemima shrugged.

"You were wearing an apron so no blood would get on you. Did you borrow it from Ivy and did she agree to throw it on the bonfire for you?"

"Let's say Ivy wasn't terribly fond of Cissie either. We certainly had that in common. The chance to get her revenge, plus the bonus of a few hundred extra pounds were enough to persuade her to help me." Jemima glanced at Ivy. "Right, Ivy?"

Ivy smiled. "My pleasure. She had it coming to her."

"She certainly did." Jemima sighed. "She never had any qualms about taking what she thought she deserved—even if it belonged to someone else. And she blamed *me* for taking things!"

"Ethan," Penelope said suddenly as the pieces fell into place. "She was trying to take Ethan away from you, wasn't she? They'd been lovers once before."

"It was all a game with Cissie. I don't think she gave a fig about Ethan—she wanted him in order to get back at me for taking him away from her in the first place. You know who I feel sorry for?"

"Who?"

"Poor Tobias. I think he knew what was going on. It was Cissie's fault—she's the one who drove him back into Rose's arms." Jemima sighed. "Cissie could afford to do what she pleased. She was the one with the money. All she ever wanted from Tobias anyway was the title."

"But you killed Tobias," Penelope said.

Jemima made a sad face. "I had to. He could have given me away."

Jemima clasped her hands together. "But I do love Ethan. Cissie would have broken his heart and I couldn't bear that."

"What about Floyd?" Penelope looked at Ivy and then pointed at Floyd, who was slouched in a chair. "Was he stalking me? And was he the one who slashed my tire?"

Ivy nodded. "We thought it would warn you off but you didn't listen. You had to keep sticking your nose in where it didn't belong. More's the pity."

"Did you pay him, too? To do those things?"

"I didn't have to." Ivy smiled at Floyd. "Right, Floyd?"

Floyd grunted.

"No, Floyd owed me," Ivy continued. "I rescued him, you see. He's the son of that wretched aunt I was sent to live with. It was a miserable life for him, too, even though he was her own flesh and blood. When I decided to escape, I agreed to take Floyd with me. I was able to get him a job working for the gardener at Worthington House. He didn't have nowhere to stay, so his lordship very kindly let him have a small room off the kitchen."

"You're not going to get away with this," Penelope said. She groaned to herself—what a horrible cliché. Bettina would never let that stand in one of her manuscripts.

"It's been lovely chatting," Jemima said, looking at her

watch. "But I'm afraid I must go. I'm sorry to miss the finale, but I'm meeting Ethan for a late lunch." She looked at Ivy then Floyd. "I'll leave you both to it."

Penelope felt her stomach turn over and a trickle of sweat made its way down her spine, giving her the chills.

She wondered if she dared to make a run for it. Would Floyd be able to hit a moving target with his knife?

It was now or never, Penelope decided. No need to make it easy on them by being a sitting duck. She turned and had almost made it to the door when something crashed down on her head. There was a momentary jolt of pain and then everything went black.

TWENTY-THREE

Penelope's head throbbed and she had a cramp in her calf. She tried to move her leg, but something was in the way. She'd been having the strangest dream and couldn't shake the odd feeling it had given her. Slowly she opened her eyes.

She was sitting in the driver's seat of her car. What was she doing in there? Had she fallen asleep at the wheel? She rubbed her head, and her hand came away with blood on it. She stared at it in panic. If only she could make the pounding ache go away she could think more clearly.

Suddenly she became aware that the car was running. What had she been thinking? She reached for the key to turn if off, but it wasn't there. Had it fallen out?

She began to search the floor of the car but then realized that was ridiculous. If the key wasn't in the ignition, how did she start the car?

She began to look around. She was parked in some sort

of shed. It didn't look familiar. She'd never left her car anywhere like it before. A shaft of sunlight was coming through
windows high up in the double doors behind her.

She rubbed her forehead. If only she could remember
what had happened.

A sharp pain tore through her head and she reached up
to touch the sore spot on her skull. The motion brought back
a bit of memory—something smashing down on her . . .
pain . . . then blackness.

She tried to grasp the fragments of thought that drifted
through her mind, which were as insubstantial as silk
threads.

She remembered standing in a room with an immense
stone fireplace. Ivy was there and so was Jemima. Had
she been at Worthington House? She didn't think so.

She was beginning to feel light-headed and had the urge
to close her eyes again and go to sleep. Trying to puzzle
things out was exhausting her.

Her head was beginning to nod when she had a terrible
realization. The car's motor was running and she was in a
confined space. She hadn't exactly been a star in science
class but she'd learned enough to know that carbon monoxide was deadly.

She had to get out.

She reached for the door handle but couldn't find it. She
felt as if her brain had been replaced with a thick impene-
trable fog. Finally she got a grip on the handle and managed to get the door open. She squeezed through the space
and stopped, suddenly doubled over with a spasm of intense
coughing.

She staggered to the double doors at the back of the
shed. She needed air. She put the flat of her hand against
one of the doors and pushed.

Nothing happened—the doors didn't budge. They were obviously locked from the outside. She patted her pockets but they were empty. She must have put her phone in her purse. She made her way back to her car where she upended the contents of her purse onto the driver's seat. She looked through the items twice but her phone wasn't there. What a time to forget her cell!

Penelope's vision was getting blurry and she squinted as she looked around the shed. She couldn't see any other way out. She had to get the doors open.

Exhaust continued to pump out the back of the MINI and the air felt as if it was getting thicker. Every breath made Penelope cough.

But she was darned if she was going to die in this shed without a struggle. As her Yankee grandmother always said, Parishes weren't quitters.

Penelope tried to stiffen her spine, but she was finding it harder and harder to stand up straight and coughing continued to wrack her, doubling her over with intense spasms.

She felt herself beginning to panic and tried to take deep breaths to calm herself down but then realized that all she was doing was breathing in more noxious fumes.

If she could disable the car's engine somehow, perhaps she would be able to shut it off. She popped open the hood and peered in dismay at the inside. She had no idea which part did what.

In a burst of anger, she slammed the hood shut.

Darn it, she wasn't going to be Jemima's third victim no matter what it took. There was no way she was going to allow Jemima to get away with murder.

Every problem has a solution even if you don't like the solution, her grandmother used to say. She just had to think hard—harder than she ever had in her life. Maybe if she imagined what one of her characters would do in a position like this—she'd always been able to come up with an answer when they had to be rescued from a potentially deadly situation.

She was beginning to feel woozy when an idea came to her. It would take courage, but what did she have to lose?

She got back into the driver's seat of the MINI, put her foot on the brake, and shifted the car into reverse. She said a short prayer that she was going to be successful, then removed her foot from the brake and transferred it to the gas.

The car shot backward and slammed into the shed doors, jolting Penelope's very bones. But the doors held.

She drove forward and then reversed again, and this time she distinctly heard the sound of wood splintering.

The crash against the door sent a jolt of pain through Penelope's head, but she wasn't giving up now. She put her foot on the gas and floored it. The MINI shot backward and crashed into the doors. The lock gave way and the doors flew open.

Penelope put the car in park and stumbled out. She didn't have the heart to look at the damage to the rear of her car. She shoved the now-splintered doors open, folded them back on either side of the shed, and got back in the MINI.

She prayed the car was still functional. She put it in reverse and carefully backed out of the shed. Her hands were shaking and her head was still fuzzy. She winced when she heard a high-pitched screech as the rear door of the MINI scraped against the side of the shed.

She managed to turn the MINI around and head back down the path toward the road. She could hear a scraping noise coming from underneath the car. It was probably her bumper dragging but this was no time to stop and look at it.

She had no idea where Ivy, Jemima, or Floyd were.

Jemima had been about to leave and was probably already tucked up in a restaurant somewhere with Ethan, but she didn't know about the other two. If they were still at the lodge, surely they heard the noise as she rammed the shed doors with her car.

She pressed down a bit harder on the gas pedal at the thought that Floyd might even now be coming after her. She had no doubt that this time he would finish the job he'd started.

Every rut in the lane jolted the MINI and sent a corresponding jolt of pain through Penelope's head. All she could think about was getting her hands on some ibuprofen and a big glass of water. Her throat was dry and her mouth felt parched.

She heard a clang and looked in the rearview mirror to see the bumper of her MINI lying crumpled on the path.

Something else now appeared to be dragging behind the car. Penelope heard it scraping the ground and when she looked in the mirror again, she saw that she was etching a furrow in the dirt.

As long as she made it to the main road, she thought. It wasn't particularly well traveled but surely someone would come by before too long.

She caught a movement out of the corner of her eye and turned to look. The Land Rover she'd seen parked outside Worthington's shooting lodge was jouncing across the uneven terrain toward her.

She was almost to the road. Penelope increased her pressure on the gas pedal, and the MINI lurched forward, the scraping sound behind her increasing with the speed. She had to grit her teeth against the pain as she hit the numerous ruts and ridges in the path.

She didn't dare look to see where the Land Rover was.

The last time she'd checked, it had been close enough for her to see that Floyd was driving with Ivy in the passenger seat beside him.

The country road that led into Chumley and the high street was now only yards away. Penelope turned onto it and the sound coming from in back of the car now became a screech as whatever was hanging off dragged along the macadam. She suspected she was about to lose her entire muffler.

The dragging slowed her speed and it was barely any effort for the Land Rover to catch up to her. Floyd rammed the back of her car and she felt a shock travel from the base of her spine up to the top of her skull.

Penelope's hands were clutched on the steering wheel so hard they were beginning to ache. Her face felt wet and she realized she was crying. Her nose was running, too. She was tempted to swipe at it but didn't want to take her hands off the wheel.

A car was coming from the opposite direction. Penelope squinted into the distance. It looked like a police car. As it got closer, she recognized the blue-and-yellow checkerboard pattern of a patrol car. What if he just passed her by? She had to signal her distress somehow. Would her trailing muffler be enough to alert the cop to her plight?

Penelope decided she couldn't let the patrol car go past her without doing something. She slowed down, quickly wrenched the wheel and angled the car so that it took up both of the narrow lanes, and slammed on the brakes.

She heard a noise and looked in back of her in time to see Floyd yank the steering wheel and drive the Land Rover off the road and into the adjacent field.

The patrol car's brakes squealed and the smell of burning rubber filled the air as the officer came to a stop inches from Penelope's MINI. His face was red with fury as he opened his door and got out.

"What on earth do you mean by stopping your car like that?" Puffs of vapor clouded from his mouth as he spoke.

Penelope fumbled for the door handle. It took all of her waning strength to push the door open. She felt her legs tremble as soon as her feet hit the ground and she carefully slid from the seat and stood up. She swayed slightly and put out a hand to steady herself.

"Blimey." The cop rubbed a hand across the back of his neck. "What's happened to you, lass? Have you had an accident?"

Penelope opened her mouth but at first no words came out, but then all of a sudden they spilled out, tumbling over one another until she was convinced that she sounded like a lunatic.

The policeman held up a hand. "Whoa, slow down, lass. You say someone was chasing you? In their car?"

Penelope started to nod but the movement set off a wave of pain.

"Yes. They were trying to kill me."

A change came over the policeman's face—a wary look of disbelief. "Kill you, you say?"

Penelope could tell he was now convinced she was crazy. She had to get him to believe her.

She pointed toward the field adjacent to the road where the only sign of the Land Rover was a rapidly settling cloud of dust.

"Yes. The man and woman in that Land Rover that cut across the field there. They were trying to kill me."

"I see." The cop stroked his chin. "I think we'd better get you to hospital." He pointed at her. "Get that head of yours taken care of. That looks nasty."

Penelope had caught a glimpse of herself in the rearview mirror at one point. There was dried blood on her forehead and cheeks and matted in her hair. No wonder the policeman thought she was daft.

"But you have to go after them." Once again, Penelope pointed across the field and into the distance. "You have to stop them. They tried to kill me." She didn't know what she wanted to do more—stomp her foot or burst into tears.

"Yes, yes," the cop said soothingly. "I'll be taking care of that. Just as soon as I get you to hospital. That's a nasty-looking lump on your head. No wonder you're imagining things."

"I'm not imagining it." This time Penelope did stamp her foot. She pointed at the cell phone on the policeman's belt. "Call Detective Maguire. He'll tell you."

A look of doubt spread across the man's face. His hand inched toward his cell phone.

"Go ahead." Penelope pointed at the phone. "Call him." She lifted her chin and glared at the policeman.

TWENTY-FOUR

❧❦❧

The policeman had Penelope sit in his patrol car while he dialed his cell phone. She didn't know who he'd called, but moments later another patrol car arrived and a tall, earnest-looking cop with slightly stooped shoulders jumped out. A few minutes after that, there was a rumble in the distance and a tow truck rattled down the lane and into view.

Penelope turned around and watched as a man in a baseball cap bustled around hooking a chain to the front of the MINI.

Shock was beginning to set in and Penelope started to shiver, just a bit at first but then so violently her teeth clattered together.

The policeman reached out and turned the dial on the heater.

"We'll soon get you nice and warm," he said as he steered the patrol car down the lane toward the high street.

Penelope leaned back against the headrest and savored

the warmth washing over her. She began to doze and didn't wake up until they were pulling in front of a multistory building with a sign out front that read *Chumley-on-Stoke Hospital* with an arrow pointing to an automatic door with the letters *A&E* over it.

"Here we are," the cop said, pulling on the emergency brake. "We'll have you fixed up in a tick. I've called ahead and they're waiting for us."

Even before he finished talking, a woman in blue scrubs came out the door, pushing an empty wheelchair.

"Here you go, love," she said as she helped Penelope into it.

Penelope started to protest as they went through the automatic door, but the nurse just tut-tutted and assured her that everything was going to be fine.

The next thing Penelope knew, she was lying on a gurney, wearing a hospital gown, and a young female doctor was asking her questions.

Penelope explained about being hit over the head and then being exposed to carbon monoxide. The doctor looked startled briefly but then quickly resumed her professional countenance. A nurse appeared to take a blood draw and then Pen was whisked away for a CAT scan.

Finally, Pen was wheeled back to her cubicle and moments later the doctor reappeared.

She pulled a flashlight out of her pocket, shone it in each of Penelope's eyes, and then had her follow the pinprick of light with her gaze.

She smiled at Pen. "We're still waiting on the results of the blood tests but you appear to have a slight concussion." She examined Penelope's head. "We're going to have to get that stitched up too," she said briskly. "It's not a terrible cut but head wounds do bleed so. I'll be right back to take care of it."

She left the room and Penelope looked around. It wasn't much more than a cubicle with all sorts of equipment hanging from the walls. There was a television mounted high up in the corner, but she didn't have the energy to turn it on.

She was closing her eyes when she sensed a presence in the doorway. The doctor, no doubt, back with her sewing kit.

When she opened her eyes, she was surprised to see Maguire standing there, his face creased with concern. He gulped when he saw Penelope.

"The constable told me what happened," he said, reaching Penelope's bedside in two strides. "You look terrible," he said and grinned.

Penelope grinned back. "You should see the other guy."

Maguire's expression became serious. "Tell me what happened." He pulled the visitor's chair over and sat down. He took Penelope's hand.

Penelope explained about Ivy and how she'd come to the conclusion that Ivy had killed Cissie Winterbourne.

"But I was wrong. Ivy was merely an accomplice with an ax to grind. She sent her cousin Floyd to kidnap me and when I got there, Jemima was waiting."

"Jemima?" Maguire sat up straighter in his chair. "Why?"

Penelope explained about Cissie and Ethan and the past that Cissie and Jemima shared.

"Ivy needed money. And besides, as I said, she had her own bone to pick with Cissie. She was more than willing to lend Jemima her apron the night of the ball and to later take it out and toss it on the bonfire."

Maguire raised his eyebrows. "What about Tobias?"

"Jemima was afraid he might have seen her with Cissie that night so she decided he needed to be eliminated."

Maguire sighed. "I have to confess that I originally agreed with the constable that the bump you'd gotten on the head must have had you imagining things. But this makes sense." He got up abruptly. "I need to send some men after Ivy and Floyd. I'll interview Jemima myself." He started toward the door but then stopped and turned around. "I hate to leave you here all alone."

Penelope shooed him out the door. "Go on. I'll be fine. I can always call Mabel or Figgy or my sister."

Maguire didn't look totally convinced, but he left and Penelope could hear him hurrying down the hall.

Figgy came to pick Penelope up when the doctors in the A&E were finally convinced she was fit enough to go home.

"You will have someone with you, I hope," the nurse said as she gave Penelope a sheet of instructions. "You have a concussion so you need to be alert for these signs." She tapped a bulleted list on the paper in Penelope's hand. "If your symptoms worsen, you'll need to come back to hospital." She glared sternly at Penelope.

Penelope promised to do as she was told and was relieved when the nurse left, drawing the curtain in back of her, and Penelope could change out of the hospital gown and into her own clothes.

There was a bloodstain on the neck of her sweater and she shivered when she saw it. The horror of what had happened washed over her anew and she had to sit down for a moment while she fought back the tears pricking her eyelids.

"Hey, what's the matter?" Figgy popped through the door. "Whoa." She came to a halt. "What on earth happened? You said you'd had an accident and needed stitches.

I assumed you fell or something. You look like you've been through the wringer."

"I'll explain later," Pen said. "All I want now is to get out of here."

"Righto. My car is outside. Can you walk? Should I get you a wheelchair?"

"I can walk," Pen said, slowly standing up. "I think." She swayed slightly. "Can I take your arm?"

Penelope linked her arm through Figgy's and they made their way out of the examining room and down the hall. Penelope took a deep breath when they got outside, hoping to get the antiseptic hospital smell out of her lungs.

Figgy carefully tucked Penelope into the front seat of the car and then went around to the driver's side.

"You'd best drive rather slowly," Pen said, wincing slightly as Figgy's front tire hit a pothole in the parking lot.

"Will do." Figgy reached over and patted Penelope's hand. "Do you mind if we make a quick stop at the Open Book? I seem to have left my phone behind." Figgy clicked on her blinker. "Besides, Mabel wants to see with her own eyes that you're okay."

They rode down the high street slowly. Gladys was standing outside the Pig in a Poke, locking the front door. She waved as they went by.

Figgy pulled up in front of the Open Book. "Wait and I'll come round and help you out," she said as she put the car in park and turned off the engine.

"Well I never!" Mabel exclaimed when Penelope walked through the front door. "You go and sit down. Figgy will make us a cup of tea and then you can tell us all about it."

Pen didn't argue and sank into one of the slipcovered armchairs, grateful for its soft embrace. Mabel kept looking at her as if to reassure herself that Penelope was all right.

"Here we go." Figgy wheeled over the tea cart. Penelope noticed a tray of tea sandwiches on the bottom shelf and realized she was starving. "Here's a nice cuppa for you," she said, handing Penelope a cup of tea.

"I hope you put plenty of sugar in that," Mabel said, pointing to Penelope's cup.

"Potted shrimp and cucumber and watercress," Figgy said as she handed Penelope a plate of the dainty sandwiches.

Penelope drank her cup of tea, downed several sandwiches in record time, and sighed with satisfaction. She felt her energy slowly returning.

"Now you're getting some color in your face," Mabel said with satisfaction. "You had us quite worried, you know."

"Are you up to telling us what happened?"

"How did you ever figure out that it was Jemima?" Mabel said when Penelope had finished talking.

"I didn't really. Jemima admitted it although I suppose I might have gotten there myself eventually."

"What about the MINI?" Figgy said.

"They've towed it to Digby's garage, but it's not looking good," Pen said. "It seems the frame could be bent—whatever that means."

"Well, thank heavens for that," Mabel said, throwing her arms in the air. "You've had more than your share of near misses. You'll be much safer on foot."

Figgy began to pick up their used cups and saucers and stack them on the tea tray. She was whistling as she did it.

Pen looked at her curiously. "You seem rather chipper for a change. Have you and Derek definitely decided to elope? Is that what has you in such a good mood?"

Figgy turned around, her dark eyes sparkling. She shook her head.

"No. I'll show you."

She disappeared into the tea shop and came back with a large white box.

"Derek brought me this today." She took the top off the box, rustled around in the tissue paper, and pulled out the contents.

Penelope caught a flash of vivid red fabric as Figgy lifted some garments from the box and spread them out on an empty chair.

Penelope and Mabel gasped.

"It's . . . it's beautiful," Penelope said.

It was a long red pleated skirt covered in intricate gold embroidery and a short top also adorned with exquisite needlework.

Figgy held the skirt up to her waist. "This is a *lehnga*. It's what a Pakistani bride wears for her wedding." She held up the top. "And this is a choli. Mrs. Kahn wore it for her wedding and she thought I might like to wear it for mine. She gave it to Derek to give to me."

"I guess they liked you after all," Mabel said somewhat dryly.

Figgy gave a sheepish grin. "I guess so. I was worried for nothing. They're just very quiet people like Derek said."

"It's lovely," Penelope said with a broad smile. "Somehow I couldn't picture you in a traditional long white wedding gown and veil, but that," she said, pointing to the outfit in Figgy's hand, "that's absolutely perfect."

Thank heavens you're okay," Beryl said when Figgy dropped her off at the cottage. "You could have been killed."

That realization had been sinking in for Penelope ever

since she'd been rescued by that constable. Every time she thought about it, it gave her the chills.

Mrs. Danvers came out of the kitchen and sashayed over to Penelope, her long tail swishing back and forth as she walked. She wove in and out between Penelope's legs and purred loudly as if to say that she, too, was glad that Penelope was safe.

"I've managed to get a fire going," Beryl said as she took Penelope's coat and hung it up. "Although I don't know how long it's going to last. Why don't you go sit down and I'll bring you a cup of tea?"

Penelope sank onto the sofa gratefully and tried to stifle the groan that rose to her lips. It felt as if every bone in her body was sore. She held her hands out to the fire—the warmth felt heavenly. The tension that was tight in every muscle began to drain away and even the persistent headache that had been hammering at her skull had started to retreat.

"Here you go," Beryl said, bustling into the room with a cup of tea and a plate with cheese and crackers artfully arranged on it.

Penelope looked up at her sister and had a sudden realization. "You're all dressed up. Are you going out or did you just get in?"

Beryl fiddled with the ends of her hair and gave a coy smile. "Going out actually." She frowned. "Assuming you'll be okay? I won't be long."

Pen smiled up at her. "I'll be fine."

Beryl cleared her throat. "I met someone and . . . he's taking me for a drink at that wine bar down the street."

"What about Magnus? You're not even divorced yet."

"I can't afford to let the grass grow under my feet at my age." Beryl shook her finger at Penelope. "And neither can you, I might add. Besides, it's only a drink. It might come to nothing."

Penelope dozed for a bit, and when she woke decided she would take her plate out to the kitchen but when she stood up, she realized she was still a bit woozy.

After a few minutes she managed to get up and make her way to the kitchen. Mrs. Danvers walked alongside her as if sensing her unsteadiness. Penelope put the dish in the sink and decided it would be best if she retreated to the couch again.

She'd barely sat down when the doorbell rang. Figgy or Mabel come to check on her?

Penelope made her slow, unsteady way to the door and pulled it open.

At first all she saw was a large bouquet of flowers, but then she realized it was Maguire holding them out to her.

"I came to make sure you're okay," he said, handing her the flowers. "I hope you like them. The only place I could get a bouquet at this hour was at Tesco."

"Thank you. Come in." Penelope's head spun a bit and she decided she had better sit down. "Sorry," she said as she took a seat. "I'm still feeling a bit wobbly."

"Can I get you anything?" Maguire said with a look of concern.

"I'm fine, thanks. But there's some white wine in the fridge if you'd like some."

"I'll get these flowers in some water as well." Maguire disappeared into the kitchen and Penelope leaned back against the cushions, her eyes closed.

She heard cupboard doors opening and closing and soon

Maguire reappeared with a glass of wine. He sat down next to Penelope on the sofa and put the glass on the coffee table.

"You gave me quite a scare," he said. "I didn't know what to think when I got that call from Constable Percy. And then when I found out what had actually happened, I nearly went crazy."

"Did you catch them? Ivy, Floyd, and Jemima, I mean?"

Maguire nodded. "We rounded up Ivy and Floyd quite easily. They were arrogant enough to go back to Worthington House." He shook his head in disbelief.

"They probably thought you wouldn't believe me."

Maguire laughed. "Constable Percy certainly didn't. But then he didn't know the backstory." He took a sip of his wine. "Lady Jemima Dougal was another matter, of course. Her husband protested vigorously to her being interviewed at Worthington House, let alone taken in to the station for questioning. We had to wait for their solicitor to arrive and he put up quite a fuss as you can imagine. But he can fuss all he wants—his client isn't going to escape justice."

"What about DCI Donovan? Did you break the news to her yet?"

A wicked smile played around Maguire's lips. "As a matter of fact, I did."

"How did she take it?"

"I was surprised, to be honest with you. She was very professional. She congratulated me on solving the case and said she'd be glad to get back to London now that this was all over." Maguire ran his finger down the condensation on his wineglass. "As a matter of fact, she admitted that I probably hadn't needed her help in the first place."

"You know what I've been wondering about?" Penelope said, tucking her feet under her on the couch. "How did Floyd get my car started when there wasn't a key in the ignition? You can't take the key out without having to turn the car off."

Maguire laughed. "Haven't you ever heard of that handy little trick known as hot-wiring?" He pursed his lips. "Although it isn't that easy in newer cars with all their computerized safety systems. They make it a lot harder for today's crooks to steal a car. Your MINI is fairly old, so perhaps it didn't have one of those systems in place. Of course, he could have broken the key off in the lock. That's been done before, too. The garage should be able to tell us."

Maguire put his glass down on the table and put his arm around Penelope. She leaned her head against his shoulder and snuggled in with a sigh of contentment.

Maguire traced Penelope's face with his finger. "There's one thing that's been on my mind," he said quietly.

Penelope turned so she could look at him. "What's that?" His blue eyes were troubled.

"I've hesitated to ask because I'm not sure I want to know the answer." He took a deep breath, his expression pained. "How long will you be staying in England?"

Penelope felt a warm rush of affection. She smiled at him. "As long as I want."

Don't miss Penelope's next adventure in

PERIL ON THE PAGE

Coming soon from Berkley Prime Crime!

Penelope Parish loved her position as writer-in-residence at the Open Book bookstore in Upper Chumley-on-Stoke, England. She never knew what to expect. One thing she certainly hadn't imagined when she'd crossed the Atlantic and set foot on these shores was to be involved in a murder. So far she'd been involved in two. But that was all behind her now, and she could focus on writing her next novel and helping Mabel Morris, the owner of the Open Book.

At least that's what she told herself.

Today they were getting ready for a book launch at the shop. Stepping into the Open Book was like stepping back in time with its low ceiling crisscrossed with wooden beams and the large diamond-paned front window. It was located on Upper Chumley-on-Stoke's high street, where the storefronts were the original Tudor and all the shops had hand-carved wooden signs hanging out front.

The book launch had been Penelope's idea and she had her fingers crossed that it would go off without a hitch. Mabel had been a bit skeptical at first about Penelope's unusual idea for the launch, but had finally come around and was now as enthusiastic as Penelope was about the event.

Odile Fontaine, an art teacher at the Oakwood School for Girls just outside of Chumley, had written a fun how-to guide called *You Can Paint* and the book launch was being combined with a wine and paint party.

The event had stirred up considerable interest and a photographer for the *Chumley Chronicle* (the weekly newspaper) had phoned to say she planned to attend and take pictures.

Odile was a member of Penelope's fiction writing group and had introduced her to Maribel Northcott, the headmistress of the Oakwood School for Girls. Maribel had in turn invited Penelope to conduct a seminar for the students there. Penelope was quite pleased that her master's degree in Gothic literature was finally being put to good use.

Of course that same degree had driven her to write *Lady of the Moors*, which, much to her surprise, had become a bestseller, so perhaps the money on her education had been well spent after all, in spite of what her mother was always saying. It was the writer's block that she'd been stricken with while working on her second book that had pushed her to apply for the writer-in-residence position at the Open Book, hoping that a change of scenery would spur some creativity.

Life in Upper Chumley-on-Stoke, a medieval town about an hour from London, had worked its magic and Penelope's second book, *The Woman in the Fog*, was due to be published at any moment.

Pen was arranging a stack of Odile's books on a display table when Mabel approached her.

Mabel ran a hand through the fluffy white hair that made her look more like a grandmother than the former MI6 analyst she'd been.

"I've cleared a space for the easels to be set up," she said. She frowned. "They are bringing the easels, right?"

"Yes. Odile is taking care of everything—the easels, paints, aprons for the participants and the wine." Pen looked toward the bookshop's tearoom, which was run by Lady Fiona Innes-Goldthorpe or Figgy as she was more familiarly known.

"Figgy is providing some desserts—cakes and cookies, that sort of thing."

Mabel nodded. "Good. Best to have something to soak up the wine." She looked around. "It appears as if everything is in order then," she said, giving a relieved smile.

The bell over the front door tinkled and Odile Fontaine, the subject of that evening's book launch, swept in. She was a fairly tall woman, although not as tall as Penelope's nearly six feet, and big-boned, with a purple beret perched on top of her head of long curly red hair threaded with strands of gray. She removed her cape with a dramatic flourish sending it swirling in an arc around her that nearly toppled the sign on one of the display tables.

She was wearing a bloodred skirt that flowed around her ankles with a purple tunic over it and a necklace of large mustard yellow beads that looked hand-carved.

Penelope took the cape from her and hung it on the coat stand near the front door.

Odile had brought an almost palpable sense of excitement into the store with her as well as a whiff of cold air. It was mid-October and the Michaelmas term was underway at the Oakwood School. The leaves on the trees were turning color and the residents of Chum, as the town was affectionately known, were digging out their cozy sweaters and boiled wool jackets.

Odile swept over to Penelope and greeted her with an air kiss on each cheek.

"Have you read my manuscript yet?" she said. An armload of silver bracelets jingled as she straightened one of her books on the display table. "I'm hoping to send it off to a publisher soon."

Not content to just publish a book on painting, Odile had taken up fiction as well and had penned a six-hundred-page contemporary romance. Penelope silently groaned. She'd been meaning to get to it and had actually read a few pages, but it was such a slog that she'd given up and had spent the time wondering how she could persuade Odile to stick to painting instead.

The door opened again sending a chilly breeze through the shop that ruffled the pages of the flyers sitting out on the front counter. A young man stuck his head into the store.

Odile glided over to him, her long fluid skirt swishing about her legs.

"I've got the gear," the young man said. "Where do you want it?"

Penelope hastened to join them. She glanced out the window and saw a large van with the Oakwood School crest on the side double-parked in front of the Open Book.

"There's a another entrance behind the shop," she said, and directed the young man to an alley that ran alongside the Open Book and led to a back door that opened into the storage room.

"Cheers." The young man gave a salute, turned around

and hopped into the driver's seat of the van just as the driver of the car behind him began to lean on his horn.

"That's Grady Evans," Odile said, as the van pulled away. "He takes care of the grounds at the school and does odd jobs for Rodney, who is in charge of maintenance. I asked him to cart my supplies over here for me."

The door opened again and a gentleman walked in. He had thick gray hair brushed back from his forehead in a wave and round tortoiseshell glasses. He was wearing a tweed coat with a velvet collar and leather gloves, which he pulled off as he walked toward Odile and Penelope.

Odile smiled and put her hand on the man's arm.

"Penelope, this is Quentin Barnes, my significant other, as the young people say." She smiled up at Quentin. "He teaches history at the Oakwood School." She turned to Quentin. "Quentin, this is Penelope Parish. This event was her brilliant idea."

Pen crossed her fingers. She hoped her idea would turn out to be brilliant.

"Will you be doing a painting?" Penelope said to Quentin.

"Heavens, no. I'm just here for moral support and to say good-bye." He gave Odile a peck on the cheek and glanced at his watch. "Unfortunately I can't stay long. I have a conference in Bristol that starts early tomorrow morning so I'm heading out tonight." He turned to Odile. "I'll be at the Bristol Harbor Hotel if you need to reach me."

"Well, I hope you can stay for a bit. I've got some of that wine you fancy." Odile took his arm and led him over to the display table where her books were piled up, waiting to be signed.

A few minutes later Pen heard Grady knock on the back door and ran to open it.

Grady sidled through the door with several easels tucked under his arms.

He was tall and sinewy with dark brown hair left long enough to flop onto his forehead. He was wearing faded and worn jeans, a plaid flannel shirt with the sleeves rolled up and work boots. Penelope could see goose bumps on his arms.

"You must be freezing without a coat," she said.

Grady shrugged. "I left my jacket in the van. I'm okay." He nodded at the easels he was holding. "Where do you want these?"

"We've cleared a space at the front of the store," Penelope said.

"Right-o."

Penelope led him toward the area where she and Mabel had decided to hold the event. They'd shoved some display tables out of the way to create a large enough space for the painting party.

"Why don't you lean them against that table over there?" Odile pointed to a spot. "You can help me set them up after you bring everything in."

Grady nodded. "I'll go get the rest of the gear." He loped off through the store toward the back entrance.

Moments later he came back with a handcart piled with cardboard boxes.

"Let's have those over there," Odile said, pointing to a spot off to the side. "Now we can begin to set up the easels."

Grady, who had briefly paused and was leaning against one of the display tables, reluctantly shoved off and began placing the easels according to Odile's instructions.

"What do you have here?" Mabel wandered over and peered into one of the open cartons.

"Paints, palettes, aprons." Odile ticked them off on her fingers. "And that last one there is the wine." She whirled around to face Penelope. "Do we have glasses?"

"Yes, no problem."

"Hello!" Figgy called as she wheeled a tea cart over to them, its wheels rattling as she pushed it across the floor.

Her short dark hair was gelled into spikes and looked as if she'd run her hands through it haphazardly, and she was wearing one of her vintage thrift store finds—a flowered peasant dress with an empire waist—a style that had been popular in the nineteen-seventies. She'd paired it with black ankle boots and large hoop earrings.

Penelope glanced at the tea cart and her stomach rumbled, reminding her that she hadn't had dinner yet. She'd been working on her third novel and had become immersed in it—something that sadly didn't happen every time she sat down to write. Her writing room at the Open Book—a small space barely bigger than a closet with a desk and a chair and nothing else to distract her—was windowless, and she hadn't seen the sun going down and darkness descending. She wondered if there was time to dash across the street and pick up something from the Chumley Chippie.

"I've made some shortbread cookies, Jaffa cakes and jammie dodgers," Figgy said, pointing to the various platters.

"What on earth is a jammie dodger?" Penelope said. "It sounds like a position on a baseball team." Penelope put on an announcer's serious voice. "And John Smith has been drafted for the jammie dodger position with the New York Yankees."

Figgy laughed. "It does rather sound that way, doesn't it? They're shortbread cookies with jam filling. They're quite lovely." She pointed to the tea cart. "There's a Victoria sponge as well and some slices of Madeira cake." She frowned. "I think that should do."

"It certainly should," Pen said, pushing her glasses up her nose with her finger. She glanced at the tea cart again, longing to grab a slice of the Madeira cake. It had become one of her favorites since arriving in England. It was like a pound cake but more moist and with a hint of lemon flavoring. According to Figgy, the Victorians used to serve it with a glass of Madeira in the afternoons and that was how it had acquired its name.

Grady, meanwhile, had set up the easels and folding chairs Mabel had rented for the occasion and Odile was organizing the paints and palettes.

Penelope glanced at the clock. The wine-and-paint participants should be arriving any minute now. She nixed the idea of running to the Chumley Chippie. A slice of Figgy's Madeira cake would have to do.

Fortunately for Penelope, she had been blessed with the sort of metabolism that made it hard to gain weight and it didn't help that she often forgot to eat until hunger finally drove her to think about having a meal.

The shop door opened again and two women entered, their faces red from the cold and their hands fluttering in excitement.

Odile introduced herself and invited them to choose a spot and take a seat.

India Culpepper was the next to arrive. She was wearing the English gentlewoman's uniform of a plaid wool skirt, twinset and a strand of yellowing pearls. She was distantly related to Arthur Worthington, the Duke of Upper Chumley-on-Stoke, and lived in a cottage on the grounds of the Worthington Estate.

The family money, handed down through generations of Worthingtons, hadn't reached India to any substantial degree, and her sweaters were likely to be darned and her shoes rather worn at the heels. Figgy kept her supplied with cookies and cakes from the tea shop at no charge and Mabel often hunted out used copies of the books India wanted to read.

But India was a proud woman as befitted the aristocrat she considered herself to be, and never complained about her lack of funds.

Penelope guessed that India's interest tonight didn't lie in wine and painting but rather in the contents of Figgy's tea cart.

Gladys arrived next, her face red from rushing across the street where she and her husband owned the Pig in a Poke, Chumley's butcher shop. She took off her coat and squealed when she looked down at herself.

"I've forgotten to take me apron off," she said, laughing, and slapping her thigh. She whipped it off quickly and hung it from the back of the chair she'd chosen next to India.

Several more women arrived, chattering like birds and fluttering around the shop. One of them went over to Odile and began chatting.

The bell over the front door tinkled as it opened and everyone's head turned in that direction. Several of the women gasped in surprise when the duchess of Upper Chumley-on-Stoke walked in. The former Charlotte Davenport, she had married the duke of Upper Chumley-on-Stoke in a magnificent ceremony at Worthington House that had been the talk of the town from the moment it was announced. Not all the talk had been positive, though—not only was Charlotte an American, but she was a romance writer and neither of those things sat well with a lot of the residents.

Charlotte was as unpretentious as they came. She and Penelope had developed something of a bond as Americans and fellow writers and had become friends.

From the moment Worthington and Charlotte had said *I do*, everyone in Chumley, as well as reporters and photographers from all the tabloids, had been on the watch for the proverbial baby bump. There had been a couple of false alarms but now Charlotte was visibly pregnant, much to everyone's satisfaction and delight.

Charlotte looked effortlessly elegant as usual with her long blond hair swept into a simple knot at the nape of her neck. She was wearing a wax jacket, jeans and a fitted navy and white striped Breton sweater that accentuated her stomach.

The women smiled at her nervously as she took a seat on the other side of India.

Finally Odile clapped her hands and everyone took their place. Quentin didn't join the group, but instead wandered around the Open Book, stopping every once in a while to pull a volume off the shelf.

Figgy opened the bottles of wine and began handing out glasses to the women. Odile accepted one, took a sip and put it aside as she concentrated on leading the class through a painting that looked like a piece of modern art.

Figgy poked Pen as she stood watching. "It looks rather like a fake Mondrian, doesn't it?"

Pen looked at the squares and rectangles of red, yellow and blue separated by black lines.

"It looks like a Rubik's cube to me."

Figgy laughed, then picked up a bottle of wine and went to refill Gladys' glass.

Penelope noticed Quentin walking toward the door as he

buttoned his coat and pulled on his gloves. He waved to Odile and left.

The audience continued to follow Odile's instructions and slowly their paintings were taking shape. Pen noticed that Gladys had the tip of her tongue between her front teeth as she concentrated on her canvas and Charlotte's jaw was set as she attempted to copy Odile's strokes.

The photographer from the Chumley Chronicle, a middle-aged woman with graying hair wearing a stretched-out red sweater, roamed around snapping pictures of the event, occasionally pausing to grab a cookie off the tea cart.

Suddenly Odile swayed and put a hand to her head. Penelope eyed her with concern.

"Are you okay?" Pen said. "Do you need some air? Perhaps the smell of the paint . . . ."

"I'm perfectly accustomed to the smell of paint," Odile said, puffing out her chest. "I am an artist after all. It was just a slight dizzy spell. Nothing to worry about."

"Do you want to sit down for a moment?"

Odile made a face and waved Penelope away as if she was a pesky fly. She adjusted her beret and turned back to the assembled audience.

"Where were we?" she said in her throaty voice, pausing dramatically with her paintbrush in the air.

Penelope glanced around the room again. The women were dutifully copying Odile's brushstrokes with varying degrees of success. India's hands shook slightly and her lines were wavy, giving the whole thing a watery impressionist look like something seen through a rain-spattered window.

Everyone seemed to be enjoying themselves and Penelope sighed with satisfaction.

Once the paintings were finished and left to dry, the ladies gathered around Figgy's tea cart, their eyes wide with delight at the array of goodies. Slices of Madeira cake or a couple of jammie dodgers in hand, they wandered among the easels admiring each other's handiwork.

Much to everyone's delight, Charlotte circulated with them, complimenting their artistic abilities and daintily munching on a shortbread finger.

"I've been craving sweets ever since . . . ." Charlotte said to the women clustered around her. She cradled her belly gently with her left hand.

Gladys threw back her head and laughed. "I was the same with my daughter Elspeth—only with me it was vegemite. I had it on toast every morning and for my tea and I even dipped crisps in it. I went through any number of jars of it. Bruce—he's my husband—thought being in the family way had made me barmy."

Their laughter was cut short by a cry from Odile. Pen looked over at her and was horrified to see her sway wildly, clutch at one of the easels sending the painting soaring, and then crash to the ground in a heap of red and purple fabric. Her beret flew off and landed several feet away.

The photographer, who had been busy munching on a piece of Madeira cake, gave an abrupt cry, grabbed her camera off a chair and hastened over. She immediately began snapping pictures, oblivious to the crumbs leaving a trail down the front of her sweater.

"Please, don't," Pen said to her and held up a hand to stop her. She knelt beside Odile. "What is it? Are you ill? Should we call a doctor?"

"I'm dizzy," Odile said. "My head is spinning."

Mabel came over and crouched down next to Pen, her knees giving a loud crack.

"And I have the most abominable headache," Odile said, rubbing the back of her neck.

"Has this happened before?" Mabel said in a crisp, no-nonsense voice. "Do you have any medication you're supposed to be taking?"

Odile shook her head. "Just so dizzy," she said again.

"When did you start feeling ill?" Mabel said.

"After I got here," Odile said. "I felt fine before. I don't know what's wrong."

Several of the women had wandered over and were clustered around Odile.

Mabel peered at Odile more closely and then turned to Pen. "Her pupils are awfully dilated. They're positively enormous. Take a look."

Pen looked at Odile and nodded her head. "Shall I call an ambulance?

"I think you'd better," Mabel said. She frowned. "I hope it's nothing serious."

As Penelope stood up and pulled her phone from her pocket, Odile's eyelids fluttered, closed and her head flopped to the side.